How To
Rob an
aRMOReD
caR

Also by Iain Levison

A Working Stiff's Manifesto
Since the Layoffs
Dog Eats Dog

HOW TO ROB AN ARMORED CAR

IAIN LEVISON

SOHO

Copyright © 2009 by Iain Levison

Published by
Soho Press, Inc.
853 Broadway
New York, NY 10003

Library of Congress Cataloging-in-Publication Data

Levison, Iain.
How to rob an armored car / Iain Levison.
p. cm.
ISBN 978-1-56947-599-7
1. Criminals—Fiction. 2. Pennsylvania—Fiction. I. Title.
PS3612.E933H69 2009
813'.6—dc22
                                    2009011309

10 9 8 7 6 5 4 3 2 1

For Samantha

How To Rob an Armored Car

CHAPTER

Mitch was watching a forty-two-inch plasma TV when the woman came up behind him. She was pretty but rough looking, hippieish, with long hair falling all around what appeared to be a brown bedsheet. He had been staring at the $1,799 price tag on the TV, knowing he would never own it, not at what they paid him to manage at the Accu-mart. He would never own it unless he stole it, and he was wondering where they kept the inventory sheets for the high-end electronics.

"Hi," she said, her tone not friendly but brusque, as if the salutation was a military call to look alert.

Mitch turned slowly from the TV. "How can I help you?"

"Are you a manager?"

Oh, Christ. One of the employees had pissed her off. It could have been any of them; none of them gave a shit. Any of them but Charles, the Nigerian, whom Mitch had

1

just sent on a mission to buy an eighth of kind bud while still on the clock.

"I am."

"I read that all your clothes are made by political prisoners in China. Is that true?"

She had an angelic smile on her face while she asked it, but she had really come looking for a fight. She was holding a candle she was going to buy, and she had to be feeling bad about coming to a superstore, a huge corporate conglomerate, to buy a cheap candle, and now she felt the need to pick a fight with a manager to make herself feel better. This way, when she told her hippie friends where she got the candle, she could also add the story of how she had argued with one of the corporate henchmen, which made her a supporter of the little guy and a friend of the environment, rather than a cheap bitch who needed a candle and was too lazy to make one herself, like the Earth child she was posing as would do.

"You'll have to ask in Clothing," Mitch said.

This happened once a week. Accu-mart was not a store with good media coverage. Every time one opened, there were protests. They were exploiting Third World laborers, they were building huge parking lots which caused a runoff of dirt and oil to enter the water supply, and they were underpaying their employees. That last one was true enough, Mitch knew. But people needed cheap shit, so the stores were always packed. If people really wanted Accu-mart to go away, they could just stop shopping there, a rule which applied to the candle-toting hippie bitch who was trying to pick a fight.

"Nice candle," he added pleasantly.

She put the candle down on a TV set, as if she had never intended to buy it, had just been carrying it around in case the lights went out. "That's how you can sell them so cheap, isn't it? You don't pay the people who make them for their labor."

"Ma'am, I really have no idea. This stuff just comes in on a truck."

"Well don't you wonder where it came from? Who made it? Because they're paying your salary, you know."

"Yeah, they are," said Mitch. These issues had been addressed in the training video, and Mitch knew what he was supposed to say. Growing global economy, market forces, people being offered jobs and earning money, as opposed to not working and earning no money, blah blah blah. The corporate response sounded hollow even to him, and he didn't care. "If someone is making money off these people, it ain't me."

She stared at him.

"Lady," he said, tired, forgetting his script. "What do you want from me? Why don't you go over to the coffee shop and say something to them? You think coffee pickers in Colombia make any money? How about the people who make your car tires?" It was burbling forth, all the stuff he thought about while he restocked floor mats and air fresheners and added up time cards. He knew it would only be a few seconds before he started casually using the word *fuck,* which certainly hadn't been in the training video, and then he would be back on the unemployment line and his half-assed health insurance would be gone and he would be cooking at the restaurant with his roommate, Doug. He took a deep breath, stopped himself, and stared at her blankly.

"You people," she said, marveling at Mitch's insensitivity. "You know, that parking lot used to be a forest." This was clearly a first-time argument for her, and she had retreated to the forest issue quickly. They usually put up a little more of a fight before they started rambling about woodland creatures and the purity of streams. "The runoff is going into the streams and poisoning our drinking water." She turned to leave.

"It hasn't been a forest since the First World War," said Mitch, levelheaded now, reciting the videotaped speech word for word. "Before we paved it over, it was a dirt field used as a junkyard by the Mulgrave Scrap Metal Company." But he was talking to her back now, and she was waving him off as she walked away. She turned the corner and went back toward housewares, probably to get another candle.

He turned his attention back to the TV, which was showing a commercial for an acid reducer. High definition, baby. He could see the pores in the actress's face. It was like someone with an acidy stomach was actually *in the room with him.* If he owned that TV, could life get any better?

• • •

MITCHELL ALDEN HAD been born with a number of gifts, but overshadowing them all was the Curse of Poor Decision Making. It was genetic. He remembered sitting in the kitchen in the house where he grew up in Queens, listening to his father talking to his business partner, who wanted to get out of the indoor air-cleaning business and invest in computers. "Dammit, I don't know how long this computer fad is going to last," he remembered his dad saying, trying to talk his partner into staying with selling Smoke-Eeters. "But as long as I'm alive, people will be smoking in bars in New York City."

These words turned out to be true. Mitch's dad died on the Long Island Expressway, six weeks before the ban on smoking in New York City bars went into effect, because of another error of judgment, this one involving a tractor trailer's stopping distance. Mitch carried on the family tradition by joining the army and getting kicked out six weeks later for failing a drug test, then going to community college and majoring in English.

Upon graduating with an associate's degree, Mitch was fired up to start the career for which community college had best prepared him, which was selling kind bud for a Canadian smuggler he had met while in jail for his second DUI.

But the smuggler disappeared and was never heard from again, and standing in the parking lot of the Wilton Community College, the mortarboard tucked under his arm and the tenth call to the smuggler going unanswered on his cell phone, Mitch looked around and saw the sign at the college job fair:

ACCU-MART! NOW HIRING MANAGERS!

Fuck it, he thought. What else am I gonna do?

• • •

MITCH DIDN'T LOVE Accu-mart, but he didn't hate it as much as he had expected to. He thought he'd cash the first two paychecks from the training program and then find a job bartending somewhere until he could hook up with a new pot contact, but soon realized that, despite its claims to the contrary, Accu-mart expected very little of him. The term *manager* was really just an excuse not to pay him overtime, because he was rarely required to make a decision, and when he did, it was scrutinized and double-checked by everyone at the store who outranked him. The training manual had flattered him by pointing out that he had been selected from a huge pool of available talent, (though Mitch had noticed that no one he had seen filling out an application at the community college job fair was not also present on the first day of training) and the hiring gurus had claimed that they found him to be the one of the bright lights of his generation. Then, perhaps blinded by the glow of his brilliance, they stuck him back in the car accessories department to rot. A few hours of inventory control and some restocking here and there, and the rest of the ten-hour shift consisted basically of just being on the premises.

Being blazingly high sometimes helped move the shift along. Today, Mitch had smoked his last buds on the way to work and had been dreading spending the last five hours of the shift straight and sober, when Charles had suggested he make a weed run for both of them. Mitch had forked over $50, leaving himself $27 to last three more days until payday. Now he was wondering if dreading your job so much that you paid the last of your money to avoid working it with all your mental faculties intact might be an indicator that it was time to get a different one.

"I wanna go home," whined Denise. "I'm sick."

Denise was Mitch's new eighteen-year-old associate. He had won her in a poker game. The department managers had been playing cards with the new-hire lists as a way of determining who got assigned where. Mitch had cleaned house and wound up taking the two Nigerians on the list (all the Nigerians worked hard and had good weed contacts) and the only attractive girl. The downside was that Denise, who was still in high school, had only applied at Accumart so she could work in the clothing department and hang out with her friends and get them discounts. She now found herself stocking brake pads and steering wheel covers largely out of view of the public, so she was constantly whining.

"You can go when Charles gets back," Mitch said.

"Nooooooo," she whined. "You sent him to buy weed." She looked at him saucily. Apparently, Charles couldn't keep his mouth shut.

"Did you at least finish stocking the order we got in?"

"Almost," Denise said, now chirpy and pleasant, sensing victory, any apparent signs of illness gone. "I just left the smelly things out. I can't stand picking up those boxes. They make your hands smell." She made a gagging face.

"All right, thanks. You've done a good day's work."

"Thanks, bye," said Denise, heading for the time cards.

"Your fifty-three minutes of service to the Accu-mart Corporation have been invaluable . . ." he called after her, but the swinging doors leading to the stockroom were already banging shut, and through the circular scratched green Plexiglas windows he could see her beautiful blonde head bending over the time cards. Dammit. Now he was sober, bored, and had no one to look at. Where was Charles?

"Where's Charles?" asked Bob Sutherland, the store's general manager, who had crept up unnoticed. Sutherland gave Mitch the creeps. He could be either bossy and demanding, constantly trying to intimidate, or jovial and overly friendly. He was also the stupidest man Mitch had ever worked for. A few months earlier at a manager's meeting, Sutherland had pointed out how well the sporting goods department at an Accu-mart in Santa Monica had done, selling surfboards. He had recommended that the sporting goods manager order ten surfboards, not taking into account that it was late fall in Wilton, Pennsylvania, over two hundred miles from any surf. The one board that had been sold since still mystified everyone. Who was that guy who bought a surfboard in central Pennsylvania as wintertime approached? The other nine took up a block of racks in the storeroom.

"I sent him to buy drugs," Mitch said.

Sutherland laughed. Today it was Dr. Jekyll. "When he comes back, give him these," he said, handing Mitch two envelopes full of forms. "There seems to be some kind of problem with his paperwork at the INS."

"Will do."

"Seriously," Sutherland said. "Where did he go?"

"Umm, I sent him to the Autocenter to pick up a case of wiper blades. Ours didn't come in."

"Well, did you call the distributor? They should just bring them over. It's their problem, not ours."

Fuck, now Sutherland was going to get on the phone to the distributor and bitch at them about not dropping off wiper blades that they had actually dropped off.

"It was really slow here," said Mitch. "I figured it would give him something to do."

"You could have had him clean the stockroom," said Sutherland, and then Charles walked through the stockroom doors.

"Did you get the wiper blades?" Sutherland asked him. This was turning into a disaster in a hurry.

Charles nodded and smiled. "Wiper blades," he said cheerfully, in heavily accented English, walking past both of them to resume stocking the aisles. Charles's English was perfect, and he actually had very little accent, but he could deflect conversations with feigned idiocy when he wanted to. Cold air from the outside had blown in with him, and Mitch smelled the heavy, warm scent of freshly smoked reefer.

Sutherland turned to leave, either not smelling it or not sure of what it was, or perhaps just anxious to go. Mitch had developed the distinct feeling that Sutherland would leave almost any conversation when an hourly employee showed up, especially one who didn't speak English as a first language. He really didn't like being around them. He babbled for a few seconds on his way out about how Mitch should make the distributors work for him, not the other way around, and Mitch nodded dutifully, as if he was learning something of great import from an extremely competent man. Then thankfully, mercifully, he left.

Mitch turned to Charles. "Damn, that was nearly very ugly," he said. "Did you hookup?"

Charles nodded, his eyes so red they looked like he had

suffered a brain hemorrhage. He smiled broadly. "It's gooooooood," he said.

•   •   •

KEVIN WOKE UP still remembering the dream. It was the most undramatic of dreams, embarrassing in its banality, but as with so many of his other dreams, he knew that because of it, he would spend the day with a vague sense of unease, of personal disappointment and dissatisfaction. Lately he had begun to wonder if this was the only emotion he ever felt.

In the dream, he had been standing in line in a coffee shop with his six-year-old daughter, Ellie. All the other people in line were young couples with children, and they were glowing with delight at parenthood, at family, at their place in the community. They seemed to sense Kevin's unease, and they regarded him with suspicion because of it. He saw young couples sitting on the plush coffee shop couches, looking at him and asking each other, in whispers, who he thought he was fooling, hanging around in a coffee shop with middle-class normal people, trying to pass himself off as one of them. When Kevin blinked himself awake and stared at the ceiling, he wasn't sure if it actually had been a dream, or if it was a memory of the last time he and Linda and Ellie had gone to Starbuck's.

As he felt Linda stir next to him, he reached over and gently grabbed her ass, not as an overture of sex but more to see what she would do. Her hand shot down and pushed him away. She had never been a morning person, but the abruptness and finality of her movements surprised him.

"Ellie's up," Linda murmured angrily, her face partly under the covers. "Could you get her breakfast started?"

Kevin hated it when Linda gave him orders disguised as suggestions, especially when he had just been about to do the thing she was ordering him to do. It was as if she thought he was a small child, like Ellie. And worse, she knew it annoyed him, so frequently she would know he was about to do something and suggest it anyway, just to piss him off. What was she expecting him to do? Just lie there and let his kid go to school hungry? A deaf man would know Ellie was up, and didn't he get her breakfast ready every day of the week?

As he got up, he pulled the covers aside quickly enough to send a cold blast of air against Linda's back. She slapped the covers back down. Kevin shivered as he groped around in the near darkness for his hooded sweatshirt. He could almost see his breath in his own bedroom.

"We can't keep the thermostat this low," he said. "I know it saves, like, a dollar a month, and that's really important, but I'd rather Ellie didn't catch pneumonia." Linda remained quiet. Kevin knew he could bait her in the mornings, get away with sarcasm and the odd dig here and there, simply because he woke up quicker than she did. The arguing part of her brain, which Kevin felt was most of it, warmed up slowly. It wasn't usually until her second cup of coffee that she started grinding away at his soul with her complaints and observations and outright orders.

"Hey," he said to the lump under the covers. "Doug's coming over this morning. I told him he could have some of those double-A batteries we got in bulk from Accu-mart."

"Goddammit," said Linda, sitting up and smacking the pillow. "Why can't you just let me sleep for ten more minutes? This is my one morning to sleep in . . ."

"I'm just telling you that Doug might come over," Kevin yelled back. "I didn't want you to be weird if he came to the door." He tried storming out to end yet another conversation with his wife by slamming a door, but one of Ellie's toys got caught in the doorway; he heard it cracking as he yanked the door back open. He cursed, not out of concern for the door, or the toy, but because the momentum of his dramatic exit had been made laughable.

"Why do your idiot friends have to come over here?" Linda asked as she slumped back into the pillows, almost whining. "I don't want them here. You spend enough time with them in that rat hole they call an apartment."

"It's just Doug," Kevin said, measured and patient, holding the bedroom door open. He was suddenly overcome by the urge to be nice. He wanted to go walk dogs today feeling positive and pleasant, not worn down, with the residue of yet another Linda argument circling around in his brain. "He's only coming over for a minute."

"Why don't you just move in with them?" Linda said, now fully awake, eyes blazing with anger, directed straight up at the ceiling. "You could all live together like a bunch of animals and smoke pot all day long. That way your daughter wouldn't be asking me where you were all the time—"

SLAM. There might have been more but Kevin didn't get a chance to hear it.

So much for having a positive and pleasant day.

• • •

"I DON'T WANT to be married to Kevin anymore," said Linda, as if she were mentioning that she was thinking about changing her brand of fabric softener. Nice weather we're having. I have to take the car in for an oil change. I think I'll get rid of my husband.

She was rooting around through her junk drawer for a pack of AA batteries, which Kevin had promised Doug he could have if he came over. Doug had come late, and Kevin had already gone to walk dogs. Linda had answered the door and let Doug in, gone to get the batteries, and then offhandedly mentioned that she was thinking about divorcing his friend.

This was the last thing that Doug wanted to hear. He had just smoked a fattie and was really enjoying his day off from the restaurant. He had just come over to get the batteries so he could fire up his remote control and spend the day baked on his couch. Though he had known Linda for years, he thought of her as sketchy and moody and hadn't been pleased when she had answered the door.

He said nothing, which Linda took as a signal to continue. "We just don't communicate anymore."

Doug knew that they didn't communicate but wasn't sure that they ever had. Linda didn't usually communicate with him either, which was why it was a surprise that she was suddenly trying to. He had been around Kevin and Linda for four years and didn't recall ever seeing them have a conversation which didn't escalate into hostility within a few seconds, though he had noticed that lately the yelling had stopped and the conversations had gotten shorter, the endings now quiet snorts of disgust. He had never seen them kiss or touch each other or say anything nice, and he occasionally wondered to himself how Ellie, their daughter, had ever gotten made. He had just assumed that things were different when he wasn't around.

"That sucks," said Doug.

"Why does it suck?" asked Linda, lighting a cigarette, staring at him.

He wasn't anticipating a question, and Linda seemed almost confrontational when she asked it. She also appeared to have stopped looking for the batteries, which was a bad sign. The exit was being cut off.

"Because . . . you and Kevin . . . are good people." He had the feeling he was being tested, and while not actually acing the test, he wasn't failing disastrously either. He didn't really know if Linda was a good person. Often when he came over to get high with Kevin, he was glad if she wasn't around, because it meant you could dump the bong water into the potted plants and put your feet up on stuff without having someone stare at you reproachfully. He thought of her as a neat freak and a nag and was fairly sure that this was Kevin's opinion too.

"I think I make him unhappy," she said. "He's just unhappy all the time."

"Oh, no," said Doug. "He'd be unhappy anyway." The comment slipped out. It wasn't the supportive, wrap-every-thing-up kind of sentence he was looking for, but it was true. Ever since they had met four years ago, when Kevin had been a waiter at the restaurant where Doug was a cook, Doug had thought of him as a grouch. It was only because Doug had shown an interest in selling off the weed that Kevin was growing that they had even struck up a conversation. Kevin, though an excellent grower, lacked the social skills and contacts for dealing and had managed to stock-pile about four pounds of high-grade White Widow in his basement. During a typical after-work half-drunk conversation, they had hammered out a deal, and a friendship was forged.

Since then, the frequency of their get-togethers had resulted in a bond forming, a familiarity which had expanded into all kinds of other activities, like drinking and playing pool and painting Kevin's house and helping each other move. Linda, though usually around, had never really become a part of these activities.

"Why is he so unhappy?" Linda asked. She looked around and threw up her hands. "We've got a nice house, a beautiful daughter. Money's tight always, but we get by. I mean, why? It has to be me."

Doug shook his head. "Some people are just unhappy," he said.

"Oh, bullshit," she said, going behind the kitchen counter and running water into the kettle. "Do you want some coffee or tea?"

Decision time. If he said yes, the conversation could eat up half the day. Women could talk forever. He knew that much from hearing the waiters at the restaurant complain. Put two of them at a table with two cups of warm liquid in front of them, and that table was shot for the shift. But the novelty of this situation was enough to keep it interesting. In four years, Linda had never wanted to talk to him before about anything, and who knew? Maybe she wasn't so bad.

"I'm not forcing you," she said, forcing him.

"Uhhh, coffee. No, tea. Tea. I'd definitely like a cup of tea."

"Have a seat." Linda went back and forth behind the counter, putting the kettle on the stove and opening and closing cabinets. It suddenly occurred to Doug that the prospect of going home and watching TV all afternoon was familiar, but had not really been exciting him, and this might not be such a bad idea after all. Hell, he thought, it might be fun to sit and shoot the shit with Linda.

"I think he changed after he got out of jail," she said. "It's like he's been depressed. That was, what, two years ago now? I've been putting up with his moods for two years." She put an ashtray out and carefully placed her cigarette in it, then said, almost conspiratorially, "You know, he still thinks you had something to do with that."

"I know he does," said Doug. "No matter how many times I deny it. I mean, if you're accused of something you didn't do and you can't really prove you didn't do it . . ."

He trailed off, hurt just thinking about it. About two and a half years ago, when Kevin had been growing a field of marijuana plants in his basement and Doug had been selling the harvest for him, it had all ended suddenly. One day, cops had come in and seized the whole lot, thousands of dollars worth of lights and fans and fertilizer, and thrown Kevin in jail for ninety days. Kevin's theory was that Doug had been busted for possession and had told the cops who was growing the plants as a condition for immunity. Doug had, in fact, never been busted, and the whole thing was a hurtful and miserable episode he was always hoping was behind them but which never actually seemed to be. Kevin would often claim it was over, that he believed him, and then the next time they were out drinking, after a shot of tequila or two, Kevin would put his arm around him and say something like, "Really, man. I won't get mad. Just tell me what happened."

Linda was looking at Doug, studying him, and for a paranoid second he thought that Kevin had put Linda up to this—have him over, make him tea, and see if he confesses. Then he decided that the paranoia was probably just the joint he had fired up on his way over. He doubted Kevin and Linda ever spoke to each other long enough to hatch a plan. But just to make sure, he added, "I didn't do it. I never got busted."

"I know, sweetie," Linda said. "I never thought you did."

Her voice was warm and friendly, revealing a side of her Doug had never noticed before, and she suddenly struck him as a person, a woman, a different entity from Kevin, with whom Doug had always associated her. It was always Kevin and Linda. For four years, he had seen her come and go and occasionally spoken to her, but she hadn't existed for him except as Kevin's accessory, much like his car or his sunglasses. He liked being called *sweetie* too.

"Why does he think I did it? I mean, after all this time, I'd admit it if it had ever happened. Does he really think I'd turn him in? Dude, you know what they do to you for dealing? It's like a slap on the wrist. I wouldn't ruin his life for a slap on the wrist, you know."

Linda looked at him thoughtfully. "You know, honestly, I always thought of you as a waste case," she said. "You're really a nice guy. I can see why Kevin likes you."

"I always thought of you as a nag."

There was a moment of silence, and then they both laughed. Linda leaned across the table and said with a conspiratorial grin, "Hey, you don't have any smoke with you, do you?"

"Yeah, I do," Doug said. "Do you have any . . . like, uh . . . fuckin' double-A batteries?"

• • •

KEVIN WAS WALKING a pit bull in the rain. The pit bull was named Jeffrey, and he belonged to a shifty doctor who lived alone in a million-dollar house in Westlake. Kevin figured the dog had not been bought for companionship, but because the doctor was too cheap to install a security system. Or maybe not too cheap. Maybe he liked the idea that, instead of hearing an impotent alarm go off, a burglar should be torn to shreds. Having been banished to the yard, even during the harsh winters, Jeffrey was usually in a state of physical neglect and starved of human contact, and was always so happy to see Kevin on his daily half-hour visits that it was often difficult to get his leash on for all the joyful bouncing around. Eyeing the sores on the poor dog's back as the rain grew heavier, Kevin wondered if the alarm system wouldn't have been a better decision for all involved.

Kevin had started his dog-walking business two years ago, purely by chance. Fresh from a ninety-day stint in jail and convinced that no one would ever hire him, he had been moping around the house when Linda had mentioned that if he wasn't going to do anything all day, he could at least walk Nicky Taylor's dog around lunchtime. Nicky Taylor was a rich divorcée who owned the dress shop where Linda worked, and she was constantly leaving Linda alone in the busy store so she could drive home and let her golden retriever out. He had done it one day, just to shut Linda up, and then the next day, then the next. Then within a week he found himself actually looking forward to it. The dog-walking provided an anchor to days which had become aimless and empty, and he found himself getting attached to the dog. Max, the retriever, was marvelously uncomplicated, had no needs that couldn't be easily met, and expressed nothing but the most sincere appreciation. After seven years of a deteriorating marriage, this was exactly the type of relationship Kevin was looking for.

Nicky had then, without asking, compiled a list of all her wealthy friends who also needed their dogs walked, and had come up with a pay scale and a schedule for him. At first, Kevin had been annoyed, picturing the two women sitting around the dress shop planning every detail of his life. Linda couldn't just leave him alone, give him time to get things figured out, get his life back together. But then he realized that the work entailed no boss and noticed that the pay scale Nicky had arranged was well in excess of anything he himself would have asked for, and he couldn't believe that he could earn a hundred dollars a day just for showing up at five or six houses and taking a dog out to shit. It kept

Linda quiet and got him out of the house, and it brought money in. Soon he found the postprison depression had lifted, and he was printing up business cards and actively pursuing clients.

The rain was turning into a downpour, which Kevin liked. He was getting drenched and it gave him a feeling of working, of earning money by battling the elements. Anyone could walk dogs in the sunshine. When the sound of the water hitting the immaculate sidewalks of Westlake became a dull roar, Jeffrey turned around and looked at him, as if he expected the walk to be cut short. Kevin nodded at him to keep moving. The dog responded with a jump of enthusiasm. Rain, shit. It wasn't so bad. They both knew it was better than going home.

When the rain let up, his worn jacket and pants soaked through, Kevin's mind wandered back to football. Specifically, he was trying to pinpoint the moment in his own football career when his life had completely changed tracks without him being aware of it. Perhaps it was the day he had started pretending that a slight bruise on his right knee was a crippling injury, or the week he had blown off football practice three times with a doctor's note so he could go over to Linda's house while her parents were out of town.

After having spent most of his childhood and early adult years imagining a superstar NFL career, and having been encouraged in this by every coach and player he had met in the high school system, it had taken only a year of playing at Western College to realize that he was, in fact, headed for the scrap heap of broken bones and also-rans. After less than a semester, the joy had gone out of it, and he had begun to notice that he was more likely to wind up as the limping assistant coach at some coal-town high school than as the guy doing shoe commercials and holding up the Vince Lombardi trophy on national television.

All the guys at Western thought they were going to the big time. They were all ex–high school stars. After practice one day, he had been looking at them, listening to their endless chatter of self-promoting shit, and he had thought of them as deluded. Then, in a moment of painful self-awareness, he had seen that he fit right in. He wasn't going to the pros, no matter what. Western College athletes wound up as gym teachers. Ohio State sent guys to the pros, and they had never called him back.

After this epiphany, things went downhill quickly. He developed a thousand-yard stare during the pregame prayer and was often daydreaming when the coach called him off the sidelines for a play. Despite his versatility as a player (he could play tight end or cornerback equally well), he found his name called less and less frequently. Finally, during a midseason practice, after being slow to respond to an order to get on the field, he heard one of the coaches say to another, "Never mind. He doesn't care." Then they quickly called a different play which didn't include him.

At the next game, when he showed up to strap on pads and tape and cleats and rub his hands with Stickum, he realized he didn't care that much if Western College won or lost. He also didn't care if he watched from the sidelines or played. The rah-rah sessions before the games, which featured offensive linemen screaming "WESTEEEEEERN!" with a red-faced mania as they banged their helmets against lockers, and the episodes on the team bus, when assistant coaches would try to get the players fired up with primal screams, made Kevin feel less like he had accepted a college scholarship and more like he had joined a cult. After the games, when all the players would go to the Easytown Buffet to load up on platefuls of fried chicken and celebrate a victory or reflect on a loss, Kevin would grab a book and head down to the local diner and eat by himself.

Which was where he met Linda. And then he dropped out of college and worked at a quarry so he could spend more time with her. And now here he was, twenty-eight years old, walking dogs in the rain. Why had that happened? Why couldn't he care about winning some football games for a college that had given him a scholarship? Why did he have to be an *individual* all the time? Maybe it was because he had been lonely at college, and Linda had been the cure for it. Maybe that was how everyone made decisions that affected the rest of their lives, by trying to solve the problem right in front of them. And before you knew it, life was slipping away and you were obsessing with all your immediate problems and . . .

Stop it. Stop thinking so much. The rain had left a fresh, crisp scent in the air which gave Kevin some energy. He turned Jeffrey around to go back home, and the dog looked at him with understanding. Jeffrey seemed to understand everything, and bore it all with a grace Kevin knew he lacked. Back to sit in the doghouse, a literal doghouse, not the metaphorical one to which Kevin felt consigned. It was one of the things he liked about walking dogs, that it put everything into perspective. He got to spend time with creatures more fucked than him.

2

CHAPTER

MITCH WAS STARING at a case of auto air fresheners. Really staring at them. He was having some deep thoughts, wondering who came up with the idea of freshening the interior of a car. Mitch's own car smelled like gas and pot smoke and mold, which was fair enough, because the roof leaked and the carpet was always damp, and he hotboxed a joint out there every day during his lunch break, and the car ran on gas. That was what an old car should smell like. He knew if he put an air freshener in it, it would smell like gas and pot smoke and mold and a chemical approximation of a pine tree, which wouldn't really be better, just different.

He and Charles had gone out at lunch and fired up a joint and Charles had told him that he had nine brothers and sisters back in Lagos, Nigeria, and two of them had been killed by the secret police. Mitch hadn't known what to say. In a way he envied Charles for having had a life so shitty that working at Accu-mart was a slice of heaven. He wished he had stories about having come from somewhere merciless and tragic. Instead, he had stories about living with a distant father while attending public school in Queens, and by comparison those stories shrieked of insignificance. Even he found them dull, and because of this, working at Accu-mart was even duller, a mind-numbing slow torture that was turning his brain into lifeless putty. Work, cable TV, smoke a bowl, sleep. Try to hide from suffering in all its many forms and wind up envying people whose families were getting killed by the secret police.

"Are you memorizing the bar codes?" It was Bob Sutherland, again. He must have crept up behind him while he was staring at the case of air fresheners. "Because when I started, I used to do that. Memorize the stock numbers."

"Yeah," Mitch said, his heart pounding from being startled. Bob-Fucking-Sutherland needed to wear a cowbell. He was going to give Mitch a heart attack.

"I noticed a pattern," Sutherland said. "Sometimes you can tell which distributor it is just by the bar code. Back when I was a department manager, you could read me the bar digits off any piece of inventory in electronics and I could tell you what it was." Sutherland beamed with pride at the memory.

"Yeah, I've noticed patterns," Mitch said, hoping he wasn't going to have to cite one. Who the fuck studied bar codes? Isn't that why you had bar codes, so you could *not* memorize them? Could this man be any less interesting?

"Hey, Mitch, your eyes are really red. Are you OK?"

"Yeah, I'm fine," Mitch said. "Just a little tired."

"You don't have pinkeye, do you? A new hire in house-wares had pinkeye. We had to let her go."

"I don't have pinkeye," said Mitch.

Sutherland leaned in and stared into Mitch's eyes, close enough to be inhaling pot fumes. Mitch could smell Sutherland's cologne. He stifled an urge to giggle while Sutherland studied his eyes.

"You and Charles always have red eyes," he said finally. "Do you think you guys might be allergic to something back here?"

"Maybe the air fresheners," said Mitch, relieved to have an excuse provided for him. "I've been wondering about that. They've been making me . . . you know . . . stuffed up."

"Do you know anything about computers?" Sutherland asked.

Cool. This was it. He was going to get transferred to the coveted computer department, where he could earn commission and work in a clean environment, and not get oil stains and dust all over him. He could talk to the pretty secretaries who asked questions about software, instead of a bunch of gruff middle-aged grease monkeys with clogged fuel filters. All because of his allergy to air fresheners.

"Sure," Mitch said. "I know a ton about computers. I've got a Dell at home with a 200 gig—"

"Why don't you help Karl with the inventory sheets then? He's got a whole stack of them he needs to punch into the computer." Sutherland walked off, calling over his shoulder, "Charles'll take care of things around here." Sutherland stopped, stared at a display of air filters, adjusted one slightly, looked happy with himself, and turned the corner, missing Mitch giving him the finger while scratching his face.

"Hey, Karl," Mitch said. "I hear you need help with the inventory." Karl was the electronics department manager, a techno-geek who could reel off specs about hard drives and operating systems and one of the few souls at Accu-mart who seemed genuinely happy, which was part of why Mitch avoided him. Mitch also avoided him because he was deeply religious and had his own marketing business, so any conversation with Karl eventually turned to how Mitch should either go to Karl's church or buy Excel-Tone housecleaning products.

"Great, great, thanks for coming by," said Karl, as if it had been Mitch's idea. "I have a stack right here. Just punch the inventory numbers into the fields with a red asterisk."

He handed Mitch a five-inch-thick stack of inventory forms, and Mitch heard angels singing. They were for the audio-visual electronics, not the computer electronics. The stock control numbers for the forty-two-inch plasma TVs were on the top of the pile.

Karl stood up and looked at his watch. "I have to be at a meeting in about five minutes. You don't mind doing this for a few hours, do you?" He sounded genuinely concerned.

Karl went to meetings, usually with the store brass. It was a sure sign he was on his way up the company ladder. Mitch had never been invited to the store meetings, probably because he spent his free time smoking pot with the hourly employees in hiding places, rather than devoting himself to the more useful practice of memorizing stock numbers. He was cannon fodder to the top management, he knew, and probably had been since day one. He was trusted with brake pads, but not with anything valuable, except accidentally. Like today.

"Sure, dude, go ahead. It gets me away from the parts department for a little while. I've got some serious allergies to the air fresheners."

"Allergies? Oh, no. Perhaps you could transfer over to work with me . . ."

"They need me back there," Mitch said, and the unspoken words hung heavy in the air. They'd never let me transfer. They need me to do the grunt work. Karl nodded.

"It's important work back there. You know, the parts department turned the third largest net profit last quarter," Karl said cheerfully, then remembered that this was the type of information discussed at the meetings with the store brass, to which Mitch was never invited. Karl quickly looked at his watch. "Thanks again. Thanks so much."

"No problem."

Karl looked at Mitch as if he was a hopeless case. "You know, we're having a church picnic on Sunday morning. There'll be some nice girls there . . ."

Nice girls. What good were they? "I'm scheduled Sundays, but thanks."

Karl left, after thanking him again. Mitch turned back to the computer. He flipped through the inventory sheets for the plasma TVs. There were fourteen of them. He punched in twelve and slipped the last two into his pocket.

• • •

"HERE'S WHAT YOU do," Mitch said. He let out a stream of pot smoke and passed the bong to Kevin. "You pull up to the loading dock, hand them that piece of paper, and they'll put a forty-two-inch plasma TV in your truck."

Kevin looked dubious. "I'm still on parole, man. I don't know about this."

"Dude, it's no-risk. You're not really doing anything wrong. Worst comes to worst, just say I gave you the slip to pick up the TV. If you don't want to do it, just let us borrow your truck. We can't use my car, because the loading dock guys know my car." Mitch shrugged. "Doug'll do it."

Doug nodded. "I'll do it. But I'd like to have Kevin with me."

"Just keep him company," said Mitch.

Kevin still looked dubious.

"Dude, it'll be over in, like, five minutes. The only thing is, you have to park in the parking lot first and switch license plates. I'll get you a fake plate. I've got one in the basement, an old Nevada plate, like from the seventies or something. You just have to put that on the car, for the loading dock security cam. Hand 'em the paper, and you've got a seventeen-hundred-dollar TV."

"And then what?"

"Well, you keep it in the basement here for a few days. We can watch a playoff game on it next Sunday. Then I'll have to give it to my landlord."

Since adjusting the inventory sheets a few hours earlier, Mitch had developed a complex plan with his roommate, Doug. Originally they had wanted to keep the TV, but they had decided that would be too risky. Then, out of the blue, their landlord had dropped by and asked Mitch, with a wink, if he could get any "discounts" from Accu-mart, and a fence operation was born. In exchange for two months' free rent, at $500 a month, he would take the TV.

Kevin stared into the bong. "What do I get out of this?"

Doug and Mitch looked at each other. They were discussing practical issues now. It was becoming a possibility. "Two hundred," Mitch said, and Doug nodded.

"You guys get a thousand, and I only get one fifth? That's bullshit. It's my truck."

They looked at each other again and shrugged. "OK, one third. Three thirty," said Mitch.

"Three thirty-*three,*" corrected Kevin. "And thirty-three cents. Point three repeating."

"Hell," said Mitch. "You know what? You can have three thirty-*four.*"

"Three thirty-five, even," Doug said. "But you have to keep me company."

They heard Linda come home, heard footsteps in the kitchen above them. She walked down the first few basement stairs and stared at the three of them, high on the couches, suddenly quiet.

"Hi, Doug," she said, then retreated back into the kitchen.

Doug waved.

Kevin looked at Doug. "Why the hell did she say hi to *you?*"

Doug shrugged.

Mitch, who also thought it was odd, quickly turned the conversation back to the issue at hand. "OK then, we do this next Monday. I'll get you the license plate tomorrow morning."

"Let's do it Friday," Kevin said. "Then we can watch the Steelers game over the weekend."

"We can't. I dated the stock slip for Monday." Mitch was glad to hear Kevin push the date ahead, because he felt that Kevin was either reluctant or only half-listening, not as involved as he and Doug. "If you give them a stock slip dated three days ahead, they might notice."

"They'll notice that we're TV buyers from the future," Doug said into the bong, and giggled at his own joke.

Mitch felt the battle plan might degenerate into giggling and joking, so he quickly added, "We have to wait until it gets dark. Like six o'clock or so. Sound good?"

Kevin was baked, staring at his own TV, which was on but muted. He was smiling, which could have been in appreciation of Mitch's excellent plan or from seven bong hits of White Widow. Mitch was watching his expression carefully. "Shit," Kevin said, and shook his head, chuckled. "Nevada license plate. You're funny, Mitch."

• • •

ON THE WAY back to their apartment, Doug and Mitch stopped at the All Night Fillerup for cigarettes and so Doug could stare lovingly at his Mexican girl. There was a girl who worked behind the counter whom Doug obsessed about, but in a year of buying cigarettes from her he had never spoken to her. He was biding his time, he explained. Didn't want to rush things. Months ago, Mitch and Kevin had made fun of him, told him she would be married with grandchildren by the time he struck up a conversation. Kevin, who despite being married, had a better way with women than either of the other two, had even offered to talk to her for him, which had sent Doug into a panic. Mitch and Kevin had just looked at each other and shook their heads, convinced it was never going anywhere, just another one of Doug's fantasies.

"Just wait," Doug had said.

"We have waited. Are you going to do something about this or not?"

"When the time is right."

"Oh, come on."

"No, seriously. Just wait."

Mitch was getting concerned for Doug, who was showing more and more of a tendency to live in his head. After getting what he felt was an unnecessary speeding ticket a few weeks ago, Doug had talked incessantly about all the things he was going to say to the judge. He was going to put the whole traffic system on trial. If he was going to pay $150, he was going to have his say, about how speed traps were just an unfair form of taxation, how the only people who benefited were the insurance companies and the tax collectors, how working people were getting victimized by an unfair power structure which could charge whatever it wanted. One hundred fifty? Why not five thousand? He had rehearsed his speech over and over at every one of their smoke-out sessions for weeks until Mitch and Kevin were rolling their eyes. Then he had gone to court on his date and quietly paid the ticket. "I just wanted to get out of there," he had explained. "The place was, like, uh, crawling with cops."

Mitch was sitting in the driver's seat, bopping his head to Def Leppard, when Doug came back to the car. Mitch turned the radio down. "Your girl there?"

"She was there," said Doug, handing him the smokes and his change.

"You talk to her?"

"She was busy. Tonight, like, wasn't the night."

Mitch nodded. Better to say nothing. Wasn't it always? They drove home, the windows down despite the snow flurries, with "Pour Some Sugar on Me" shaking the glass and bolts of the car.

• • •

"MITCH, DO YOU know anything about computers?" Apparently, when Mitch had answered that question the previous day, he had been in stealth mode, invisible and inaudible. Sutherland's employees frequently found themselves in stealth mode when they were talking to him, the real conversation going on behind Sutherland's eyes, the employee's existence unnoticed.

"Yes. I punched in all the inventory sheets yesterday."

"You don't seem . . . to have any allergies today." Sutherland stared into his eyes.

"They usually don't kick in till after lunch." Mitch lifted a heavy case of tire bolts, placed them on a stack, and turned to face Sutherland. Why did this guy keep dropping by? Car accessories could run itself. It was almost as if Sutherland was lonely.

"I need you to contact the Webmaster," Sutherland said. "I want you to have him call me. Set up a time when we can talk."

"You mean the guy who runs our Web site?"

"No, no, no. The Webmaster. In Washington. If it was the guy who ran our Web site, I could do it."

Mitch made a face. "The Webmaster of which . . ." He trailed off, aware that he had gone into stealth mode again.

"I usually have Karl do it, but it's his day off." Sutherland walked away, clearly irritated by Mitch's inability to follow. "Use his office. I'll open it for you."

The Webmaster in Washington? What the hell did that mean? And since when did Karl have his own office? Karl was a department manager just like Mitch. Was Sutherland calling the computer office Karl's "office"? Mitch's office was an alcove in the stockroom, more of a design flaw than an actual room, and it was furnished only with two filthy crates that he and whomever he was talking to could sit on while eating snacks.

He sat down in the computer office and tried to figure out what Sutherland was talking about. Then he played FreeCell for forty-five minutes, just to get warmed up for computer work. Then he called Karl at home.

"Dude, sorry to bug you on your day off."

"No problem, Mitch. What can I do for you?" On his days off, Mitch would sleep in, wake up, smoke a bowl, maybe do laundry by dinnertime. His appearance and demeanor for the whole day was that of a bear just awakened from hibernation. Mitch imagined that Karl was sitting at a breakfast table, wearing a pressed shirt, his pretty wife serving him eggs Benedict with homemade hollandaise. The table would be laid out with fresh fruit and breads, the sun shining through a picture window.

"Sutherland just asked me to call, like, some Webmaster guy in Washington."

Karl laughed. "Yeah. He thinks the Web is like the post office. You know the way there is a postmaster general? He thinks there is a Webmaster general. A politician or something who runs the Internet. I've explained it to him like three times, but he just doesn't get it. What he really means is the Web site administrator."

Mitch laughed. "So I'll just call him?"

"Yeah. His number's in my Rolodex."

"Thanks, man."

"Have a good day. Say, we're having a sales meeting for Excel-Tone products at my house on Monday evening—"

"I've got to work, man. Thanks anyway."

"Take care."

Mitch hung up, leaned back in the chair, and folded his arms behind his head with an evil smile. Sutherland thought there was a Webmaster general in Washington. Hee-hee-hee. How amazingly stupid was this guy? He could supposedly run a multimillion dollar enterprise, but he didn't understand even the basics of the Internet. Mitch thought for a few seconds. What was the name of that guy that had worked in the one-hour photo department? Dave Rice. Dave Rice had left to finish a four-year degree and was now in law school at Georgetown, in Washington, D.C. Dave Rice had been a cool guy. Maybe he wanted to have some fun. Mitch searched for Rice's name on the Internet, found it easily, then picked up the phone.

• • •

THE PHONE WAS ringing, and Doug wondered who the hell was calling at ten to eight in the morning. The debt collectors had to wait until eight. It was a state law. Doug didn't know state capitals and hadn't read a book since high school, but he knew about regulations for debt collectors, and about pharmaceuticals, and he could answer any trivia question about rock bands from the eighties. Things that mattered.

If it was after eight, he would have let it ring, but he figured this might actually be important. Maybe the nursing home calling about his grandmother. He got out of bed, grumbling, tripping over a box of recycling Mitch had left outside his room. It was Doug's week to take out the trash. OK, Mitch, I get the fucking point. Now there were plastic soda bottles and empty milk cartons all over the floor.

"Yuh," he mumbled grumpily into the phone.

"Good morning. Did I wake you up?" He recognized Linda's voice; she sounded upbeat and alert. Was she serious? How many people who worked in restaurants would be awake at this hour?

"Yuh," he said.

"I'm sorry. You want me to let you go back to bed?"

"No," he muttered and flopped onto the couch, curling up in a fetal position. "It's OK. I'm up now. Wassup?"

"Are you working today?"

"Not till four."

"I want to take you shopping."

Doug let this sink in for a moment. He had never really been "shopping." Occasionally he went to the mall when he had specific things he wanted to buy, but it was a chore, like laundry or brushing your teeth. It wasn't an activity one looked forward to. "OK," he said.

"Really?"

Apparently, Linda had expected an argument. Hell, it was something to do. And since he had hung out with her in her kitchen, he had realized that Linda was a lot cooler than Kevin made her out to be. He certainly didn't want to get involved in their marital difficulties, but he figured he could be friends with both of them. Plus she got high, which was a big surprise to Doug, as she had never joined them in their basement smoke sessions. "Yeah," he said. "Why not?"

"I dunno. I thought guys hated shopping."

Doug shrugged, aware that the gesture wasn't visible over the phone. "I don't really even know what you mean by shopping. But I'll try it."

Linda laughed. "You don't know what I mean by shopping? We're going to buy you some clothes."

"I have clothes."

Linda laughed again. "What time do you want me to pick you up?"

"How about one . . . thirty," he added quickly, to give himself another half hour of sleep.

"I have to pick Ellie up from school at two. How about eleven?"

"Eleven?" Shit, that was like the middle of the night.

Linda heard the dismay in his voice. "OK, eleven thirty."

"Awright." Linda sounded cheerful and it occurred to Doug how different that was. He spent too much of his time around cheerless people: Mitch, Kevin, the cooks at the restaurant. There was a definite need for some kind of cheer in his life, even if it involved getting up before noon.

Unable to go back to sleep, Doug grabbed a cigarette and sat on the back porch and wondered what to do with his life. The Navaho believed that your life calling just came to you. He had seen that on the Discovery Channel. Why wouldn't his calling come to him? It sure wasn't cooking at a corporate restaurant. He had been there four years now and his wage had only gone up two dollars and at least three other guys had been promoted to kitchen manager without a thought even being given to him. "You're our best grill man," his boss always told him. "We can't afford to lose you." He could work every station on the line blindfolded, could do all the food ordering when the kitchen managers were on vacation, but the management would fight him if he ever asked for a quarter more an hour. Doug was convinced they would move him up if he cut his hair, but that wasn't going to happen.

The truth was, he didn't care that much, because he knew that the restaurant wasn't his calling. It was something else, something he couldn't put his finger on. It was around him; it was near; it was getting closer. He could feel a personal epiphany about to burst through, if he could only get some kind of a sign. The Navaho got their signs when they were thirteen. He was twenty-six. He should have had two already. Where the hell was it?

A traffic helicopter flew low overhead, its rotor beating like a bass drum, breaking the quiet of the morning. Maybe that was it. Maybe he should be . . . a chopper pilot. That would be cool. Wearing one of those helmets and talking into those mikes that extended out in front of your mouth, flying hot traffic reporter chicks around. Or maybe he'd be a personal chopper pilot for some billionaire and fly him down to the Bahamas a few times a year and stay in a hotel. Or maybe he could get a job with the Coast Guard, rescuing people who had taken their yachts out in bad weather. No, not the Coast Guard. They were always busting pot smugglers. And they drug tested. But still, being a chopper pilot was definitely something to think about.

He was going to look into it. And he was going to talk to the Mexican girl this week, and tell her he was going to chopper pilot school. He finished the cigarette and stubbed it into an ashtray, which was overflowing.

He could feel some weird psychic energy flowing up from somewhere, a rush of enthusiasm for a life he knew he should be having, and his brain began to whir, exploring his options. The restaurant had a program for employees who had been there over two years, in which they paid 50 percent of tuition. He could apply that to chopper pilot school. This was going to work out great. This was it. Things were about to change.

Chopper pilot. Of course. Why hadn't he thought of it before?

●   ●   ●

BOB SUTHERLAND WAS walking around the Accu-mart at midnight, checking the displays, adjusting the vacuum cleaners on the top shelf so they faced sideways, not straight out. People wanted to know what a vacuum cleaner's silhouette looked like, not what it looked like when it was coming at you. They bought vacuum cleaners for their clean, sleek look, not because they vacuumed floors. Why couldn't the housewares staff recognize that? Why did he always have to walk around at midnight and shift things so they looked more . . . buyable?

It exasperated Bob Sutherland that his staff always seemed to lack that sense of what made a customer want to buy. They would come in unshaven or with their hair everywhere and stand around talking in groups until they saw him coming, and then they'd scatter like mice, off to perform some menial task, which they would halt the minute he was out of sight. They liked to complain about their wages, he knew, because he could eavesdrop on them with the surveillance cameras. They didn't know that some of the cameras had audio. Rather than try to get better wages by showing some enthusiasm, they'd sit around and bitch about their hernia operations or having to work two jobs and how tired they were all the time, and they'd just shelve the vacuum cleaners any which way. If it wasn't for him always walking around, checking, adjusting, fixing, the whole place would just go to hell in a few hours.

Sighing heavily, he retired to his office and slumped in his Healthy-Back office chair, watching the laser printer quietly pump out the daily sales reports. He flipped back through his caller ID and noticed a call from Washington, D.C. His brow wrinkled. Who could that be? He picked up the receiver and checked his messages.

"Mr. Sutherland, this is Ken Spargenbergerluger, the Webmaster General, here in Washington, D.C. We just wanted to let you know that if you have any problems with your Web site, you should contact your own Web administrator, not us. Please tell that to your employees. OK, dork?"

Click.

Sutherland's heart was pounding. Had a government official just called him a dork? His hand shaking, he hung up the phone. Then he picked it up again, then put it back down. He took a few deep breaths. Think, he told himself. This might not be as serious as it first seemed. He listened to the message again, and he noticed that the voice sounded distantly familiar. He couldn't place it, but he had the distinct feeling that perhaps, just maybe, one of his typical miserable employees might have had something to do with this.

He took the employee phone list out of the drawer and studied it. When he got to the bottom of this, he told himself, there was going to be hell to pay.

3

CHaPTeR

VERY CAREFULLY, KEVIN filled the eyedropper with bleach and slipped it into his right front pocket so that the nozzle pointed out through a tiny hole he had cut. Now, with a little bit of pressure applied on his thigh, he could spray bleach out with his urine stream, right into the cup he was expected to piss into. A few drops of bleach would ruin any chance of a positive result on the drug test, but you had to be careful not to spray in too much or the urine would reek of bleach. To insure against that, he had eaten asparagus for the last two days, so the urine would definitely have some kind of weird odor, and the addition of bleach would just make the smell even odder. The more factors you could throw in, the better. Hopefully, the lab people wouldn't know what to make of it. There goes Kevin, the guy with the weirdest smelling piss you ever encountered. Does he smoke pot? Hard to say.

For the first six months after he had been released from jail, Kevin had actually been pot-free, but then resentment rather than craving had taken over. Who were these people to tell him what he could and couldn't do when he was alone and off of work? They had taken nearly all his money and locked him up for the whole summer, for indoor gardening. Why wasn't that enough? Five grand for the lawyer, $2,500 for fines, $600 for court counseling. He'd even had to pay administrative fees for getting released from prison. The discharge paperwork had cost him $120, which must have meant it was either typed up by someone with a doctorate in office work, or it had been printed with solid-gold toner. But who would say no to that expense if it was all that stood between you and freedom? While paying his debt to society, he had managed to accumulate a significant debt to his credit card company.

It was, he figured, all about money. The counseling for which he paid the $600 was group therapy, in which he had been made to sit in a room with three junkies and a bored psychologist, listening to the junkies' tales of child abuse. Whenever it was his turn to speak, Kevin would offer, "I just got busted for growing pot in my basement. I've never been abused." Until, of course, the local police got their hands on him, but a mention of that would have resulted in more counseling—and more fees.

Kevin had realized fairly quickly that a game needed to be played. He didn't just need to pay fines and serve time;

he needed to be grateful for their help. At the end of each session, he would thank the psychologist profusely, perhaps even ask him for advice that he didn't want. Sure enough, the psychologist pronounced him cured after only five sessions, instead of the ten the judge had assigned, though, of course, half the money was not returned.

Kevin screwed the cap back on the bleach bottle and got out of his car, dropped some quarters into the parking meter, and went into the municipal court building. Through the metal detector, past the row of young black men in orange jumpsuits chained to a bench, up the cinder block–motif stairwell, through the heavy steel door marked PAROLE AND PROBATION. The office staff was behind a window lined with chicken wire, in case any of the parolees got rowdy, though the atmosphere was never one of typical government chaos. It was subdued, polite, and quiet. These were people who had gotten out and weren't going to jeopardize their freedom with unsightly displays of emotion before a court clerk.

Aware of the intimidation factor, the clerks were brutal. They never made eye contact with the parolees and barked orders at them through the wired glass. A heavyset, middle-aged woman with glasses and stiff black hair didn't even look up at Kevin as she snapped, "Name?"

"Kevin Gurdy. I'm here to see—"

"Have a seat."

Kevin sat down on the black vinyl bench with two young

black men, who were staring straight ahead. After a moment, the woman lifted her head and said, "Jackson."

Kevin and the two men looked at each other.

"Jackson," she repeated, her voice rising with irritation at this delay. "Who's Jackson?"

"I think he went out to go look for a water fountain," one of the men said.

"Well, go get him. If he isn't here in thirty seconds, I'm marking him down as absent."

The man got up and went out into the hall to look for Jackson, returning with him inside a minute. Jackson, another young black man, who had clearly just been to the restroom, was still buckling his pants.

"Mr. Jackson," she hissed. "'Have a seat' means have a seat. It doesn't mean go wandering around the court-house."

"I just had to—"

"Officer Deakins is ready for you," she interrupted, her voice high with anger, as she shoved a piece of paper through a slot in the chicken-wire window. She turned her back to Jackson as he retrieved the paper, then buzzed the door leading into the back office, which Jackson opened.

"Hunt?" she snapped.

Again no one responded. "All right," she said, and began to fill out paperwork, dooming Mr. Hunt to a return to jail.

"Gurdy?"

Kevin stood up quickly, and she looked at him for the

first time, her attitude almost imperceptibly changing as she noticed that he was white. In his months of coming to parole appointments, Kevin had detected a definite pattern of racism from the office staff. The white women were often slightly less horrible to the white parolees. The black women were equally horrible to everyone, except for the younger ones, who were sometimes civil to the young black men. They would grow out of it.

"Yes, that's me," said Kevin. The woman shoved a slip of paper under the glass and buzzed the door.

"Officer Poacher," she said, as if Kevin didn't know. He walked back through the parole office, past cubicle after cubicle of young black men sitting in rickety institutional chairs, explaining their lives to bureaucrats who were sitting, bored, behind tiny desks. Corrections Officer Poacher was one of the senior parole officers, and he had an actual office all the way in the back, a cramped mess of scattered paperwork and half-open file cabinets, forms spilling out of every drawer.

"Have a seat, Gurdy," Poacher said when he saw Kevin. He turned to a file cabinet behind him and pulled out Kevin's file. "How've you been?"

"Fine," Kevin said. He wondered if he was supposed to ask the question back, as one would do in any other social situation, or if it was an official question to determine Kevin's state of mind. One had to be very careful what one said in a parole interview. To give a hint of any negativity might start the officer asking questions. If Kevin sighed and said, "OK, I guess," Poacher would start digging around about why life wasn't perfect and whether this meant that Kevin was going to return to his life of crime because of the stress. In a parole interview, you couldn't have problems. As far as Poacher was concerned, Kevin's marriage was wonderful, his dog walking business was about to get him on the cover of *Money* magazine, and the thought of growing or smoking marijuana was so repulsive as to make him want to vomit.

"How're things at home?" Poacher asked, without looking up from the file.

"Great, great," said Kevin, nodding, trying to force a smile. "My daughter just got picked for the lead in the school play." Kevin had made that up on the spot, because he had learned that it was always good to mention Ellie. Sometimes it triggered Poacher to talk about his son, who was fourteen, and then the interview became an unfocused mess of two parents babbling about their kids for a half hour, which was what Kevin wanted. Stay away from topics like drugs, crime, and prison, have a court-mandated chat, and get the hell out of there.

"Really?" said Poacher, so brusquely that Kevin knew it wasn't going to work this time. Actually, it hadn't worked in over a year. Poacher had become more reluctant to discuss his son as time had passed, and Kevin had pieced together that Poacher was going through a bitter divorce and may have lost custody. In fact, Poacher's general aura had deteriorated significantly since Kevin had been assigned to him.

Poacher flipped the file shut. "You staying off drugs?" he asked.

Kevin nodded. "Yes, absolutely."

"Honestly?" Poacher stared into Kevin's eyes, and it unnerved him. Did the man know something? Had he been peering through Kevin's basement window? Was this the time to confess or to act unsure? Gut instinct told him to lie.

"Absolutely," said Kevin. "No drugs." He was going to add something else, but then remembered that he had recently heard on the Discovery Channel that interrogators often noticed people were lying because they overexplained. Brief answers were best. There was a silence between them, during which Kevin repeatedly stifled the urge to do just that—start babbling and overexplaining. The Discovery Channel knew its shit.

Poacher reached in a drawer, and Kevin felt certain he was going to produce one of the little clear plastic pee cups for the drug test, but instead he pulled out a form.

"I'm a busy man," Poacher said. "I've got fifty-six parolees assigned just to me."

Kevin crossed his legs, a gesture of comfort and relief at the conversation going off on this tangent.

And then it happened.

The rubber bubble at the top of the eyedropper in his

pocket compressed as a result of the action, squirting bleach through the hole in Kevin's pocket and all over his balls.

Kevin knew what had happened right away. He felt the liquid trickling through his pubic hairs, like little insects running around down there. He kept his expression frozen and remained still. For the first second, the liquid was cool. Then it began to feel warm.

"So what I'm going to do," Poacher said, "is wrap up your parole. You seem like a good guy, a family man. I don't really see a reason to keep making you come back in here for your monthly visits. You've come up clean every time we've tested you and . . ."

Poacher kept talking. The warmth had turned to heat, then burning. It felt like someone was holding a lit cigarette to his nut sack. Kevin tried to beam with glee at what Poacher was saying, but instead felt his face freeze in a death grimace as sweat broke out on his forehead. Then the powerful odor of bleach hit him. He and Poacher were only a few feet apart, and Kevin was sure Poacher was about to sniff the air and wonder what the smell was.

Oh god, MY NUTS ARE ON FIRE. Kevin gritted his teeth. Finally, he couldn't take it anymore, and he grabbed his balls and tried to shift them around, his eyes watering as a great rush of air came out of him, his mouth wide open as if he were singing a silent opera.

It was amazing. Poacher didn't even seem to notice. He was still babbling about what a stand-up guy Kevin was and how it was a waste of resources to keep making him come in, how he had obviously learned his lesson. Kevin tried nodding in agreement. How could he end this? Could he claim a bout of diarrhea and run to the bathroom? Mercifully, the phone rang. As Poacher answered it, Kevin quickly signaled that he was going to the restroom, and Poacher nodded.

Reeking of bleach and grunting in pain, Kevin tried not to run past the desk staff, tried not to slam the buzzing metal door behind, doing his best to act like a guy who had decided to hit the men's room on his way out. Once out in the corridor, he broke into a full sprint, and once inside the men's room he ran to a sink, unzipped his jeans, and splashed handfuls of water from the running faucet over his burning nuts.

Relief. With each handful of water, the pain lessened. He became conscious of his surroundings again, suddenly aware that his jeans were now absolutely soaked, as were his shoes and socks. He didn't care. He would just have to tell Poacher he had slipped and fell, or something. The pain had stopped.

Then he became aware of someone else in the men's room, and looked up to see a young black man, maybe eighteen, at the next sink, staring at him.

The kid turned and took a paper towel out of the dispenser, and without looking back at Kevin, he said, "Man, you all fucked up."

• • •

"HOW WAS YOUR parole visit?" asked Linda when he returned home. Sometimes Kevin thought she was hopeful that he would be carted off back to jail, and the house would be all hers again. There had been so many changes in the decorating scheme when he had returned from his ninety-day stint that he was unsure if he had been welcome back in his own home. Linda was sitting at her desk and going over bills, a pose in which Kevin had learned conversation was unwelcome unless she initiated it, and even then it should be kept brief.

"Fine. I don't have to go back. I'm cured." He kicked off his shoes, pulled off his soaked jeans and underwear, and took a towel from the hall closet. Standing naked from the waist down, he began toweling himself vigorously, careful not to rub his raw, burned scrotum.

"What happened to you?" Linda asked. The shock in her voice made Kevin look down and he noticed that his pubic hair had turned white.

"Oh Christ," he mumbled. He stepped into the bathroom and turned on the shower.

Linda burst out laughing. It was a sound he hadn't heard in a long time. He set the water to cold and stood under the stream, shivering at first. Then the coolness of the water began to soothe his steaming crotch, and he gasped in relief.

Linda banged on the door, still laughing. "What the hell is going on with you? Why are you all white?"

"I'll be out in a minute," he yelled, irritated at the interruption.

There was silence. Ten minutes later, when Kevin emerged from the bathroom, Linda was back at her desk, looking at the bills. He felt better now, physically and mentally, and he watched her as she wrote a check, hoping she was still as lighthearted as she had been a few moments earlier. It had been a long time since he had seen her amused. It had been a long time since he had been free from the court system, too, and he felt like it would be a good day to go out and celebrate.

"I'm free," he said to her back. "They let me off parole today."

"Yeah, I heard you," Linda said, not looking up. "Am I supposed to say congratulations?"

"Shit," he said, annoyed. "I thought maybe we could go out and celebrate tonight, but I guess not."

"Celebrate?" She sounded incredulous.

"Yeah, celebrate. But fuck it."

"Celebrate." She shook her head in awe and laughed coarsely, not happily, the way she had been laughing earlier. "What should we tell the waiter when he asks what we're celebrating?"

"Is that what bothers you? How it looks to the waiter?"

"Where would we even get a sitter this late? And we

can't afford to go out, not this month. Have you looked at the bills lately? Do you even live on the same planet I'm on?" She turned back to the paperwork dismissively.

Kevin put on clean underwear and some loose-fitting shorts, in a hurry to leave. He had thought from her reaction to his bleaching that she might be in a lighter mood today, that he could share a moment with her. Clearly, it wasn't the case, and now he just wanted to get away as fast as possible. He had a round of dogs to walk at four thirty, and even though it was barely three o' clock, he grabbed his keys and headed for the stairs.

"I'm not the one who told you to grow pot in the basement, Kevin," she called after him. Kevin wasn't able to slam the door before she finished the sentence.

• • •

"BOB SUTHERLAND WANTS to see you in his office," said Melissa, the office manager. She sounded mad, and Mitch knew right away he was in trouble. It was odd, the way secretaries adopted their boss's anger as if it were their own. What the fuck had he done now? Mislabeled a display of lug nuts, perhaps? Permitted Charles to work seven minutes of overtime? Melissa was gone before he could even acknowledge her and he figured it was bad. Oh, shit, maybe they had found the missing invoices for the high-def TVs.

"Ooooh, that no sound good," said Charles.

Mitch stood up and stretched. He and Charles had just

finished an entire load of inventory. They had lifted, sorted, and stacked a tractor trailer's worth of Accu-mart's crap, and Mitch was in the mood for a break, not an interrogation. He sighed and handed Charles the clipboard.

"I might not see you again," he said, suddenly aware that being fired was a possibility. He waved a hand at the dirty, oil-stained warehouse with candy and potato chip wrappers scattered across the vast floor. "Maybe tomorrow, all this will be yours."

Charles looked concerned. "Why? What you do, man?"

"I didn't do anything," Mitch said, practicing his excuse. "I might have made some inventory mistakes."

Charles said nothing and Mitch realized he would have to do better. Inventory mistakes? Didn't sound right; too political, too guilty. It was something a congressman would have come up with. I have no idea what happened to those invoices . . . I never saw them. Better. That would be his lie, and he would stick to it, then throw the invoices out when he got home and bag the whole stupid TV-stealing idea, and maybe this thing would blow over.

Melissa was in Bob Sutherland's office when Mitch got there, with a tape recorder and a microphone, which Mitch found odd. She was staring right into the microphone, not making eye contact with Mitch. Sutherland was reading a file, pretending not to notice Mitch had entered the room. This was not going to be a happy-smiley type of meeting.

Melissa, a stiff-haired and efficient woman in her fifties

who in the past had bonded with Mitch over their only earthly connection, a nicotine addiction, and who was now pretending not to know him, turned to Bob and said, "OK, it's ready." She hit a button on the tape recorder.

"You're being taped," said Bob Sutherland.

"I'm being taped?"

Mitch turned to close the door, and Sutherland said, "No, leave it open." Mitch saw rage and hurt and offense in his face and put on the mystified expression which he had decided would be his best defense. That and, of course, continually repeating that he was not good with detail-oriented tasks and he maybe might have made a mistake.

"You're a real piece of work aren't you, Mitch?" Sutherland said.

How did one answer that? Neither denial nor admission really moved things along. Mitch just stared.

"Can you explain this?" Sutherland asked. He handed Mitch a sheet of paper with thousands of tiny numbers written on it. About halfway down, one ten-digit number was highlighted, and Mitch immediately recognized it as the telephone number of Dave Rice, the guy he had called about pretending to be the Webmaster general. He tried to piece together how Sutherland had started with this and somehow wound up with knowledge of the stolen TV invoices. How did *this* incriminate him? Best to just act ignorant.

"What is it? It looks like a sheet with phone numbers on it."

"Quit playing around, Mitch," Sutherland snapped. "You know what it is." Sutherland leaned back in his chair, and Mitch noticed Melissa was staring at him with what appeared to be hate. He smiled at her and her expression did not change. He might still be able to save his job if he gave the right answers.

"There's a number highlighted," Mitch said, trying to sound helpful. His brain was firing in every direction, trying to figure how Sutherland, the world's stupidest man, had been able to find the missing invoices from Mitch's conversation with Dave Rice. What was going on?

"Why don't you tell me about that?"

"About this number?" Mitch stalled.

"Yes. About that number." Sutherland leaned farther back and glared at Mitch malevolently. It was intimidating, all the hate in the room. "About how that number got called from Karl's office, on his day off."

Sutherland was enraged but he was also enjoying himself. Was a demotion coming? Could Mitch possibly be demoted any lower? Was there a cleaning closet he could be made to work out of or a hidden department of the Accu-mart more dirty and mind-numbing than auto accessories to manage?

"I . . . think it's the number of a friend of mine," Mitch said and for a second he imagined that they might just be mad because it was a long distance phone call, and he could offer to pay for it, and the matter would be behind them. Then he imagined something else: that Dave Rice had called and pretended to be the Webmaster general, as they had agreed he would and Sutherland had not been amused. Other more severe scenarios presented themselves: Dave Rice using the word *asshole,* as he had been prone to do when he'd worked at Accu-mart; Dave Rice telling Sutherland he was stupid. Also prone to that. Now that Mitch thought about it, having Dave Rice play a joke on Sutherland might not have been the most excellent idea.

"So this number is the number of a friend of yours?"

"Uh . . . yeah."

Mitch was aware of a person in the hall outside the opened door; his main thought was embarrassment that they would overhear this conversation. He had an impulse to get up and close the door but when he turned his head to look, he saw it was one of the store security guys. It struck him that Sutherland had arranged to have a store security guard outside the door to escort him off the property after their "discussion," which gave Mitch the sudden confidence of a man with nothing to lose.

"Mitch," Sutherland began, toying with him, Mitch now knew. "We've put a lot of time and energy into developing you—"

"You're the stupidest fucking douche bag I've ever worked for," said Mitch quickly, aware that his time was running out. He said it pleasantly but Sutherland was on his feet in a flash as if he had been expecting it, his face flushed. "Jesus Christ, Webmaster general? Seriously, are you retarded?" This last sentence was lost under the high-volume screeching of Sutherland screaming at Mitch to get out, which drew an instant response from the security guard, who rushed into the office as if Mitch were wielding a gun. The security guy was about a hundred pounds overweight and in his midfifties, and the excitement of the moment had him red in the face.

Mitch looked up at him. "What are you going to do, have a heart attack and fall on me?"

"Let's go, NOW," the security guy said in his roughest voice. Mitch had never had a problem with the guy, who was, Mitch suspected, borderline retarded and spent most of his time in the electronics department watching TV. He didn't want his last act as an Accu-mart employee to be an assault on a man who was most likely handicapped, so he rose gracefully and slowly, careful not to show any signs of hostility. Maybe the security guy had overheard his retard comment to Sutherland and had taken it personally, or maybe he was trying to impress Sutherland and Melissa with his brute efficiency, because he grabbed Mitch's shoulder unnecessarily and pushed him toward the door.

"Easy, you fucker," Mitch snapped.

"GET HIM OUT OF HERE!" bellowed Sutherland.

Customers and store employees were now being drawn to the scene and when Mitch walked out of the office, everyone was looking at him. Denise, his pretty high school hire, who had come in to pick up her paycheck, stared at him, shocked. Despite the situation, a huge grin broke out on his face. He turned back to show it to Sutherland.

"See ya," he said pleasantly.

The security guard pushed him in the back, and Mitch turned to him. "If you touch me again . . ." he said, the grin disappearing as he felt a surge of raw fury and the man backed off. Now that they were outside the room, without anyone to impress, the guard was meek again.

"You have to leave," he pleaded, red-faced and sweating.

"I'm leaving."

And he did. When the doors opened in front of him and a wave of cold air enveloped him, it was the refreshing air of freedom.

"Thank you for shopping at Accu-mart," said the automatic recording.

"Go fuck yourself," said Mitch, and he stared with loathing at the small speaker over the door. A middle-aged woman, who had clearly heard him cursing at the speaker, stared at him with disapproval as she walked into the store.

"Thank you for shopping at Accu-mart," the speaker said pleasantly.

"Eat shit and die," Mitch said to the speaker

Another woman entered.

"Thank you for shopping at Accu-mart."

Mitch turned and walked to his car.

4
CHAPTER

"HOW COME YOU don't have a girlfriend?" Linda asked. "You're such a nice guy."

Doug wasn't sure he was comfortable with the question. They were driving home after a shopping trip to the mall, during which Linda had insisted he buy a shirt that he knew he would never wear despite her enthusiasm about it being "so in-style." It was a dark green, striped monstrosity that Doug thought made him look like either an attention-seeking hipster or a Hispanic drug dealer, neither of which was a look he was going for. In fact, in his clothing choices, he wasn't going for anything except affordable, which this wasn't. He had laid out forty-two dollars for the shirt, mostly because he hadn't wanted to hurt Linda's feelings, but also because she had hinted, obtusely, that it would increase his chances of becoming sexually active again. But at $9.50 an hour, which is what he made at the restaurant, he calculated that, with taxes, he would have to pick up five extra hours this week to compensate for the damned thing, which would have to be on Sunday morning, the brunch shift, the only shift any of the other line cooks would willingly surrender. So on their ride back home, he had been secretly fuming that because of their little shopping trip he was now going to have to work Sunday morning, and then Linda, whom he had only recently decided was a decent human being, was suddenly asking him a personal question that he didn't want to answer, or think about.

"Uh . . . dunno," he said.

Linda was regarding him with amusement. "Is there anyone you like?"

Doug was staring out the window, watching the town go by. On days like this, wintry and wet, Wilton looked dirty and the snow that everyone said looked so beautiful when it was falling had been shoveled into exhaust-blackened piles at the edge of every parking lot. All the supposedly beautiful snow ever did was showcase all the environmental damage caused by everyday events like driving, and the cold and moisture made the diesel fumes from buses and trucks hang heavy in the air, giving Doug the feeling that the town wasn't dying as much as it was being killed.

"I don't want to date anyone here," he said.

"In Wilton?"

"Yeah."

"Why not?"

Doug grunted and pointed out the window as if to say, Look at this. Don't you want to escape? Linda just laughed, seeing it as an attempt to change the topic, and asked again.

"I've been thinking about moving out West," Doug said finally.

"I thought you were going to be a chopper pilot."

"Yeah. Out West."

Linda rolled her eyes. "You need a girlfriend."

"Why?" The conversation was making Doug defensive and he was starting to see why Kevin was always complaining that Linda was a nag. She seemed to have a need to constantly improve everyone around her.

"So she can get your shit together."

"My shit is together."

Linda laughed again and Doug smiled. He figured that she had improve-yourself conversations with Kevin all the time, that she did it instinctively, and it was nice for her to have one with nothing at stake. It was like a cat practicing its predatory skills by playing with a toy.

"What about that girl at the convenience store?"

"Awww, man. Kevin has a big mouth."

"What? He shouldn't have told me about that?"

Doug grunted.

"Are you blushing?"

"No."

She regarded Doug cheerfully for a second as she pulled

onto his street. "I think you should go into the convenience store and ask her out. Wearing that shirt."

Doug was playing with the door handle, indicating a desire to escape the vehicle. "I gotta go to work," he said.

Linda pulled up outside his apartment and, to Doug's surprise, shut the engine off, giving him the impression he was supposed to ask her to come in. He didn't think it would be a good idea as Mitch's car was in the driveway and Mitch never had a good thing to say about Linda, and, besides, he had to be at work in an hour.

"Mitch is home," Doug said, hoping she would get the hint.

"Yeah, I know." Linda was looking at him again, more intensely than he liked, the fact that he found her pretty all of a sudden just adding to his discomfiture. He had noticed that at the mall the salespeople they had spoken to had considered them a couple, and he had realized that he missed that feeling, the feeling of being seen as part of a unit. How long had it been since he'd had a girlfriend? Coming up on two years now, he thought. His last girl-friend had been a waitress at the restaurant, a seemingly shy hippie girl who had inexplicably turned into an obses-sive and domineering motormouthed bitch after just a few months, and her subsequent decision to move to New York City and not invite him to come had sent him into a black hole of emotional devastation which had lasted for over a year. Even thinking about her now, or hearing her name,

Annalisa, sent him into a funk. Mitch, noticing this, had eventually dubbed her The One We Don't Speak Of. It was an attempt at a joke, but Doug found the terminology strangely helpful, as if it was the actual mention of her name which caused pain.

"Honestly, I never really liked The One We Don't Speak Of," Mitch had offered one day while they were getting high in a field outside Wilton, looking at the smokestacks of the metal-refinishing plant belching soot into the sky.

"Her name's Annalisa," Doug had said, and knew that it was over, that he might still care but that he had survived because saying the name didn't cause a stab of misery anymore. The misery had been experienced and it had left. There was no sense of victory, just relief. Not the pure type of relief that causes happiness but the type of relief you might feel if you had driven off the road, crashed through a guardrail, plummeted into a ravine full of alligators, and then realized that, physically, you were OK. You still had problems, but things could be worse.

And here was Linda, suggesting he plummet back down into the ravine.

"I have to pick up Ellie," Linda said, her voice suddenly heavy. Doug thought she was sad, that she wanted to say something else, and he was going to ask her if she was OK but then she added, "I want you to promise me something."

"OK."

"Promise me you'll wear that shirt. Just once."

Doug was strangely touched by the request. She must have known he hadn't intended to.

"OK," he said. "I promise."

"Promise me you'll put it on and go ask out that girl at the convenience store."

"Awww, fuck." He looked at her and laughed, then noticed she was about to cry, and he didn't have any idea why. "OK, OK," he said. "I swear."

She gave him a sad smile. "Call me," she said.

"OK."

"No, really."

"I will." He had no idea why she wanted to spend time with him but she seemed so serious about it that it made Doug feel cheerful by contrast. He wanted to make a joke to lighten the mood but nothing funny came to mind.

"I have to go pick up Ellie," she repeated suddenly.

"Oh . . . OK." She'd seemed so needy a second ago and now she was throwing him out of the car. He stepped onto the sidewalk. "I'll call you."

"OK," she said, as if it was his idea. She started the car again, looking out her window into the street to check if it was safe to pull back out into the street. "Bye," she said as he shut the door and she peeled off.

Doug watched her car fly down the street.

• • •

"WHY DON'T YOU come work with me?" Kevin asked as he packed the bong. They were sitting in Doug and Mitch's living room. Night was falling and Mitch was lying on the couch with his shoes off, staring at the ceiling. Doug had just left for work. He had ignored Kevin when he had come over, which both Mitch and Kevin had found strange.

For Mitch, the energy from the emotional turmoil of being fired had worn off and had been replaced by a vague sense of relief that he would never have to look at Bob Sutherland again. Then it had been replaced by a fear that he wouldn't be able to come up with rent or money for the bills or gas or car insurance, that the few things he had were about to be taken away. Between bouts of relief at not having to get up and go to work the next morning, he was envisioning himself homeless, begging for change, producing a rollercoaster of emotion that he figured only a good blast of kind bud smoke could alleviate.

"Walking dogs?"

"Yeah, man. I need help. If I had help, I could expand the business. Linda's always all over my ass to expand the business."

Mitch thought about walking dogs for a living. He liked dogs. He liked Kevin. He sat up. "OK, I'm in."

Kevin looked at him quizzically. "You thought this through in two seconds?"

Mitch shrugged. "Yeah. What's to think about?"

"Well, for starters, it's like the mail. Rain or shine or snow or hundred-degree heat. No calling out. You call out, the dog'll piss and shit all over the floor and the people won't want you back."

"I don't call out. I never called out at Fuckyoumart."

"All right then. Why don't you come walk a few dogs with me tomorrow morning at seven."

"Dude, I just got fired. Gimme a day off to relax."

"Pussy," said Kevin. "You want to walk dogs or not?"

"Damn, you'd think a guy who just got fired might get to sleep in one fucking day."

Kevin laughed and drew a big, gurgling hit out of the bong. "All right, man," he said, eyes suddenly red and heavy, his speech slowed, a permagrin stuck to his face as he handed Mitch the bong. "We'll give you a day off. Seven thirty Thursday."

• • •

THURSDAY MORNING, KEVIN took Mitch around to each house he would be assigned, introducing him to the dog and giving him the instructions for walking and feeding and tips about the dog's behavior. Mitch committed it all to memory: Don't let the immaculately groomed Shih Tzu in Gatesville out through the kitchen door or he'll crap on a $10,000 rug. Make sure Hans the dachshund get his Cosequin tablets. Don't play with Rex the Rottweiler, because they're trying to train him to be more obedient. Kevin had prepared papers with each dog's name, address, and instructions, showing an instinct for organization Mitch would never have suspected he possessed.

When they got to the house with Jeffrey the pit bull, Kevin said, "This guy's a jerk. He leaves his dog outside in all kinds of weather, and I don't think he feeds him regularly." Kevin opened the gate, and Jeffrey came bounding up to him, then noticed Mitch and stopped short. Mitch looked at the dog's powerful build and massive head, an evolutionary development that had only one purpose—to crush bone. He felt a strong urge to step back behind the gate and slam it shut, but he stood his ground and was rewarded immediately with a tail-wagging frenzy.

"He likes you," Kevin said.

Mitch wondered what criteria the dog had used to come to that decision. It was, he thought, a system of evaluation completely different from Bob Sutherland's, who was always looking to find fault, always studying you as if to figure out your angle. This dog just saw him with Kevin and that was it. He had passed the interview. Oh, you know Kevin? Great, you're in the club.

They walked Jeffrey, then went inside the house to get him a bowl of food. The house was one of those old, stone mansions with a kitchen the size of Mitch's apartment. Mitch walked around the kitchen, admiring the granite counters, the butcher-block island, and the copper-finished pots hanging from the racks above it. So this is what a rich person's house looks like, he thought.

"Dude, are you listening?" asked Kevin.

"Yeah. Something about water."

"Dude, you have to take this seriously. You have to fill his water bowl before you go and he keeps the food in this closet here."

"I'm taking it seriously," said Mitch, and he was. Then he stepped on the lever of the garbage can to pop the lid, meaning to throw a used Kleenex away, and noticed a small piece of paper sitting atop the pile of trash. Kevin continued talking as Mitch extracted the paper from the pile and held it up, still dripping what looked like orange juice.

"What the hell are you doing?" Kevin asked.

"Dude, do you know what this is?"

Kevin came over and peered at it. "It's a piece of paper with some letters and numbers on it. And it's not yours. Could you stop going through this guy's trash and listen to me for a second?"

"36-L-18-R-22-L-9-R-5," Mitch recited. "This isn't just letters and numbers. It's a safe combination."

Kevin stopped walking around the kitchen filling the dog's bowls. "It's a what?"

"A safe combination. Does this guy have a safe?"

"Shit, I don't know. I've never been anywhere in the house except the kitchen." Kevin walked over and looked at the paper. "OK, even if this is a safe combination, so what? It doesn't concern us." He tossed the slip of paper back in the trash can.

Mitch immediately picked it back up and put it in his pocket. Kevin was staring at him.

"What?" Mitch asked.

"Dude, do me a favor, OK? Don't go wandering around this guy's house looking for his safe."

"I promise not to."

"Really?"

"This week."

"Dammit, look—"

"Kevin, man, listen. Why do you think this was in the garbage? Huh? Answer me that."

"I don't know. What difference does it make? I've been doing this shit for a year and I don't usually go through my client's garbage."

"'Client'? What are you, a lawyer?"

"That's what I call them. They're my clients."

Mitch sighed. "Anyway, I figure it was in the garbage because he just had the safe installed. Has there been anyone working in the house in the last couple of days?"

Kevin thought for a second. "There was a locksmith here yesterday. He was doing some work back there in the den, or the living room, or whatever it is." Kevin pointed to one of the opulently decorated, paneled rooms off the kitchen.

Mitch nodded. "What do you suppose he was doing back there?" There was silence for a second while Kevin looked concerned, then curious, then concerned again. "Let's at least have a look."

Kevin finished filling Jeffrey's bowl. "Do what you want," he said, resigned. "But take your shoes off."

Mitch took his shoes off and stepped over the dog gate into the den. There was a huge cherrywood desk in front of a brick fireplace, and Mitch was struck by the grandeur of the room. Persian rug, leather bound books on inlaid shelves—rich people had some really nice shit. He wondered if they ever appreciated it or if it was just meant to impress, or intimidate, the dog walkers, the maids, the locksmiths, and the plumbers. Perhaps spending gobs of money on opulent rubbish was a way of giving a straight-up middle finger to all the people like him who couldn't afford things like wrought-iron fireplace pokers and Waterford crystal. He picked up the fireplace poker and looked at it. Probably cost hundreds, he thought. No Accu-mart crap in this house.

Most of all, though, he noticed the smell of freshly cut wood, and there were some splotches of sawdust to the right of the Persian rug. Someone had cut a wall stud right near there. He looked at the walls and saw no marks. Then he touched the gilded frame of a painting and it swung outward. He laughed. Could this shit be any more James Bond?

He was looking at the pristine stainless-steel knob of a safe. Behind him, he saw Kevin standing in the doorway of the den in his stockinged feet.

"You're a menace," Kevin said, but Mitch heard grudging respect in his voice.

Mitch gently pushed the painting back against the wall, aware that his heart was pounding. "Let's go walk some more dogs," he said.

• • •

THEY WERE IN line behind two other cars at the Accumart loading dock, and Doug was getting nervous.

"Dude, I don't think this is a good idea," he said. Kevin knew Doug thought that because he had been repeating it like a mantra since they had switched the license plate on the truck an hour earlier. The nonstop doubtful mumbling had only made Kevin want to bring him along even more, both because of a sadistic impulse to make Doug face his fears and a genuine desire not to steal the TV alone.

"Good idea or not, man, we're doing it, OK? We're in line."

"It's not too late to just pull out of the line and go back," Doug said.

Kevin put the pickup in park. "Look," he said, holding the invoice up in Doug's face. "In two minutes, I'm going to hand this piece of paper to the guy on the loading dock, and we're going to get a TV. And when I do it, the whole thing is gonna go a lot easier if the guy sitting next to me in the passenger seat isn't covered in sweat and freaking out. OK?"

"OK," said Doug, softly.

"Just be cool."

"OK, I'm cool." He seemed cool for a second, then he said, "But you're on parole."

"What the fuck are you bringing that up for? Besides, I'm not on parole anymore. I got released on Wednesday." The loading dock workers waved the next car up, so that Kevin and Doug were next.

"Hey, congratulations, man. That's cool."

"Thank you. That's more than Linda had to say about it."

"What do you mean?"

"Bitch couldn't even congratulate me, you know?"

Doug felt a flush of anger at hearing Linda called a bitch but stopped himself from saying something in her defense. For reasons that were not available to him, he didn't want Kevin to know he and Linda had gone to the mall the other day, or that they had ever even spoken without Kevin around.

"Mitch congratulated me," Kevin said.

"Mitch is crazy," said Doug, in an effort to change the topic by bringing it to a subject they agreed upon.

"Damn, man, we were at one of my clients' houses the other day, and—"

"Client?"

"Yeah, that's what I call them. The people whose dogs I walk. Anyway, Mitch wanted to break into this guy's safe."

"Mitch can crack safes?"

"No, dumbass, Mitch can't crack safes. He found the

friggin' combination in the trash can. The guy had just had the safe installed and he was memorizing the combination. You believe that shit?"

Doug laughed, glad to have his mind taken off what they were doing. "It's probably less risky than this," he said cheerfully, which was, of course, the wrong thing to say, as it reminded them they were in line to steal an $1,800 television.

It was quiet in the car. And it was their turn. The car in front of them drove off and the loading dock workers waved Mitch and Doug forward.

"Keep cool," said Kevin, not looking at Doug. He rolled down the window and pulled up next to a well-built man in sunglasses and an Accu-mart T-shirt.

"Hi," he said, handing the man the invoice.

"Hey. Thanks." The man took the invoice and went up on the dock and disappeared from view.

"Shit, where'd he go?" asked Doug.

"Settle down."

"I'm glad we've got that fake license plate on," said Doug.

They were silent for a few seconds as they listened to the loading dock workers call out to each other. Then one called, "Forty-two-inch flat screen. Got it."

Kevin and Doug looked at each other. "That's us," Kevin said.

Two huge doors burst open and a man wheeled a giant white box up to the edge of the loading dock. Two other muscular men hopped off the dock and put the box in the bed of Kevin's truck. One of the men came around the side.

"It's a big load. I don't know if you want to tie it down or what," he said to Kevin.

"Hey, how you doing?" Doug said, trying to be friendly and not suspicious. The dock worker gave him a strange look and then a perfunctory nod.

Kevin stifled a wince, then said to the dock worker, "I'll fix it over there in the parking lot, thanks."

"Sure. I just need you to sign something," the guy said and disappeared from view again.

"Shit," said Doug. "Where's he gone now?"

"Dude, will you stop acting weird?"

"I'm not acting weird. Hey, don't sign your real name."

"I'm not an idiot. I'm not gonna sign my real name."

"That's how they caught the Boston Strangler. I think."

"What the fuck are you talking about? Are you telling me the Boston Strangler signed documents after he was done strangling people?"

"Maybe it was Ted Bundy. I dunno." Doug was babbling nervously and it was starting to make Kevin nervous. He should have come alone. But then he'd be alone.

The guy rounded the corner bearing a clipboard, and Kevin tried to act like he wasn't in a hurry to take it and sign and drive off.

"That sucker's a real work of art," the loading dock guy said, handing Kevin the clipboard. "It's really not that heavy either. Those thin screens, they're like eighty pounds now. A few years ago the lightest high-def was minimum two fifty. The sound quality on it is awesome and if you hook it up to a Cerwin-Vega subwoofer you can get—"

"Hey, we gotta go," said Doug, who was now visibly sweating. "Thanks a lot."

The loading guy gave Doug another odd look while Kevin pretended he didn't know he had a passenger.

"Yeah, I got a Cerwin-Vega subwoofer at home," Kevin said, handing the dock worker the paperwork.

The guy started to ramble about subwoofers for a few more seconds, then he turned and waved to the next car behind them. "You guys have a great night." He slapped the side of the pickup and Kevin gave the gas pedal a gentle nudge.

"Holy shit, dude, we did it."

"We did it," said Kevin, driving off through the parking lot. It was getting dark, just the time that Mitch had said would be best. The loading dock was busiest at around six P.M. Mitch had been right about everything. It had been so easy.

When they pulled out onto the street, Doug was becoming almost manic. "We did it! Holy shit, man, we did it!"

They high-fived and began talking excitedly. They recounted each second of the experience they had just shared and laughed about Doug's mention of the Boston Strangler. When they pulled into the driveway, Mitch was waiting for them, businesslike.

"Oh, man, it was so easy," Doug yelled as he got out of the truck. It had just occurred to him that, as rent would be paid with this TV, there was no reason to pick up the dreaded Sunday brunch shift now to compensate for his buying the green shirt.

"Keep your voice down," said Mitch. He bent down and began unscrewing the Nevada license plate which, fortunately, hadn't gotten them pulled over. Mitch slapped Kevin's real plate back on.

They took the TV into the cramped living room, wrestled it out of its packaging, and Doug and Kevin connected the cable. Then they all sat down and stared as the forty-two-inch screen came to life.

"Man," Kevin said, reclining on the worn sofa in Doug and Mitch's ratty wood-paneled apartment, with its stained, once-white carpet and its walls gray with pot smoke, "this is the life."

"For another two days," Doug said. "Then we gotta give it to the landlord."

"Let's just pretend it's ours for forty-eight hours."

"Cool."

They settled back and stared at the screen.

• • •

THE NEXT MORNING, winter arrived. It was Mitch's first full day of dog-walking by himself, and he found that the job he had imagined was hilariously easy could, if done in a blizzard, be as much of a nightmare as inventory day at Accu-mart.

His first dog of the day was a St. Bernard named Duffy who considered the blizzard a gift rather than an irritation. Two hundred pounds of playfulness, he bounced around on the icy sidewalks, chased snowflakes, and pulled Mitch into a gutter, nearly spraining his ankle. At that point, Mitch decided that, as Duffy seemed reasonably obedient, it would be safer for all concerned if he was just let off the leash and allowed to run a little by himself. Mistake number one.

The second Mitch unsnapped the leash, Duffy, who was familiar with the sound, motored off around a corner and was gone, leaving Mitch standing in the snow-covered road, leash in his hand, listening to the gentle hiss of the snowfall.

Feet crunching in the snow, Mitch walked to the corner and looked in the direction the dog had disappeared. At the far end of the block, nearly disappearing in the light fog, he could see a St. Bernard's ass bouncing up and down as it grew steadily smaller.

Dammit! What did a dog walker do in this situation? Go home and wait for the dog to return on his own? Kevin, who had left strict instructions never to let the dogs off their leashes, might not be the best person to ask. Surely Kevin would understand if Mitch told him about nearly spraining his ankle in the gutter, right? Mitch tried to imagine Kevin's reaction to the gutter story and decided that empathy might not be Kevin's strong suit. He began jogging after Duffy. Mistake number two.

He almost immediately slipped and fell on the ice. Powdery snow covered his face.

"Shit!" Mitch screamed. He got up and was angrily shaking himself off when his cell phone rang. It was Kevin. "Shit," he said again, and decided not to mention Duffy's disappearance.

"Dude, check this out," said Kevin. "I opened the safe."

"The safe at Jeffrey's?" Mitch was flush with relief that Kevin hadn't called to check that everything was going well. "What's in it?"

"Pills, man. Boxes and boxes of pills. He's got, like, everything. Hydrocodone, OxyContin, morphine. Shit, I've never seen so many pills. The guy must be a drug dealer."

"Isn't he a doctor? Maybe all that shit is legal."

"Damn, man. You gotta see this safe. It sure as hell ain't legal."

Mitch wondered why Kevin had called about this. The other day he had seemed freaked out by the idea of even looking for the safe and here he was opening it and talking excitedly about its contents. Was he planning to become a drug dealer the week he got released from parole? For his part, Mitch didn't really want anything to do with pills.

"Any weed in there?" he asked.

"Nah, it's all pharmies. Nothing good."

"Doug'll like it. Doug likes pharmies. Give him an early birthday present."

"I'm not going to turn him into a pill head. Besides, I'm not taking them. I just looked inside."

Kevin had sounded almost hurt by the suggestion that he might steal the pills, but Mitch had noticed that ever since they had stolen the TV, he seemed to have developed a fascination with criminal behavior. They had gone for a ride to the store to get beer and along the way Kevin had pointed out houses that might be easy to break into, doors that didn't look secure, mailboxes that might be full of information that could be used to steal identities or credit cards. He had even pointed out a bank and said that it was situated perfectly for a robbery, as there were streets and alleys weaving off in every direction. He had actually sounded like he knew what he was talking about and it made Mitch think that perhaps his time in prison had not been a total waste.

"Well, I'm gonna finish up here," Mitch said. He was aware that his lack of interest was disappointing Kevin, but he was worried about how far away Duffy might be getting.

"Just thought you'd like to know," said Kevin.

Mitch heard a thundering in the snow behind him and turned around to see that Duffy had returned and was bounding toward him. The dog jumped right into Mitch's midsection and knocked him sprawling into the gutter, sending the cell phone sailing off into the snow.

"Goddammit!" Mitch screamed. But he'd had the presence of mind to grab the dog's collar on his way down, so although he was lying in the snow with a minor head wound, he at least had Duffy back. Duffy thought they were playing a game and nudged Mitch back into the gutter, which was filled with icy water, every time he tried to rise, until Mitch finally started screaming straight into the dog's friendly slobbering face. Then Duffy shook the snow off himself, his head flying back and forth, and the gobs of drool that had been dangling from his jowls went splattering into Mitch's eyes and mouth.

The phone, which had hung up on Kevin when Duffy knocked it out of his hands, rang again. It was Doug.

"Wassup, dude?" said Mitch. "I thought you were at work?"

"Dude, I got fired."

"What?" Doug had worked at the restaurant for four years and despite his continual claims of having goals (like becoming a chopper pilot) Mitch had thought it was Doug's fate to work there forever. He imagined Doug at age fifty, the head grill cook at last, his pay bloated to twelve or thirteen dollars an hour, making him the highest-paid grill cook in town. Mitch pictured him wandering back and forth behind the line in late middle age, saying things like, "I'm thinking about starting night school to become a welder," or "Soon I'll fill out an application to learn massage therapy at the community college."

"Well, not fired exactly, but the restaurant closed. I guess you could say 'laid off.'"

"It closed? It's been there for, like, twenty years."

"I know. I just went in and it was padlocked."

"Shit," Mitch said in amazement. "Dude, that sucks."

"Well, listen. I was wondering if you could ask Kevin if he had any jobs walking dogs."

Doug had been out of work half an hour and he was already panicking. Mitch knew the feeling. The dog-walking job was taking up half as much time as Accu-mart had and was likely to earn him half as much money, too, so Mitch had problems of his own without his friend asking for half the work. If being mauled by a fun-loving St. Bernard was the best thing he had going, maybe Kevin's enthusiasm for the safe-opening might not be a bad thing, he thought. The three of them needed to get together and talk.

"Let's all talk tonight. At our place."

"Sounds good," Doug said, thinking he was being offered a dog-walking job, not a safe-cracking and drug-selling job. "And hey, man, thanks."

"Sure." Mistake number three.

Doug hung up the phone in a panic. He had been panicking for close to ten minutes, ever since he had pulled up outside work and seen the waiters milling around outside the chained doors. The general consensus among them had been that it was fucked up.

"This is fucked up," one of them said.

"It's *so* fucked up," another agreed.

There was a note on the door saying that the restaurant would reopen in a few months and thanking customers for their business. There had been an employee meeting a few weeks earlier and none of the managers had bothered mentioning the fact that the restaurant was going to close, which was the most fucked up thing of all.

"I can't believe they didn't give us any warning," one waiter said. "Man, that's fucked up."

Doug hadn't heard the words *fucked up* used so much since his last appearance at traffic court, where a group of his fellow citizens had sat around in the same type of shock, thunderstruck by the realization that they were losing a lot of money and there was nothing they could do but accept it. It occurred to Doug that four days of paid vacation, along with his tuition assistance, which had been the basis for his dream of chopper school, were all gone. That was it. No warning, just gone.

He got back in his car and watched his breath steam up the windshield for a few moments, then called Mitch, who had sounded vague and out of breath. He wasn't sure Mitch appreciated the gravity of the situation but at least he had promised to talk about it later.

He started the car up and pulled back out onto the snow-covered road and hadn't gone more than fifty yards before a cop car pulled up behind him.

"You know your tags have expired," the cop said. Doug's

view of expired tags was that the little numbers in the corner of his license plate didn't affect how well the car drove, so the tag renewal money had gone to repairing a fuel pump. Besides, the money for insurance, which the car had to have before you could get your tags renewed anyway, had gone toward new brakes, so the car could pass inspection, that is, if the inspection money hadn't gone to repairing a cracked window so he didn't get pulled over for driving with a cracked window.

How could Doug respond? He could say, "Yes, I know," and get a lecture on personal responsibility, or "No, I didn't know," and get a lecture on vehicle awareness. It wasn't as if the negative answer would instantly solve the problem. The cop wasn't going to slap his hand to his head and say, "Oh, you didn't know? That's OK then. Glad I could bring it to your attention so you can get it taken care of sometime soon." No, Doug knew a hefty fine was coming his way. He handed the cop his license and said nothing.

"Your inspection has expired and your insurance has expired," the cop said after sitting in his car for ten minutes. He handed Doug a stack of paperwork and explained each document while Doug stared blankly, suppressing the desire to scream, which would only have made things worse. "This is for no inspection; this is for no registration; this is for no insurance." Doug saw the numbers on the tickets and saw they added up to over $400, which was exactly the amount he had almost saved up to take care of all the problems the cop was ticketing him for. "I can't let you drive this vehicle," the cop finished.

"Why not?"

"It's not legal."

"How am I supposed to get home?"

The cop shrugged. "I can't let you drive this vehicle." He walked back to his car, his feet crunching in the snow, and then sat in it, idling the cruiser as if daring him to drive away.

Doug sat and stared at him in the rearview mirror. He looked down at his cell phone and thought about calling Mitch. Mitch would come and pick him up, but he doubted that Mitch had taken care of his inspection and registration, either, so calling him would be like luring him into a trap. How long was this asshole going to sit behind him? How bad could this day get? He'd had no idea when he went to work that within an hour he would have no car and no job.

Then he remembered Linda. He needed a ride but he realized that he also really wanted to talk to her. It was almost as if he had missed her the last few days, which was weird, because he had known her for years. He picked his cell phone up off the seat and dialed her number.

5

WILTON, WHILE NEVER beautiful, could be at least photogenic after a snowfall. The three gray brick smoke-stacks of the metal-refinishing plant with the snow-covered mountains as a backdrop made a decent photograph for a freshman arts major trying to capture man's inhumanity to nature. Over time, this had become Wilton's purpose. Flocks of Penn State students would come down every spring to catch a black-and-white image of a strip-mined valley or a withered ex–coal miner dying of black lung disease on his disintegrating porch. From the gutted earth of the quarries just outside the town to the abandoned coal mines, some of which were permanently on fire, Wilton was a picturesque icon of poverty and environmental rape.

The citizens of Wilton had done their best to act their part as poor environmental rapists. For decades, they had lived large off the environment, until, in the late seventies,

Mother Nature had run out of resources for them to plunder and given the town a big middle finger. The mines closed; the quarries filled with rainwater; and only the metal plant remained. Within a decade the town had shrunk by half and most of the downtown buildings were empty shells, giving politicians who wanted a job a chance to make some bullshit pledges about "revitalization" of Wilton's center. Of course, these promises never amounted to anything, because nobody wanted to pour money into a half-dead coal town whose glory days were long gone and whose tax base was primarily welfare recipients, but the citizens fell for it time after time. Denial of their own hopelessness was the only bond that the community had left.

Doug remembered the excitement that had gripped the town when the Accu-mart had opened. Here it was, at last, the Great Revitalization! Other businesses were sure to follow—Best Buy, Circuit City. Soon there would be a tech-retail corridor right outside the town, drawing people from as far away as Lake Erie, the papers guessed. In fact, the only other business that had followed the Accu-mart had been a Kentucky Fried Chicken, which had been knocked down after three months of existence by a tractor trailer loaded with scrap metal sliding off an icy road. The KFC Corporation had decided not to rebuild; the Great Revitalization had officially stalled.

"I think the best thing to do is leave," Doug said, looking out at the smokestacks from Avery Hill, where Linda had driven after she had picked him up. The vantage point was an odd choice, because Avery Hill had a reputation as a lovers' lane, but when she had produced sandwiches and sodas and mentioned that she came out here all the time, Doug had relaxed.

Linda was eating a chicken salad sandwich on rye bread and staring through the windshield at the smokestacks and the lightly falling snow. She wordlessly offered Doug the other half of her sandwich.

"I don't like rye. But thanks." Doug sighed. "It's not like this everywhere."

"Where would you go?"

"Aspen."

"Aspen? You mean Colorado? What would you do there?"

"Cook. They have lots of restaurants there. Or be an environmentalist."

"An environmentalist? I thought you wanted to be a chopper pilot."

Doug was annoyed that Linda had brought the chopper pilot idea up, because it made him seem flighty. He *did* want to be a chopper pilot, dammit, but how could you get people to understand that you could be more than one thing? You could be an environmentalist *and* a chopper pilot *and* a cook if you had enough money and time for training, and he was already a cook, so that was one out of three.

"The thing is," Doug said, "that there are so many possibilities. Like, I could be a chopper pilot in Aspen, or a
cook in Aspen, or a cook here, or an environmentalist in,
like, Peru, or a heart surgeon. Or anything. It's like, there
are so many possibilities. If you pick one, it means you can
never pick one again. You only get one shot and what if you
fuck up? What if you pick heart surgeon and after three
years you're like, 'Man, I hate hearts. I'm so sick of looking
at fucking hearts,' you know?"

"You think you could be a heart surgeon?"

"Shit, I don't know." He pulled a knob on the passenger
seat and leaned back to see the black cloth of the SUV's
ceiling. "Why? You don't think I'm smart enough to be a
heart surgeon?"

"No, that's not it," Linda said so forcefully and sympa-
thetically that Doug really believed her and really believed
that she did think he was smart enough to be a heart surgeon, even though he himself knew he wasn't. He didn't
want to be a heart surgeon anyway. But it was nice to hear
her say it and he had the thought that no one else he knew
would have said that to him. Mitch would have laughed at
him and told him to get a job unloading trucks at the farm-
ers' market. Kevin would have asked him if he wanted to
steal another television.

"No, it's just that I didn't think you ever wanted to do
anything like that." She smiled. "Don't be so sensitive."

Doug was warmed by the smile, which was something he

didn't see on her face very often, and was going to tell her she had a nice smile but then he thought it might sound like a come-on. By the time he had processed this thought, he realized they had been making eye contact for several seconds. The type of eye contact that happened just before a first kiss. But that wasn't going to happen, because she was his friend's wife and he wasn't the type of guy who—

Linda leaned over and kissed him. He didn't mind the chicken salad breath.

• • •

KEVIN WAS WALKING Butch Rogers at the Wilton Dog Park, a remnant of the days when Wilton had civic pride. Two decades ago, the citizens had pitched in to fund a fenced, four-acre park on the outskirts of town, which over time had become a fenced, dog shit–covered wasteland with a lone tree still standing in it. Whatever type of tree it was, Kevin thought, it must be a type that thrived on dog pee.

Butch Rogers was a spiky-haired terrier of some sort, easily terrified and desperate to please, and Kevin liked taking him to the dog park because the presence of other, bigger dogs made Butch piss himself with fear. Ostensibly, Kevin could claim to the owners that he was "conditioning" Butch, "socializing" him, or some other sort of dog psychology crap that his rich clients loved. But the truth was that Kevin found it entertaining to make the dog freak out with terror. He couldn't help wanting to punish the dog for being a pussy. If Butch would just stand up for himself once, Kevin had decided, the nightmarish trips to the park would come to an end. He just had to stand his ground one time in the face of an Australian shepherd or a mixed breed as scrawny as he was and it would be over; Kevin would resume walking him in the peaceful neighborhood around his home. But no. Butch saw a small child playing with a Super Ball about fifty yards away and he ran and hid behind Kevin's legs, trembling.

"Butch, you're a pussy," he told the dog as he leaned down to attach the leash, ready to go home. Behind him, he heard the clink of the metal gate, indicating someone new was coming into the dog park and had most likely over-heard the comment. He straightened up, looked around, and saw a man he remembered from prison standing right behind him with a Doberman pinscher.

Kevin was never sure what to say to people he recognized from prison. Usually there was a mutual decision to ignore each other and go on your way. What were you going to talk about? The toilet paper shortage of July 2005 or the time one of the inmates had found an actual turd in the meatloaf in the mess hall, resulting in the dismissal of the entire kitchen staff? This time, however, the man was filling Kevin's whole field of vision, and they were looking right at each other, so it was too late.

"Hey," said Kevin.

"Hey," said the guy and unsnapped the Doberman's leash.

The dog bounded over to Butch, who cowered even lower and began to tremble even more violently as the Doberman gave him a few bored sniffs before darting off.

"How's tricks?" asked the guy, whose name Kevin couldn't remember. He did remember what the guy had done: some kind of computer fraud. Kevin only knew that because he had heard the guy bitching in the mess hall one day about the provisions of his sentence, which included a year of counseling and a lifetime ban on using computers, which indicated to the guy that the judge had no faith in the counseling. "If I have to pay for a year's worth of counseling, why not take away the ban when the counseling is over?" he had complained.

"Things are pretty good," said Kevin. "I walk dogs." He had meant to convey that he ran his own profitable dog-walking business, but instead he sounded like a retarded kid stating the obvious. It didn't matter, because the guy clearly had something on his mind.

"Hey, weren't you in for, like, stealing cars?"

Kevin shook his head. "Nah. I got pot possession. And manufacture."

"Because I know a guy who'll pay great money for a Ferrari," the guy said. "He really wants a Ferrari and he'll pay big bucks."

Kevin nodded, aware that this guy wasn't listening to anything he said, just talking. Perhaps a bit manically. Perhaps he was wired up on a chemical of some kind. Perhaps the Doberman, who was doing laps around the dog park, had gotten some into his system too, though sometimes dogs were just like that. Half curious, Kevin asked about the Ferrari deal.

"This Italian guy I know. He wants to steal a Ferrari for his girlfriend. It's all he ever talks about. This bitch, she's going nuts bugging him for a hot Ferrari. She's like, if you're such a big mobster how come you can't get me a Ferrari on the cheap, you know? So then I saw you, and I knew you were in for boosting cars, and I thought I'd let you know about it," the guy said.

Kevin nodded sagely. Despite having just denied being arrested for stealing cars, this guy seemed set on the idea that Kevin was an experienced car thief, so he might as well go with it. "Do you have this guy's number?" he asked.

The guy pulled out his cell phone, and Kevin copied the number and all the information. As he was driving Butch back home, he began fantasizing about stealing a Ferrari. Twenty grand cash, the guy had said. That would pay all his bills for months and maybe he and Linda could go on vacation, get things back together, like old times. He'd get a sitter for Ellie for two weeks and they'd go down to the Caribbean. He'd put Mitch in charge of the dog-walking business and, for the first time in his adult life, actually get to relax. Prison, money worries, they'd all be behind him. Burning his balls with bleach, getting kicked off the football team, stealing TVs from Accu-mart—all of it would melt into the past.

He could be a good husband and a loving father and every-thing would be like it was supposed to have been, before all the details of reality started fucking everything up.

• • •

HAVING SEX WITH your best friend's wife on the weed-covered shoulder of a road overlooking a metal-refinishing plant was about as seedy as it got, Doug figured. That was it, rock bottom. You could sell smack cut with battery acid to junior high school kids and still look down your nose at a guy like him. That morning he had woken up thinking of himself as a citizen of the world and perhaps a future chop-per pilot but now he was carless, unemployed, and the shit-tiest human being in town.

One thing was for sure—Kevin couldn't find out about this. But Kevin had just called and said he was coming over and wanted to talk to Doug and Mitch about something, and he was going to have to sit there and listen to Kevin with the smell of his wife's perfume still on his shirt. He suddenly pulled off his shirt as if it were covered with biting insects.

"What are you doing, dude?"

He and Mitch were sitting in the den, watching some video compilations of people injuring themselves in humorous ways or, in the case of the current video, pets injuring themselves or their owners. Mitch, who had con-trol of the remote, was watching it as if it were some kind of career-training video, as if his new job walking dogs required that he spend a few hours a week on home study, learning about a German shepherd's tendency to chew up a wedding dress or a cat's fondness for slamming its head into a window while a bemused bird watched from the other side.

Sitting in the recliner shirtless, Doug shrugged. "I have to take a shower before Kevin comes over," he said.

"You have to what?" Mitch was hardly paying attention, his eyes riveted to the screen where a playful Rottweiler pup was pushing a toddler around on a tricycle.

Doug got up to take a shower and Mitch suddenly looked away from the screen. "You're taking a shower for Kevin? What, are you guys, like, gay now or something?"

"Man, I'm not taking a shower *for* Kevin. I just want to take a shower. Is that OK?" Doug slammed the door to the bathroom but he could still hear Mitch call to him:

"Hey man, if you wait a while, maybe Kevin'll join you."

Doug got into the shower and cranked up the heat and the pressure, as if he could wash away his sins. The only way to make this right was to do something good for Kevin. Something that involved loss or suffering for himself equal to the loss or suffering he had caused in others. He strained to remember the book on Buddhism he had read in his senior year in high school. He had liked it. The paper he had written on it had been his last A. It had been the last book he had read too.

Maybe he could buy Kevin a present. No. What the fuck was he thinking? Mitch had already made a comment about them being gay because he wanted to wash Linda's perfume smell off himself, so if he actually bought Kevin a present, it would open the floodgates of ridicule. Not to mention the way Kevin would probably react. Given the fact that Doug had known the guy for four years and had never been moved to buy him anything before except a pack of cigarettes, suddenly showing up at Kevin's door (which, of course, was also Linda's door) with a lavish gift might arouse his curiosity. And what would Linda think? Shit, shit, shit. This was all wrong.

He heard Kevin come in downstairs and could hear the muffled sound of Kevin and Mitch talking. He shut off the shower, toweled himself off, and listened to their conversation. They were talking about how he and Mitch would have to go grocery shopping now that Doug could no longer bring food home from the restaurant.

Surprisingly, the sound of Kevin's voice did not fill him with anxiety. Instead, he found it oddly reassuring, as if the idea of Kevin were more menacing than Kevin himself. Perhaps this life of deceit that he had just embarked on would not be as terrible and karma-destroying as he had first imagined. He would do something nice for Kevin but he didn't know what yet. Not a present though. He could take his time and figure something out. He felt himself calming down and emerged from the shower to go downstairs.

"Hey, dude. That sucks about your job," Kevin said as he saw him coming down the stairs. "Here. Maybe this'll help." Kevin tossed him a dime bag of weed. "It's mostly sticks and stems, but I thought it might ease the pain of unemployment."

Oh Christ. Kevin had bought *him* a present. It was supposed to be the other way around. Kevin was such a good guy and Doug was a sneaky slime-bellied snakeass of a human being who slept with other men's wives while they worked hard for money to buy weed for him.

"I . . . I can't take this," Doug said miserably, then thought what an idiot he sounded like. This was far more suspicious than simply saying thanks and firing up, which is what pre-sex-with-Linda Doug would have done. He shook his head and was relieved when he realized that his sheepish refusal had been interpreted as depression over losing his job.

"Hey man, it's not a big deal," Mitch said. "You'll find something else real soon. Don't worry about it. The rent's paid because of the TV deal anyway."

"I may already have something for you," Kevin said slyly, sitting on the sofa and putting his feet on the coffee table. When Kevin came over, he seemed to relish the lack of tidiness, the informality. He could plunk his feet on anything and Mitch and Doug didn't care. Or at least, Mitch didn't. Doug was frequently scraping bits of dried mud from Kevin's boots off the coffee table but today definitely wasn't the day to say anything. He sat down next to Kevin and began packing a bowl.

"Have something for me? You mean dog-walking?"

"No. I already got Mitch for that and I only need one other person. This is more money less work." Doug and Mitch leaned in and Kevin paused for a moment, enjoying their curiosity. "You guys wanna steal a Ferarri?"

Doug stared at him. "Huh?"

"I wanna steal a Ferrari," said Mitch.

"I'm serious, man. I know this guy who'll pay, like, twenty grand cash for a Ferrari. It should be an hour's work. At the most."

"Sounds good," said Mitch. "Where do I sign up?" Ever since they had stolen the television from Accu-mart, Mitch and Kevin had developed a whole new respect for theft, which disturbed Doug. The morning after the theft, Mitch had been reading the paper and happened on an article describing the arrest of a bank robber. Mitch had held forth on the idiocy of the man's crime, concluding that he should have robbed electronics and flogged them as they had done. Based on his one experience with crime, he seemed to have appointed himself the local criminal genius. But to be fair, Doug thought Mitch might have had a flair for it.

"I don't know anyone who has a Ferrari," Doug said. "And they have, like, security systems and shit."

"How do you know this guy?" Mitch asked.

"From prison."

"Great," said Doug. "You can't trust those people."

Mitch and Kevin stared at him. "I'm one of those people," Kevin said. "I was in prison."

Shit. He had meant to be nice to Kevin and now he had wound up insulting him. He had insulted Kevin and *slept with his wife on the same day.* "Sorry," Doug said.

"I ran into this guy in the dog park," Kevin said, ignoring him. "He seems to think I'm someone else, some dude who stole cars. Anyways, he put me in touch with this other guy who'll pay twenty grand for a Ferrari. And at first I thought, what the fuck do I know about stealing cars? Then I remembered high school."

"High school?" asked Doug, trying to sound interested but actually waiting for a good place in the conversation to point out that Kevin had gone insane. He would point it out nicely. Maybe that could be the nice thing he did for Kevin—save him from a five-year prison term for doing something stupid.

"Yeah, man. I went to high school about an hour from here. I worked weekends as a valet at this super high-end restaurant, parking cars. Dude, there were Ferraris in there every night. Rolls-Royces, all that shit. And you know what? We left the doors unlocked and we put the fucking keys under the mat. That was ten years ago but I bet they still do."

"Sounds like a plan," said Mitch, as if they were discussing buying concert tickets or a pickup softball game. Doug winced. Did these guys not realize what they were talking about? This was a crime, punishable by years, not days, in prison. This was the last thing Doug needed. He began to shake his head, was about to beg out of the whole deal, when a sudden, horrible thought struck him. What if this was the nice thing he was supposed to do for Kevin? Not talk him out of it but participate enthusiastically. The laws of karma dictated that you scored more karma points for doing something you didn't want to do, something repugnant to you but pleasing to the offended party. This certainly qualified.

"OK," said Doug.

"Really?" said Kevin, who had obviously been anticipating resistance. "You're in?"

"Yeah." Doug looked into Kevin's eyes and saw not suspicion or anger or betrayal, all the things Doug knew he should be feeling, but pleasure. Pleasure at having his friend Doug along for the ride, part of the team. This was it, though, Doug thought, the one thing. Once this was over, they were square.

Oh, and no more sleeping with Linda.

• • •

MITCH LIT A cigarette and looked at the snow falling over his backyard. Kevin had left and Doug had gone upstairs to be moody and depressed, so he was getting a chance to enjoy a moment of solitude amid the rusted tools and piles of broken PVC piping on his back porch. A year ago, in exchange for half a month's free rent, Doug and Mitch had renovated the kitchen's ailing plumbing, a job which had taken a day, but the cleanup process was in its thirteenth month. At the end of that day, Doug, flushed with the success of the home-repair job, had resolved to become a plumber.

So they were going to steal a Ferrari. Twenty grand for a day's work. It was odd, but it seemed like a job to him. Only, unlike working at Accu-mart, this was something he could really get into. He would make decisions and be a part of a team, not a worker ant who constantly had to be reassured of his own importance with platitudes and false-hoods. There would be no motivational posters, no time cards, no uniforms. There would be no Bob Sutherland, no endless hours of boredom, no need for a lunchtime pot break. Just exciting and productive work, good pay, and the knowledge that he was one of a select few chosen to do the job, which were the only things he had ever wanted from his employment. Accu-mart had provided none of them.

He wondered if he would have a knack for it. He knew Kevin would be the perfect partner, smart and aggressive, but he was surprised that Doug seemed so interested. He would have imagined that Doug would have just shrugged the whole thing off and gone looking for another cooking job, leaving him and Kevin to split the money. Mitch thought that the fact that he had lost his job that day might have been a factor. Maybe Doug had wanted in on the job because he was worried about his bills. But that theory didn't quite make sense, as Doug wasn't one to really worry about his bills. Mitch usually had to remind him to pay them, and if he didn't handle the rent, they both would have been evicted a long time ago.

"You have to pay your credit card bills every month," Mitch remembered lecturing Doug once after discovering about five late notices stuffed into the couch. "If you don't, it will ruin your credit score."

"Why are they keeping score of how often I pay my bills?"

Mitch had begun to explain the system to him, incredulous that a twenty-six-year-old man didn't already know about this. But, it turned out, he did. He had simply applied his own logic to the system and wanted an argument to test it.

"So they're keeping score on me so if I get a high score I can buy a house?" Doug had asked.

"Yes," Mitch had answered suspiciously.

"What if I don't want a house?"

"Eventually, you're going to want a house."

Doug had shaken his head. "I'll never have a house," he'd said without regret. "Neither will you. We'll never own houses. They just like to keep score on us. They keep score on all of us but we'll never own houses."

In truth, Mitch couldn't help feeling Doug was right but he wasn't willing to let go of the idea that he would one day own a house. He just knew he would, one day. He wasn't sure how but just over the next hill there were good things waiting to happen. He was certain of it. Sure, the credit system was fucked, the credit score just a number that indicated how willing you were to participate in a rigged game, but that was no reason not to try.

So maybe Doug wasn't worried about bills but for some reason he was finally taking some responsibility and joining up for the Ferrari mission. It seemed ironic that the first time in months that Mitch had felt respect for Doug was when the guy decided to commit a felony. Maybe Doug was changing, turning into a different person right in front of them. Maybe he was finally joining them on Planet Earth.

Good things were waiting to happen. Soon, with the proceeds from the Ferrari, he could clean up his credit, maybe even apply for a gold card. Then on to other good things. Maybe one day he would even get a nice suit and perhaps get a Ferrari legally and drive it up to his house, which he owned. He and Doug would both own houses and they would live near each other and go over to each other's houses and smoke pot all day and play beer pong and not have to worry about anything because they were such efficient and excellent car thieves that they never needed to work crappy jobs. But they would, of course, occasionally help Kevin with his dog-walking business. Dogs were cool and how else would they explain all their money to the IRS?

The door opened and Doug peered out. He looked better, less moody, less beaten by life, as if he had had a good cry. "Hey man, you wanna play beer pong?"

Mitch got up from the worn couch and tossed his cigarette into the snow. "Sure, dude. I'm gonna kick your ass."

6
CHaPTeR

THE ROAD TO Eden, Kevin's hometown, was beautiful, snowy, and desolate. The roads were icy and Mitch and Doug were getting anxious about Kevin's lead-footed driving, as they were both crammed into the death seat of Kevin's pickup and unable to fasten the seatbelt.

"Dude, you could maybe slow down?" asked Doug, hoping not to cause offense. He found it hard to make eye contact with Kevin but he didn't think sleeping with someone's wife gave them the right to kill you in an auto accident. Mitch, who Doug had thought was too high to care, mumbled something in agreement.

But Kevin was lost in thought. Seeing the roads he grew up on had made him gloomy and thoughtful and he would occasionally point out random things along the way, things which had some long-lost personal meaning for him, making him the world's most boring tour guide.

"Me and Willie Wright used to play down there," he said, seeming wistful, as he pointed out a drainage ditch. Mitch looked down into the ditch, trying hard, for Kevin's sake, to find something interesting in there. He felt he should ask a question but the moment passed as his dope-soaked brain searched for the right one. A block farther on, Kevin pointed out a tree. "That's where Katie Feld broke her arm."

Instead of asking about the details of her injury, Mitch asked the first question that occurred to him. "Was she hot?"

"She was six years old, you asshole," Kevin said. Mitch burst into a fit of giggles, which caused Doug to start giggling, and they both went into convulsions of laughter on the bench seat of the pickup as Kevin snorted with disgust.

"You guys are morons," he said. "You'd better get your shit together because we're almost there."

They pulled off onto a gravel road in the thick of the woods and Mitch wondered what type of a high-end restaurant would be in such a location, apparently in the middle of a forest. Kevin seemed to anticipate the thought, because he said, "This place is really cool. It's a remodeled farmhouse. We should go to dinner here one night."

Which was pure fantasy, they all knew. It was an hour from Wilton and a trip to McDonald's usually had all three of them checking their wallets. Eating out had become a luxury that they just read about and saw on TV. And besides, if you stole a Ferrari from a restaurant's parking lot, it might not be a great idea to use the proceeds eating there, since that would increase the likelihood of being seen by a busboy or valet parking attendant who might have noticed you lurking around in the woods prior to the theft.

So much of their lives were made up of that kind of fantasy, Mitch thought, so much time wasted with comments like that one. We should go to dinner here. Yes, we really should. It would be awfully nice, wouldn't it? Perhaps we should have our butlers make reservations for seven-ish. It was all part of the same brainwashing—him obsessing about paying his credit cards on time so he could one day buy a house and Kevin suggesting a dining-out experience at the priciest restaurant in their part of the state. They had eaten it up, all the shit they had been fed about having a future. Their future was to work or starve, and the work was getting harder to come by.

Kevin pulled into the parking lot, which, despite the freshness of the snowfall, had already been plowed and most likely would be again before the restaurant opened at four o'clock. They looked at the ornate woodwork on the porch, the sign with a layer of snow neatly balanced along its narrow edge. A Mexican man wearing an apron emerged from a basement door and began shoveling the snow off the steps, paying no attention to the pickup truck idling in the otherwise empty parking lot.

"That's Jorge," said Kevin, full of awe. "He's the dishwasher. Jesus, I can't believe he still works here."

"Where else would he go?" asked Mitch, looking around at the woods and motioning toward the dying town they had driven through to get there. Kevin was still staring at the dishwasher, lost in a reverie of nostalgia. He snapped himself out of it and looked across the parking lot.

"See back there? All the way back against the tree line?" He pointed to the far end of the lot. "What we gotta do is hide in those trees over there, as far as we can from the front of the restaurant. On busy nights, they park the cars all the way back against the trees."

"How can we be sure they'll park the Ferrari back there?" asked Mitch.

"We can't."

"How do we know what nights the Ferrari will be here?" asked Doug.

"We don't."

There was silence. "Look, guys," Kevin said patiently. "We're gonna make over six grand apiece, OK? We gotta put a little bit of work in."

"Like what? Whaddya mean, work? You mean we gotta hide in those trees in the middle of winter until a Ferrari shows up?" Mitch was getting annoyed now. He'd just spent an hour in the cramped pickup with Doug's leg crammed against his, putting his foot to sleep, and he had the good seat. He could only imagine how uncomfortable Doug must have been, straddled over the stick shift, and now it was starting to look like the plan involved coming out here on a nightly basis for god knows how long, and lying in a snowy bush all night. He didn't mind stealing cars. That was the fun part. But he hadn't signed up for night after night of freezing his balls off in a forest.

"Yeah, that's what I mean," said Kevin, as if he were talking to his six-year-old daughter.

"Dude, let's just steal the first car we see. This is fucked up."

"I don't mind," said Doug quickly.

"That's the spirit," said Kevin. "Dude, there are like three guys who come here all the time who drive Ferraris. Seriously."

"That was ten fucking years ago," snapped Mitch. "They could all be dead by now."

"OK, there's more," said Kevin, talking only to Doug now. "We have to wear business suits."

"Business suits? What the fuck are you thinking?" said Mitch.

"Business suits," said Doug thoughtfully.

"Yeah, business suits. If we get out and walk around in this parking lot the way we're dressed right now, in jeans and these shitty jackets, the valet guys'll be on us in a flash. They'll start asking all kinds of questions. But if we're wearing business suits, they'll leave us alone."

"So I have to squat in a bush for a week wearing a business suit," said Mitch. "Dude, fuck this. Let's just go rip off that doctor with a safe full of pills."

"Pills?" asked Doug. "I hadn't heard anything about this. What's this about pills?"

Kevin ignored him. "Mitch, man, what the fuck is the matter with you? You won't spend a few nights getting your precious little hands dirty for over six thousand dollars? Fine. Fuck it. Me and Doug'll do it. That'll be ten grand for each of us. We don't really even need three people anyway."

"Yo, you guys, what's this about pills?" Doug said. "Do you know someone who can get pills?"

Surprised at how easily he was being cut out of the deal, Mitch began to backtrack. "Dude," he said patiently, "I'm just a little surprised. I thought you knew exactly when and where we could find a Ferrari. I didn't think it was going to involve a lot of detective work."

Despite having run a booming pot-selling operation with Doug, Kevin wasn't sure enough of his intelligence to go into the car-theft business with him alone and felt more comfortable about the three of them working together. He, too, began to backtrack. "Well, I can't say for sure what night we'll get a Ferrari," he said, "but we'll get one. The plan is good."

"The plan is good," Mitch agreed, skeptically.

"OK then," said Kevin. "Do you guys have business suits?"

"What's this about pills? Why won't you guys answer my questions about pills? I know you've got pills," said Doug.

"We don't have any fucking pills," said Mitch. "I was kidding."

"You weren't kidding. I distinctly heard you talking about stealing pills."

"Well, if we're talking about stealing them it means we don't have them, right?"

"Do you guys own business suits?" asked Kevin again

"Yes, we have business suits," Mitch half-shouted.

"What kind of pills?" said Doug. "OxyContin? Can you get some OxyContin? Seriously. Do you know how long it's been since I've been able to get ahold of OxyContin?"

Kevin looked across at Mitch and rolled his eyes. Neither one of them gave Doug a straight answer as they drove back to Wilton.

• • •

ON THE DRIVE back, Kevin was thinking about a guy he had met in prison named Eddie Dars. They were in the common room one afternoon, which was really just a huge cell, and as they were the only two white men in the room at the time it was only natural that they gravitated toward one another. Eddie was playing chess by himself and had invited Kevin over and taught him some moves. Kevin had been intrigued by the game. Then the conversation had turned to sports, and they discussed the Steelers and the Dolphins in great depth. Eddie really knew his football, knew the colleges attended by the whole Steelers offensive line, the histories of the coaches. They had laughed sometimes as they talked and Kevin had gone back to his cell thinking, I've finally found a friend in this place.

Kevin found out later that same day that Eddie Dars had raped seventeen women. Not one, not two. Seventeen. The guy was a fucking maniac. After a week of jail, this was the first actual *criminal* Kevin had met and up until that moment it had not occurred to him that the prison's ostensible reason for existence was occasionally valid. Among the black kids who had driven through white neighborhoods with bags of weed, the drunk drivers who didn't have connections to get them out, and the junkies who had failed to show enough respect to the judges and police, there were some *actual criminals* mixed in. This was an eyeopener for Kevin. It turned out that Eddie Dars was only in the minimum-security prison because he was attending court dates in the county and would be headed back to maximum-security prison at the end of the month to serve out a fifty-year sentence. And Kevin had picked him over all the others as a friend.

What did that say about him, Kevin wondered? He knew that he himself was a well-grounded fellow—normal upbringing, popular in high school. Yet in his personal choices he always seemed to gravitate toward the fringes. How else would he have wound up in a car with these two, Continually Complaining Mitch and Pillhead Doug, planning a felony? Was he just like them? He *felt* normal and he figured that if people saw the three of them together they would see him as an ill fit. But he did fit. He got along with them.

He knew the fact that he got along with them annoyed Linda. There was always something about his attraction to the fringes that had bugged her. He hadn't decided to grow pot in his basement for the money, though the money it generated hadn't hurt. He had grown the pot because he knew he would start meeting people like these guys. He had felt that he was about to sink into a middle-class hellhole, and Linda had already started going to PTA meetings. Real PTA meetings. Kevin had thought that the PTA was just a *Saturday Night Live* joke, a symbol of domestication and middle-class family life, like white picket fences. He hadn't thought there was actually a PTA. But there was and Linda had found it.

So that was it; he was doomed to spend the next fifty years hanging out with married couples and going to dinner parties at other people's houses and talking about the cost of gutter replacements and the best way to seed a lawn. Some of the people he met when he was forced to go to a dinner party and reexamine his lost youth were younger than him. One cheerful neighbor named Hank, in his early twenties and dressed in khakis and a sweater (which was almost as bad as going to a PTA meeting), had suggested that Kevin needed to aerate his lawn and spent a full half hour giving him horticulture tips. While Hank had been rambling, Kevin had decided that a little horticulture might not be a bad idea.

He had sat down at the computer the next day and

bought lights and seeds online, built a partition in the basement, and told Linda that he was setting up a "workshop" for himself. Rather than buy a padlock to keep her out, he had decided to make her think that whatever he was doing in there was just so boring that she wouldn't care to enter. She wanted him to have hobbies, so he picked the most boring hobby he could think of—sculpting—and ran with it. The space behind the partition became his "sculpting room." Linda never asked why a sculpting room required ten kilowatts of power a day, nearly doubling their energy bill, nor why it emitted an eerie glow visible under the panels of the partition at all hours of the night, nor why fans could be heard constantly running in the sculpting room, nor why he never produced any sculptures. His lack of sculpting output could always be blamed on sculptor's block. But finally, when he had felt it was time for him to produce something, anything, he had gone to the Asian market and bought a raw wood sculpture of an Easter Island–style mongoloid with a huge head. Linda's comment when he showed it to her had been, "Yeah, I saw that at the Asian market."

It had gone on that way for months. Linda never asked questions. She must have known all along what he was up to. Must have. He went to dinner parties (when forced to by Linda) and the conversation one night had turned to basement remodeling. I'm going to hook up a high-def sound system in mine; I'm going to get a weight room set up; I'm going to get a sports room/pool room/guys-only room with a bar and a Beer Meister, blah blah blah. They were all talking about brand-name appliances and how great it was going to be when their basements were all finished and how everyone was invited over, and Kevin had only one thought: you guys are never coming over to my basement, unless you want to sample some Afghan sativa hybrid under 320-watt sodium lights. The thought had made him smile to himself, which the other guys had ignored, because they were used to him smiling to himself and never saying much and they didn't really like him anyway.

On the way home, Kevin had repeated some of the conversation to Linda, holding it up as an example of why these parties were a form of torture for him. Linda had missed the point. "Why don't you bring them over and show them your sculpting room?" she had asked. But Kevin had detected a trace of irony in her voice, disguised as innocence. She knew. She had known along. But, he thought as he drove through the wooded, windy roads back to Wilton, she had let him do it without bothering him.

And he suddenly realized why. She had let him do it because it must have seemed to her that it was the only thing that made him happy. That's what a miserable prick he had been. And that's what a good wife she had been. But things had changed, Kevin knew. Linda just wasn't that worried about his happiness anymore.

"What are you thinking about, dude?" Doug asked him. "You're looking all deep and shit."

"Nothing."

"No, seriously. What are you thinking about?"

Kevin looked out the window at the fields of blue spruce, snow hanging from their drooping branches, as he took another turn at an uncomfortable speed on the icy road. Doug and Mitch said nothing, having resigned themselves to helplessness. "I'm thinking about Linda," he said.

Doug froze. He had wanted a nice, personal conversation, something to kill the time on the ride, but he certainly didn't want to talk about Linda. Not with Kevin. In fact, not with anyone.

Kevin misinterpreted his silence as an opening to keep talking. "I think I've been a shitty husband," he said. "I wonder if it's too late."

Doug was staring through the windshield, eyes wide, mouth clenched shut. Kevin looked over at him and figured the expression was due to his driving.

"Dude, I'm not driving that fast. I know these roads."

Everyone in the truck was silent. No one said another word until they reached Wilton.

• • •

THE FOLLOWING DAY, Mitch walked Jeffrey the pit bull and when he got back to the client's house, he found himself tempted by the safe. He knew how much Doug loved pills and he figured that, if there were some loose pills in there, he might grab a handful for him. Fuck it, he thought, let the guy have some pills. He'd had a shitty week, getting laid off and all. Only he'd have to make up a story about where he got the pills so Doug wouldn't bug the crap out of him for more.

Mitch took off his shoes, stepped over the dog gate, and tiptoed carefully back into the den. The adrenaline rush from the illicit action made his hearing alert and sensitive, aware now of the steady hum of the huge house's central heating and even the noise of his heart thumping as his unsteady fingers pulled the gilded frame of the painting forward. He looked out the window at the snow-covered front lawn, nearly a hundred yards of pristine whiteness between him and the street. Even if the doctor came home early, Mitch figured he would have plenty of time to slam the painting shut, run back to the kitchen, and put his shoes back on before the guy made it into the house.

Mitch twirled the knob to each number in the combination. On the final number, his nervousness made him turn the dial several digits too far and when he cranked the small lever, the safe didn't open. He cursed, took a deep breath, and started over, then froze as a car turned the corner at the top of the street and drove past. Shit. He took another deep breath and started a third time. Hadn't Kevin opened the safe? How hard could it be? This time, when he cranked the lever he heard a hydraulic hiss and the door came loose. He swung it open.

Inside were about a dozen small mailer boxes and what looked like several thousand dollars in cash. The cash was stacked in piles about six inches high. Kevin hadn't mentioned the cash. Was the cash new or had Kevin just not mentioned it? If he asked Kevin about the cash, then he would have to admit to Kevin that he had opened the safe. Which was OK, Mitch decided, because Kevin had opened the safe. And besides, he wasn't really stealing; he was doing a good deed for Doug. He grabbed one of the stacks of cash and looked at it. It appeared to be all twenties, not hundreds, as he had assumed. Still, it was quite a sum. Then he grabbed a mailer box and flipped it open.

It was filled with loose pills, all the same, white and round. He grabbed twenty or so and shoved them into his pocket. As he was doing this, one of the pills fell on the hardwood floor and bounced onto the rug. He looked down and didn't see it. Shit, he thought. It had rolled under the desk. He shut the mailer box, put it back, and closed the safe. Then he carefully let the painting swing back in place over it and got down on his hands and knees to look around under the desk. There it was. He picked it up and stared at it, clean and white and pure and shiny, and without thinking, he popped it into his mouth and swallowed. Let's see what Doug is always talking about, he told himself.

Mitch stood up, looked around the room to make sure nothing had been visibly disturbed, and as he was backing out of the room, he noticed two obvious impressions in the dust on the hardwood floor where his knees had been when he had knelt down to get the pill. He tiptoed back over and swirled the dust around with his sock. Then when he backed up, he saw the dust from his sock tracked on the rug. He picked up some dust lint with his hands and mussed the carpet, and this time noticed the streak marks he had left in the carpet while mussing it. Then he decided he was just being stupid; nobody examined their carpet when they came into a room. He turned and left.

Mitch ran back into the kitchen, put his shoes on, and locked the kitchen door on his way out. He waved goodbye to Jeffrey, who was huddled, freezing, in his doghouse, half-frozen snot dangling from his nose. Jeffrey stared at him forlornly as he peeled out of the driveway.

• • •

MITCH DROPPED TWO of the pills on the table in front of Doug, who was watching TV while cleaning a bong. The effect on Doug was electric, as if awakening him from slumber with a gunshot. He sat up, instantly alert, as he took the pills and examined them.

"Dude, what're these?"

"I don't know. You tell me."

Eyes focused and expert, Doug turned a pill in his hand and then held it up to the light coming through the window into their dingy living room. "Hydrocodone," he said, as if pronouncing a discovery. "These are the good ones. Seven-point-five milligrams." He looked at Mitch beseechingly. "Can I . . . eat it?"

"Yeah, man. It's yours."

Before Mitch had finished uttering the short sentence, the pill was in Doug's stomach. "Thanks, dude. Where'd you get it?"

"Never mind."

"Do you have more?"

Oh, for god's sake. He had created a monster. He was about to empty his pockets, dump the twenty or so pills he had all over the coffee table, but then had an evil impulse. Doug was suddenly like a trainable dog, begging for treats. Mitch was aware of an almost total power.

"That's it," Mitch said. "I took one myself and saved two for you. All I'm feeling is itchy, like I've got fucking ants in my shorts."

Doug laughed. "They make you itchy," he said. "But you get a little high and a little speedy."

. Which was true. Within minutes of popping the pill, Mitch had suddenly found he had energy and a real interest in dog-walking. He could see how these things could be addictive, until the ants in the shorts effect had started, and by the time he was walking Duffy, his last dog of the day, he was scratching himself raw. Still, the extra energy might be nice if he was going to spend the evening sitting behind a bush in the freezing woods dressed in a business suit.

"Are you ready to go steal a Ferrari?" Doug asked. "Kevin just called. He said he'd be over in a little bit."

"I guess we have to go put on suits."

"I guess."

"I think the suits are a stupid idea."

"Kevin says we should wear suits," Doug said, as if reminding him of the teachings of their cult leader. Mitch picked up on something in the tone of his voice. Over the last two days, he had noticed that Doug had been particularly reverential toward Kevin, careful to not interrupt him or disagree with him. Nothing specific, just a vague change in attitude. It was definitely a change from his regular behavior. Two weeks ago, Mitch remembered Doug cursing Kevin for failing to return a CD he had lent him, and before that, mentioning that Kevin might be a little too enthusiastic about the idea of stealing the television and that perhaps they should spend less time with him because he seemed to be turning into a criminal. But this week every word that fell from Kevin's lips had to be stringently adhered to.

"Dude, what's going on with you guys?"

Doug stared at the television, not saying anything, and Mitch leaned over him, slowly putting his head between Doug and the TV set, which was showing a commercial for toilet-cleaning products.

"Duuuuuuude, I've got pills," Mitch taunted. "Talk to me," he sang. "I'll give you another piiiiiiiiiiiill."

Doug said nothing, but continued looking toward the TV, clearly stressed and focusing harder than ever on a foaming liquid which was making a toilet bowl so clean that it sparkled.

"Have you joined Kevin's cult or something? Is there something going on between you two I don't know about?"

"Nothing," said Doug. Then he added, "I don't want to talk about it."

"Ah-hah! So there is something. What don't you want to talk about?"

"DUDE, IT'S NOTHING!" Doug yelled, and his voice was filled with such anxiety that Mitch was taken aback. Doug was so easygoing and relaxed and this outburst so uncharacteristic that Mitch instantly sensed joking about pills was not the right way to go about having this conversation. But he was also baffled. He knew both these guys pretty well and hadn't really noticed anything unusual between them, other than Doug's reverence. Kevin had been acting normal. For Kevin.

His head still hanging jauntily in Doug's view of the TV screen, Mitch began to piece the situation together. Kevin had been acting normal and Doug hadn't. Which meant that whatever it was, Kevin didn't know about it. Doug had, therefore, done something to Kevin. What? Stolen something from him? Nah, Doug would never steal stuff. At least not by himself or from someone he knew and liked.

"Dude, did you do something to Kevin?"

Doug got up from the couch, not making eye contact. His voice was shaking slightly as he said, "We should put on suits." Then he ran up the stairs, which was also uncharacteristic. For a tall, thin man, he was surprisingly slow moving and bursts of energy were usually signs that something was very wrong. The last time Mitch had seen Doug move very quickly was when his grandmother had suffered a heart attack.

"Hey man," Mitch called after him. Doug was at the top of the stairs and when he turned, Mitch noticed his eyes were red rimmed as if he was going to cry. Shit, Mitch thought, something serious is going on. He decided he didn't want to know. He reached into his pocket, pulled out all the pills, and showed the handful to Doug. "I'll leave these here for you on the coffee table."

Doug nodded and almost smiled in gratitude.

"Don't overdose yourself, you pillhead."

"I won't." This time he did smile. "Thanks."

• • •

MITCH LOOKED GOOD in a suit. His suit fit well and had been expensive, over two hundred dollars, and he wore his hair in a short, military cut, as did many men who wore suits regularly. When he had looked at himself in the mirror before they left, he'd had the thought that, had he made different decisions with his life, this would be the way he looked every day. What decisions could he have made differently? Not smoking pot in the army would have been a start. He could have finished his six-year stint and gotten GI Bill funding to get into a real, four-year school. He could have graduated with a degree in finance and gotten a job on Wall Street or gone on to law school. He was certainly smart enough. The image of himself, crisp and professional, as he posed in front of the mirror on his way to steal a car, filled him with a sense of regret over his lost opportunities.

Doug, on the other hand, was never meant to wear a suit. His hair was long, his expression more artistic and dreamy than alert, and his "suit" was an ill-fitting sport jacket with nonmatching dress pants that he had bought at a thrift store for his grandmother's funeral. His appearance was that of a small boy who had been dressed for church and would run off and play in mud if you didn't keep your eyes on him. Mitch had to stop himself from wincing when he saw him.

"Dude, you need a new suit."

"Fuck it. What're you, like James Bond or something?"

"I'm more James Bond than you."

"You look like . . ." Doug searched for a derisive comparison and found nothing.

"Good comeback," Mitch said.

"Yeah, uh, eat me."

"Good comeback again. You're like Oscar Wilde with this shit."

Before the conversation could deteriorate into abuse and

cursing there was a knock on the door. It was Kevin. It was Ferrari time.

THE PLAN REQUIRED that Kevin park the pickup out of sight of the restaurant and, as soon as Doug and Mitch were in the Ferrari, pull out onto the gravel road and lead them to the drop-off point. Kevin couldn't park his pickup in the parking lot because one of the valets might think it looked suspicious and take down his license number. So the pickup was parked about a hundred yards away, on a small gravel access road that led to a now defunct quarry. The minute a Ferrari pulled into the lot, Doug and Mitch were to call Kevin and he would drive back out to the road. Doug and Mitch were to stride over to the Ferrari and, bold and unobtrusive in their business suits, drive it out of the parking lot to the road, where Kevin would be waiting.

What the plan hadn't taken into account was the fact that to get to their stakeout point from the pickup, Doug and Mitch had already had to walk through a forest in their business suits, meaning their dress shoes were caked with freezing mud. They had also neglected to consider that business suits were not very warm. So while Kevin, fully dressed for the weather in a heavy down jacket and blue jeans, was waiting in the truck for a cell phone call alerting him that a Ferrari was present, Doug and Mitch were standing behind a tree, freezing, with ice forming on their feet.

"Dude, this sucks," said Doug.

Mitch had taken to the work. There was a lot to be said for working outdoors. He had been enjoying the adventure of it, the concealment, which gave the mission an air of great importance. Who concealed themselves if their work was unimportant? Then Doug had ruined the moment by complaining.

"It's cold," Mitch agreed. He had brought with him a cheap pair of opera glasses, which had been in the apartment when they had moved in. He put them up to his eyes and examined the parking lot, which was perfectly visible with the naked eye.

"Dude, do you really need those?"

"It'll give us more time. To call Kevin. With these, I can see a Ferrari the minute it comes up the drive."

"Whatever. I can't feel my feet."

"Why don't you go wait in the truck with Kevin?"

Doug was quiet for a second. "No. Then you'll talk shit about me, about how I didn't help."

"These things are cool," said Mitch, ignoring him and holding up the opera glasses. "You can see the hostess through the window. She's hot."

"I don't care," said Doug.

"Dude, if you're gonna be a bitch, seriously, why don't you go wait in the truck?"

They froze and ducked as they heard the noise of an approaching car. Mitch put the opera glasses up to his face, but they had fogged over. He polished them with his wrist as a car came into the parking lot and pulled up beside the little valet hut. It was a BMW. Mitch looked at it through the glasses and said, "BMW."

"Dude," Doug said, shivering. "I can see that from here."

They watched as the valet parked it about three spaces from the door. Somebody was apparently paying a valet to walk eight feet. Even if it had been a Ferrari, it was parked so close to the valet booth that the valet would notice any-one who approached it, and he would be sure to notice two half-frozen, wet creatures with their feet caked in mud emerge from the woods and get into it.

"Dude, this ain't gonna work," said Doug.

Mitch was surveying the situation like an embattled para-troop commander, his breath frosting in the air as he swung the opera glasses back and forth across the parking lot. Doug asked idly what the fuck he was looking at. He had to admit, Doug had a point. "It's not gonna work unless the parking lot is full," he said.

"These business suits were a bad idea," Doug said.

Yes, Mitch had to admit, they were. The deception of wearing business suits was all well and good but after you had been crouching in a wintry, outdoor environment for several hours, a business suit just made you look more con-spicuous. All soiled and muddy and coming out of the woods in suits, they would look more like survivors of a plane crash than jaunty guests heading into the Eden Inn. And besides, they were freezing.

They knocked on the window of the pickup. The truck was idling and Kevin was sitting in the warm cab reading the paper, a steaming thermos of cocoa in his hand.

"You comfortable enough?" asked Mitch as Kevin rolled the window down. "Need, like, a foot rub or something?"

"What's up, jerkoff?"

"We're scrapping the plan," said Mitch. "This business suit bullshit is ridiculous. If I'm waiting in a bush all night, I need to be dressed for the weather."

"Y-Y-Yeah," shivered Doug.

"We're going for speed not deception," said Mitch, his paratroop commander persona returning. "There're two ways we can do this. One, deception, where we get in the door by looking like we belong there, or two, speed. Just spring out of the forest and take the goddamned Ferrari while the valets are busy. What're they gonna do? Leap in front of it to save the car? Then we speed off."

"We decided this," said Doug.

"Besides, look at him," said Mitch, pointing at Doug, who was shivering and wet, his soaked long hair clinging to his cheeks. "He looks even creepier than usual."

Kevin looked at Doug. "All right," he said with a nod. Doug's appearance was enough to win the argument. These two were never going to pass for business people, or even people who had any business in the parking lot of the Eden Inn. He leaned over and opened the passenger door and they got in.

"We're going commando," said Mitch. "Comfortable, warm clothes we can move fast in."

"Doesn't that mean you're not wearing underwear?" asked Doug.

"What?"

"Going commando."

"No, it means quick and well prepared. And dressed for the damned weather."

"I think it means no underwear," said Kevin.

"Bullshit. I never heard that."

"I'm going to wear underwear," said Doug.

Kevin pulled out onto the road for the long drive back to Wilton, the snow starting to fall silently on the tree-lined roads, his two friends bickering in the seat beside him, and thought: This is so much better than a PTA meeting.

7
CHaPTeR

DOUG WAS FLIPPING through the classifieds and found himself drawn to a particular ad promising wealth for the writing of children's books. According to the ad, there was a virtually bottomless market for children's books and no real skills were required to write one. Doug allowed himself a moment of reverie as he imagined being an admired children's book author and realized it was a fantasy he had had before.

Two years earlier, while working at the restaurant, Doug had found himself staring at the lobsters in the tank and imagining writing the story of one that escaped. He had wanted the story to be happy and have the lobster make it home to Maine, where he would be reunited with his family. Standing over the hot grill, sweat dripping into his eyes, he had been suddenly thrilled at the idea of being a writer of children's books and the next day he had sat down to write one.

At first, everything went well. The stage was set, the lobster escaped, and he went off on his happy way to Maine. Annalisa had said she loved it and waited eagerly for the next installment. But as the story developed, the lobster began to change perceptibly, from a happy escapee to a morose and violent drifter. At his best the lobster was aimless; at his worst he was hell-bent on revenge. Despite Annalisa's admonishments to keep the story light, Doug continually had the lobster running into trouble. By the time the lobster had been arrested for selling nitrous hits at a Phish show and had stabbed a lizard at a truck stop following an argument about leftover fast food, Annalisa had finally persuaded him to give up the story for good.

"You're weird," she had said, but her voice had lacked the saucy delight that had been present when she had made the same observation at the beginning of their relationship. It had been the final weeks and now Doug wondered, as he sat and read the classifieds, if he hadn't thought of the lobster story as a device to keep her attracted to him, an attraction he knew was waning. He stared blankly at the ads, not reading them, wondering what Annalisa was doing now. Right now at that very moment. Waiting tables at some other corporate restaurant, telling all her tables about moving to France, and getting an advanced degree in poetry writing probably. And maybe banging one of the cooks. She liked cooks. Banging other waiters was just so *jejune*. Or *passé*. Or *coup d'etat.* Or something. He was shredding the edges of the newspaper with his fingers.

On the kitchen table was his final paycheck, which had arrived in the mail that day. One hundred ninety-eight dollars. That was it. That was all he had going for him. He had just lost his job and his car and most likely his license, and he had slept with his friend's wife, and all he had to show for his life was a check for $198. And a handful of little white pills that Mitch had given him. He took another one.

The phone rang. It was Linda, the call he had been dreading. He had so many things he wanted to say to her, serious things about right and wrong and betrayal and friendship, things that had been circling madly in his mind for the past few days. He wasn't used to keeping secrets and he hated the feeling that he might make an errant comment to Mitch or Kevin. Skills of deceit were not in his DNA.

"How are you?" she asked. Her tone was cheerful, which he wasn't expecting. He had imagined their next conversation would be a somber rehashing of events, full of admissions of shame and phrases like "never again." Instead she sounded happy, energetic, and friendly, which made Doug nervous.

"I'm good," he said, wondering how to play this. Maybe she just didn't want to share her angst on the phone.

"I was just wondered how your day was going," she said pleasantly, not sounding at all angst-ridden. "I miss you. We haven't talked in a couple of days."

Doug wanted to point out that prior to two weeks ago they had never talked at all. Accidentally having an affair with his friend's wife was one thing, but having her call up and pretend it had never happened was not only insulting, it was confusing. What was this about? Should he join her in the pretense that they were just friends? Yeah. He should. Maybe that was the answer and Linda had figured it out. If they both pretended they had never had sex, maybe the whole thing would just go away.

"Yeah," Doug said. He could hardly say he missed her too, because that was some weird schmaltzy shit you said to your girlfriend, not to your friend's wife while your roommate was watching TV ten feet away, wondering who you were talking to on the phone. He tried to think of something mundane to say, some insignificant detail of his day which he might offhandedly mention to a friend but nothing occurred to him except, "I've been thinking of writing a children's book."

"Really?" Linda sounded genuinely enthusiastic and Doug realized how nice it was to make new friends, because they weren't sick of you yet. To new friends, an announcement of your new life plans was a novelty. It wasn't put into the context of a dozen previous announcements which might not have come to fruition. New friends accepted your announcements with the excitement that you had when you made them, and they understood that when you announced your life plans, you were deadly serious and totally committed, at least for the duration of the announcement. "What's it gonna be about?"

For want of a new idea, Doug told her about the lobster, and while he was telling her he began to relive the enthusiasm that he had felt upon his first venture. Perhaps writing children's books was his real calling after all. This was the second time he'd had this idea. Maybe that was it. You had to wait to get your calling twice. He told Linda the whole lobster story the way he had imagined it originally, with a joyful escape and a happy reunion. She was charmed.

"Write it!" she said and Doug was so happy to hear the support in her voice that he forgot he had just slept with her, and all the anxiety that went along with it. "I'll read it to Ellie. We'll make her your focus group."

Doug was about to respond when Mitch, dressed in a camouflage jacket and his baggie pants, walked into the kitchen. "Dude," he said, "let's go. It's Ferrari time." He opened the refrigerator and took out a beer. "Who you talking to?"

"A dude from work," Doug said and instinctively put his head in his hands. Mitch stared at him.

"Hey Kevin, man, you want a beer?" Mitch called out into the living room, alerting Doug to the fact that Kevin was in the apartment while he was talking to Linda on the phone.

"Nah, man, I'm driving." Kevin came into the kitchen. "Wassup, Doug? Get your coat. We gotta get going. We got a Ferrari to steal."

"Is that Kevin?" Doug heard Linda ask.

"Later, man," Doug said into the phone and hung up, praying that the phone had been tightly pressed against his ear and that her voice had not echoed around the kitchen, giving clues to her identity, or even to her sex. To the phone lying inert in its cradle, he said, "Talk to you later, dude," with an emphasis on the last word, clarifying once and for all that he had, in fact, been talking to a man.

Doug and Mitch went out into the snow, dressed warmly this time, and as they were waiting on the steps for Kevin to finish using the bathroom, Doug turned to Mitch and said, "Dude, do you ever think that no matter how much you try to make your life simple, it just keeps getting more complicated?"

Mitch lit a cigarette. "Yeah. I guess. Maybe. Why?"

"I don't know, man. I just hate when shit is complicated."

"What's complicated?" Mitch looked at him. "Who was that on the phone?"

Doug was desperate for a change of direction in the conversation, even though he himself had just started it. "I've decided I'm going to write children's books," he announced.

"Didn't you do that once before? About a lobster or some shit? And the lobster turned into, like, a hardened criminal or something."

"He was just a petty criminal," said Doug. "And this time it'll be different."

Kevin came outside and they got into the truck, which was warm and smelled of cocoa. "Linda thinks I'm walking dogs," said Kevin, "and she made me some cocoa. I brought it along for you guys."

Linda knows you're not walking dogs, Doug thought. Another thing that was his fault.

"Cool," said Mitch as they pulled out of the driveway. "Doug's gonna write children's books."

"Didn't you do that once before?" Kevin asked. "About a suicidal junkie lobster?"

"He wasn't suicidal, man. He just had some problems. And he wasn't a junkie. He just sold nitrous hits. And this time it'll be different." You couldn't discuss anything with these guys because they were always bringing up the past. Shit, how would they like it if Doug kept bringing up the fact that Kevin got arrested and sent to prison or that Mitch had been fired from a shitty job?

Kevin shrugged. "Ready to go steal a Ferrari?"

"Ready," said Mitch.

"You ready, dude?" Kevin asked, looking at Doug.

Doug stared moodily out the window, so Kevin asked him again. And again. Finally, Doug responded that he was ready and Kevin pulled a fat joint out of his pocket and said, in a long, slow drawl, "Awwwwwright."

• • •

THE NEXT DAY, Kevin really was walking dogs, and he was thinking about the fact that there weren't as many Ferraris on the road as there used to be. But he was also thinking about Linda. Linda had said something to him about Ferraris when he had gotten home late the previous night. It had been their fourth fruitless night of staking out the Eden Inn parking lot and as he headed toward the bathroom, Linda had mumbled something about Ferraris in her sleep.

"Wozzis about Ferraris?" she'd mumbled as he tiptoed through the darkened bedroom.

Kevin took it as a sign. Linda had said the magic word. Maybe she was some kind of good luck charm. He stopped in the bathroom doorway and looked at her, half asleep, or completely asleep, and dreaming about Ferraris.

"Ferraris," Kevin said, wanting to hear more and to determine her state of consciousness.

"Yuhferrarizzz," she mumbled and dozed off again. Damn! It was definitely a sign that next time they went there would be a Ferrari. A beautiful red Ferrari just waiting for them, the doors unlocked and the keys under the mat. Now if only he could convince the other guys, who were getting pissed with the whole plan and had started to doubt if anyone in the whole county even had one of the damned things anymore.

Maybe he was just thinking about Linda that morning because he could smell her. Today he had taken her car, rather than his truck, because her smaller Toyota was easier on gas and the car, he noticed, had a strong odor of her perfume. He pulled into Scotch Parker's driveway and shut off the engine.

Scotch Parker was a Scottish Terrier who was kept in the garage of a million-dollar house because Mrs. Parker had supposedly developed an allergy to him. Kevin didn't believe it. He got the feeling that the dog really belonged to Mr. Parker and her shoving Scotch in the garage was just the type of passive-aggressive shit that unhappy married couples did to each other. Antagonism-by-pet-treatment, Kevin knew, was a phenomenon far more common than nondogwalkers would ever imagine.

He opened the garage door and immediately noticed that Scotch was lying dead on the floor.

"Shit," he groaned. He went over and looked at the dog's little mouth and saw a green puddle by his inert, partly open jaws. Antifreeze. He could even smell it. He looked around the garage and noticed it all over the floor. They must have had a leak, and the dog had lapped it up. Then Kevin remembered that as long as he had been coming there, over a year now, he had never seen a car in the garage. This wasn't a leak; someone had intentionally poisoned the dog.

Enraged, he dialed 911 and waited in the driveway for the cop car, chain-smoking. He knew that what he should be doing was calling the owner, Mrs. Parker, who was at work, but he had the distinct feeling that she was the one who had done it. Little Scotch did bark a lot, so it could have been a neighbor or just a local vandal, as the garage door was always unlocked, but Kevin was secretly hoping the cop might find some clue that implicated Mrs. Parker right off. Mr. Parker, who loved the dog, had been on a business trip for weeks.

The cop car pulled into the driveway and Kevin was disappointed to see the cop was young and innocent looking. Not the kind to immediately notice clues. He had been hoping for someone brimming with confidence and competence, like the CSI team from television, toting bags of sophisticated electronics and weird machines and sprays. This was just a kid with a clipboard. Kevin pointed out the dead dog and watched as the kid walked aimlessly around the garage.

"You think the dog ate some antifreeze?" he asked after a few seconds.

Drank, Kevin thought. You drink antifreeze. It's a liquid, you idiot. "Yeah."

"Hmmmph," the cop said. His eyes darted around, and from his expression, Kevin guessed there would be no CSI team. This guy was trying to figure out the best way to get back to his cup of hot coffee without getting stuck with hours of paperwork. "Are you the owner?"

Kevin explained that he was the dog walker, hoping that this information would not be the legal paperwork loophole that nullified the whole case. The kid was transfixed by his clipboard, trying to think up an exit strategy.

Finally, he jotted down a few notes and asked, "What is it you want me to do?"

"Investigate," Kevin said, as if the answer was obvious. "The lady who lives here, she did it." He knew better than to let his voice show too much emotion, or he would be in the back of the cop car himself in no time. Make a fuss and the cop would run *his* info through the system and find out he had a record, and then he'd have to get Linda to pick him up from the police station. So, with extreme calm, he added, "You know, check out the neighbors, examine the scene, ask questions."

"If I ask anyone if they did this, they'll just deny it," the cop said.

Kevin was trying to keep himself from getting visibly annoyed. "You know," he said evenly, "I've seen a lot of cop shows. And I've never seen anyone on *Law and Order* say, 'Hey guys, if we investigate this murder, the people who did it will just deny it.'"

"Those shows are about people who got murdered, not dogs," the cop said, equally evenly.

"I thought you guys protected and served," said Kevin, letting his rising anger show now, which caused the cop to walk toward his car.

"We protect and serve people, not dogs." He got in and started the engine. Then, apparently feeling he had been too harsh, he rolled the window down. "You can investigate but you'd have to pay for it yourself. I mean, you could fingerprint that container of antifreeze but a fingerprint test is, like, five hundred dollars. And if it was the lady of the house, all it would prove is that people touch their own antifreeze."

Utterly deflated, Kevin just stared at the cop as he drove out of the driveway. He called Mrs. Parker at work and listened to her fake the emotion of shock for a while, then ask him if he could dispose of the dog's body. So he put little Scotch's body in a trash bag and placed it in the back seat of Linda's car, then drove off to walk his next dog.

• • •

WHEN HE GOT to Jeffrey's house, Jeffrey was alive, which was nice, and the shifty doctor who owned him was home, which wasn't. Kevin groaned as he got out of the car. The last thing he felt like right then was face-to-face contact with another human being. Part of the reason he enjoyed his job was that such contact was a rarity.

"Hi," said the doctor, whose name Kevin could never remember because the checks he got for dog-walking were from a pharmaceutical firm. The doctor was a young man, early to mid thirties, and he had the slicked back hair and fit appearance of a stereotypical eighties stockbroker, reminding Kevin more of an extra from the movie *Wall Street* than of a health care professional. He also seemed too young to own this magnificent house, but hell, Kevin knew very little about how much doctors got paid.

"Hi," Kevin said, trying to fill his voice with exhaustion to dissuade further conversation. Jeffrey bounced up to him and Kevin greeted the dog, hoping to get him leashed and be on his way.

"Come inside for a second," the doctor said. "I want to talk to you about something."

Shit.

Kevin went into the house, which was at least warm. It felt good to get out of the elements, if only for a few moments.

"Take your shoes off," the doctor said brusquely. He had a manner about him that dissuaded argument of any kind. "Come back here."

Kevin spent a good two minutes unlacing his boots, then went into the den, the same room where he had opened the safe a few weeks before. There was no way the doc could have found out about that, Kevin thought. Besides, the guy looked cheerful, not like someone about to begin a conversation about home invasion. There was a fire going in the fireplace, and the doctor sat down behind his huge cherry-wood desk and pointed Kevin toward one of the ornate European-style red felt chairs.

"I have to ask you something, Kevin, and I hope you won't take offense," he said, leaning back in his chair, folding his hands across his stomach as he put his feet on his desk.

Kevin shrugged. "Go ahead."

"You were in prison for a drug charge, is that right?" The question caught Kevin off guard, but it was asked with such self-assurance and directness that Kevin could hardly take offense. How the hell did this guy know that? Obviously, as Kevin's job entailed access to people's houses, his prison record was something he preferred to conceal.

"That's right," Kevin said. "How did you know about that?"

"I give you the keys to my house, I'm going to run a background check on you," the doctor said, as if it was the most obvious thing in the world. "I have a lawyer who handles these things." Kevin figured that he was about to get fired, which would mean he had lost two clients in one day. Fine, dickhead, go get yourself a dog walker with no criminal record, he thought. It was a competitive business, he knew, and there was no shortage of dog walkers with clean backgrounds. He waited calmly for the news of his dismissal.

"That intrigues me," the doctor said and looked at Kevin expectantly.

"How so?"

"Well, I'm curious. About, you know. What exactly you did."

Kevin leaned back in the chair, aware that snow was dripping off his jacket onto this guy's antique furniture, which made him feel even more out of place. "Look," he said. "It was a long time ago. If you want to get someone else to walk your dog, that's cool with me." He got up to leave.

"Whoa, whoa, whoa," said the doctor, motioning for him to sit down, and what was supposed to be a friendly smile, but to Kevin seemed like a cheap salesman's grin, flashed across his face. "No, no, that's not it. I still you want you to walk Jeffrey. I'm just curious."

If he still wanted him to walk Jeffrey, that made Kevin an employee again, so he had to tame himself and remember his manners. Having lost the freedom of the freshly fired, he said, "I dealt marijuana." He decided he wouldn't mention the growing.

"Did you grow it?"

"Yuh."

"Because it says here manufacture and possession."

"Damn. You got my rap sheet?"

The doctor took his feet off the desk and sat up straight in his chair, pulling it closer to the desk. "Kevin, I've got a problem. I was hoping you might be able to help me out with it."

Kevin knew what it was right away. The freak was going to ask Kevin to deal off the thousands of pills he had in the safe. Obviously, Kevin couldn't let on that he knew the guy had thousands of pills in a safe, so he had to sit there for five long minutes while the doctor went on tangents about Medicaid and the health care system, and how this somehow caused thousands of white pills to wind up in his safe. It was far too complicated for a non–health care professional like Kevin to understand, the doctor explained delicately, but perfectly legal. This last part he said with a death grimace meant to be a trustworthy smile.

"I just don't know that many people who would buy these," he said. "I figure someone who knew the streets might be able to help."

"I don't know much about pills," Kevin said, his mind whirring. He did know one fact, though, and that was that it wasn't "perfectly legal" to have your dog walker sell them. To the doctor, Kevin knew, a guy who "knew the streets" was really just a euphemism for a scumbag. It might even be on his to do list: Find a scumbag. Kevin really didn't want to have anything to do with this but maybe Doug would. Not that Doug was a scumbag but he had just lost his job, and he loved pills. "But I know a guy who does. I should introduce you to him."

"No, no." The doctor waved his hands about, shaking his head, a neurotic gesture which belied his bossy confidence of moments ago. "No, I don't want to meet people. I'm sure you understand how sensitive this is. But there's a lot of money to be made."

"All right. I'll deal with him. I'll talk to him about it tonight." Tonight was going to be another Ferrari mission and, judging by the developing tone of revolt among the troops, probably the last. Perhaps the offer of pill retail work would ease the pain of staking out the parking lot in the cold.

They shook hands and said their goodbyes. Kevin still could not remember the doctor's name. "By the way, doc, what's your name?"

"Doctor Billings," he said. "Jeffrey Billings."

Kevin nodded, and they shook hands, meaninglessly, again.

Sometimes, you only needed to know one fact about a person. The freak had named his dog after himself.

• • •

DOUG WAS SITTING in a tree, thinking about whether or not his thing with Linda was really Kevin's fault. He was deciding it was. He knew that Kevin was still not 100 percent sure that Doug had not turned him in to the police, and perhaps the constant distrust Doug felt from him was what caused him to act dishonestly. Had Kevin trusted him more, he wouldn't have slept with his wife. There, that made perfect sense.

"Dude," Mitch said. He was a branch higher up in the tree. They were looking out over the wintry parking lot, waiting for the Ferrari that would never come. Mitch was handing down the joint and Doug took it. They had been smoking pot in the tree for over half an hour and Doug was so high he no longer really felt up to the task of stealing a Ferrari, should one actually show up. In fact, every night they had been out there since the first one, that had been the situation after half an hour, and Doug was secretly relieved when each mission ended in futility. And he had been doubly glad when Kevin had suggested on the way out there that this plan might not work after all, which meant he had performed his karmic duty, by trying to help Kevin steal a car, without the personal disaster of being arrested for it. He was, as they said, off the hook

As time had gone by on their stakeouts, they had learned things. They had watched the valets so closely for so long they felt like they knew them. There was the Italian-looking dude, the fat dude, the gawky kid, and the girl, who worked Fridays and was kind of cute. They had watched her through binoculars and her appearance and attitude as she waited around with the other parking attendants had filled half an hour of conversation time. The Italian-looking dude was not nice, and Doug and Mitch had gathered from random words drifting across the windswept parking lot that the others thought he was not sharing tips. From their tree, they had spent an evening watching him very closely and had actually seen him putting money straight into his pocket when the others weren't around.

"Let's go down there and punch him," Mitch had said and for a moment it had seemed like a good idea. Then they had remembered their mission, which was to sit in a tree and wait for a Ferrari. A wait that in a few hours would be over, Doug remembered, and then he could go back home and look for a real job, working a grill at another corporate restaurant, one that he could get to without a car.

Mitch's cell phone rang, a loud, high-pitched sound that must have been audible to the diners in the restaurant and certainly, Mitch thought, to the two shivering parking attendants standing out front. He distinctly saw the Italian-looking dude look back into the forest to see why a tinny version of a Grateful Dead tune was coming from the trees and bushes. He fished it out and saw Kevin's number.

"Shit dude, don't call me. I'm on stakeout, remember?"

"Dude, why don't you just put it on vibrate?"

"Because I'm wearing gloves. I can't push the little buttons," he whispered angrily. "What do you want?"

"We might have to go home soon. Linda just called. I think she knows I'm not out walking dogs."

"Shit, man. I'm not going home without a Ferrari," Mitch whispered. "We've invested too much time in this already." Doug looked up from his branch, droopy-eyed. Damn, he looks stoned, Mitch thought. He looked happy too, and Mitch figured it was because Doug didn't really want to steal a Ferrari. Damn them both. Mitch would steal the thing by himself.

Then Mitch heard angels singing. A Ferrari had pulled into the parking lot.

What a beautiful sight. For a full five seconds Mitch admired the car, its smooth lines, its stunning bright red color, beautiful even under the faded yellow lights of the Eden Inn parking lot. Mitch felt his heart pounding, felt his senses awaken and sharpen as his inner commando was unleashed. He put the cell phone in his mouth as if it were a combat knife and slid noiselessly out of the tree.

He heard Doug mumble "fuck" under his breath.

He took the cell phone and wiped his saliva off it and put it to his ear. Kevin was talking about something.

"Dude, the fox is in the henhouse," Mitch whispered.

"What?"

"This is it. Go time. The fox is in the henhouse." He hung up and put the cell phone back in his pocket. Behind him, Doug fell out of the tree like a dead elephant.

"Dude," Mitch whispered. "Keep it down." On an adrenaline high, Mitch turned around to look at Doug, whose body language was screaming reluctance. It was too late for him to back out now. It was a five-minute walk back to Kevin's truck, through brush and thickets and there was no way Mitch was going to wait. "We're going in."

The gawky valet was talking to the Ferrari's owner, who was probably telling him to take special care of it or some such crap. The kid was going to drive it eighty feet. Mitch didn't think there was much to fear. Well, except for the Ferrari thieves lurking in the trees. The Italian-looking dude had gone around to the other side to open the door for a stunning blonde and Mitch watched intently as the couple went inside. The gawky kid started to get in the car, but the Italian-looking dude stopped him, almost pushed him away. What was that about? While he was trying to figure it out, Mitch's cell phone rang.

It was Kevin.

"Dammit, what? I told you they can hear the ringing."

"Dude, put it on vibrate."

"Whaddya want?" Mitch whispered forcefully.

"What the hell are you talking about, a fox or something?"

Mitch sighed heavily, the sigh of a man surrounded by idiots. "I said, 'The fox is in the henhouse.' OK? There's a goddamned Ferrari in the parking lot."

"Really?" Kevin was now showing the interest that Doug clearly lacked. "Why did you say something about a fox?"

"Dude, it was a code. OK? I thought you might have figured that out."

"How would I have known that? If you're gonna use a code, maybe we could agree on it first. Didja ever think of that?"

"Do you want me to steal this goddamned car or don't you?"

"Steal it," Kevin said and hung up. Mitch put the cell phone back in his pocket and turned to Doug, who was looking through the bushes out into the parking lot. "What's going on over here?"

"Dude, I think they're fighting over who gets to drive the Ferrari."

And they were. The Ferrari was idling in the parking lot with the driver's side door open while the Italian-looking dude and the gawky kid were yelling at each other over who got to drive it eighty feet. Finally the Italian dude, who was shorter but stockier and more muscular, pushed the gawky kid away from the car and got in.

"That guy's a jerk," Doug said.

"Let's spring out of the bushes and beat the shit out of him," Mitch said.

"Let's just steal the car," said Doug, with a touch of resignation. Mitch realized he was right. They hadn't waited in the snow for five nights to punch a valet, no matter how much of a dick he was.

The valet drove the Ferrari very slowly at first and Mitch figured the kid was going to park it right next to the last car in line. But just as he pulled up to the space, he hit the gas and took it around the lot, as if looking for a better space. Clearly, the kid wanted to take the car for a joyride and was trying to spend as much time in it as possible without doing anything that would cost him his job. He circled the parking lot twice as Mitch trembled with annoyance.

"I'm just gonna jump him and smash his face in," Mitch said. "This is bullshit."

"Easy, man," said Doug. "Here he comes."

The valet pulled the car into a space not more than twenty feet from them, all the way at the edge of the parking lot, and parked it diagonally. That must have been the instruction the owner had given the valets, to park the car well away from every other car. What a tool, Mitch thought. Then he noticed that the Italian-looking dude was not getting out of the car, nor even turning the lights off. Instead, he had cranked the radio, enjoying the sound system at full blast. Mitch could hear the lively beat of rap music and saw the kid bouncing around in the driver's seat.

"I hate this guy," whispered Mitch. Doug said nothing. The kid continued bopping around in the seat. When the song finally ended, Mitch heaved a sigh of relief. Then another song began and the kid started bopping again, this time singing along, turning the radio up so loud that the Ferrari began to vibrate.

Mitch's cell phone rang. Hiding behind a bush in a commando crouch, he fumbled it out of his pocket, cursing. It was Kevin. "What now?" Mitch demanded.

"What's taking you guys so long?"

"The damned valet won't get out of the car. He's listening to music."

"Well, I'm sitting here idling in the road. I can't sit here much longer."

Mitch had an idea. From watching the valets, he had learned that they always took cars in rotation. Another car was pulling into the lot right then, a BMW, and the gawky kid was opening the door for the driver. That meant the Italian dude was up next. The only way to get him out of the Ferrari was to have another car pull into the parking lot, and who knew how much longer it would be before that happened?

"Listen, Kevin, I need you to drive into the parking lot and act like you're going into the restaurant. Pull up out front. That'll get the kid out of the car."

"I'm not coming in there. What if they get my license plate?"

"Otherwise you're gonna have to idle in the street all night," Mitch said, and hung up.

The gawky kid parked the BMW and went back to his station. The Italian kid stayed in the Ferrari.

Mitch could see headlights through the trees, coming down the restaurant's long driveway, and then Kevin's truck pulled into the parking lot. Immediately, the Ferrari's engine and radio shut off and the door opened. The Italian kid, who had been watching the restaurant in the rearview mirror, tossed the keys onto the floormat, slammed the door, and ran back to greet Kevin.

"Finally," said Mitch.

Kevin had stopped to ask the gawky kid a question. It made a great distraction. Mitch and Doug wriggled out of the bushes and low-crawled over to the Ferrari. Mitch was on the ground by the driver's side door, and he still had a clear view of the valets and of Kevin's truck, idling at the restaurant's front door. He was sure Kevin could see him as he got into the Ferrari. Doug quickly hopped in the other side, and Mitch found the keys and fired it up.

"Keep your head down," he told Doug, as he put it in reverse. No clutch pressure at all, the gears just seemed to slide into each other, and the steering wheel was equally smooth. I guess there's a reason why you pay all this money, Mitch thought as he shifted into first and hit the gas. The car pushed forward, and he felt the power, increased the acceleration, and burst out of the parking lot. A puff of fly-ing snow and smoke followed them.

"Yee-haw!" Mitch screamed. As he'd roared past Kevin, who was making conversation with the two valets, he had seen them notice the flying Ferrari screaming off into the night. He had caught a glimpse of the Italian kid spinning his head back to where the car had been just moments before. Then the scene had disappeared behind the trees and the driveway had opened up before them.

"Shit," Doug said. "We gotta wait for Kevin. He knows where we're going." Kevin had arranged for them to take the Ferrari to a garage that was less than two miles away, but Mitch and Doug had never thought to ask for directions. The plan had always been to follow Kevin, who was sup-posed to be waiting in the street.

Mitch pulled over in the darkened, tree-lined driveway, waiting to see Kevin's lights behind him. Nothing. Apparently, when Kevin had seen them steal the car, he had just sat there, idling, and continued talking to the valet. Mitch rolled the window down, stuck his head out, and peered back down the driveway, as if that would somehow hurry Kevin up.

"Shit, the cops are going to be here in two or three min-utes. What the hell is he doing?"

Doug sat in the passenger seat, petrified. They could hear the idling of the Ferrari's powerful motor and felt the fresh, cold air of the woods in winter. Silence. No Kevin.

"He does know we just stole a car, right?" Mitch spat.

"I mean, does he realize this is against the law?" Mitch was aware of sweat breaking out on his forehead despite the cold.

Doug said nothing. He was staring straight ahead.

Finally, Mitch saw headlights as Kevin's truck came out of the parking lot, speeding toward them. He felt pressure lifting from his chest and was aware of being able to breathe again. The truck went flying past and Mitch gunned the Ferrari and fell in behind it.

Kevin didn't even stop when he reached the road, just spun right, throwing up a cloud of dirt and sticks, which bounced off the front end of the Ferrari. Bet the dude who wanted his car parked away from all the others wouldn't have been too happy about that, Mitch thought with an evil laugh. Kevin had his gas pedal to the floor; they were climbing up to ninety miles an hour. The Ferrari was in fourth gear and barely feeling it. Mitch started screaming.

"Whoooooooohah!" he yelled, and looked over at Doug, whose face was contorted in worry, or misery. "This baby can fly!"

"Just . . . just watch the road," Doug said, his voice shaky. "Ice." He was trying to fasten his seat belt, but couldn't find the end of it, and he was wriggling around in his seat. It was annoying Mitch.

"Dude, just sit still!"

Doug said nothing but, mercifully, did sit still. Up ahead,

Kevin put on his turn signal, and a few seconds later, they turned onto a small road, then took another turn, and then Kevin pulled up another tree-lined driveway deep in the woods. This was a nice long one too, and at the end was a large shack big enough to be a two-car garage. There was a light on inside.

They had come up the dirt-and-gravel driveway so fast that smoke and snow and debris filled the air as Kevin jumped out of the truck and ran up to the door of the garage. He rang the bell, and as he waited, Mitch could see his breath puffing up into the air. He was panting.

"Dude," said Doug. "I wanna get out of this car."

"Go ahead," said Mitch. "Ask Kevin where he wants me to park it."

Before Doug could move, a burly man in coveralls with a handlebar mustache answered the door. He was holding a welding torch in one hand and looking around the parking lot as he greeted Kevin. He saw the Ferrari and put the torch down, and came over to greet Mitch.

"Wow," he said, his feet crunching across the snow. "This one's a beaut. A 599." He turned to Kevin. "You took the LoJack out, right?"

Kevin froze. Mitch froze. Doug got out the car and said, "Hey."

LoJack. Mitch and Kevin both knew what it was. Until that second, it had never occurred to either of them that the Ferrari might have an antitheft device that might need to be disabled, a device that at that moment was probably madly signaling to anyone who cared to know where it was.

LoJack, Mitch thought. Well, I'll be damned. He could see by Kevin's expression that he was thinking much the same thing.

"No," Mitch said finally when it became obvious that Kevin was too thunderstruck to answer.

The burly guy jumped back from the Ferrari as if it had tried to bite him. "You gotta get this thing outta here," he said.

Kevin nodded.

"NOW!" the guy screamed. "Go!" He began waving his arms frantically, backing away from them. "There'll be cops crawling all over me in ten minutes! Get the fuck outta here!" He ran back inside his garage and slammed the door.

Mitch was still sitting in the idling Ferrari and he looked up at a downcast, deflated Kevin standing over him. "Where do you want to take this thing?" he asked.

Kevin stared at his shoes for a second before snapping out of it. "We gotta dump it somewhere," he said.

They stared at each other, the forest quiet except for the sound of the idling Ferrari. A feeling of calm control came over Mitch as his inner commando took over once more.

"I got an idea," he said, aware there was no time for debate. "We passed a steep hill on the way here. Those hills have truck ramps that lead off into the woods. You know, for when trucks lose their brakes? We park the

Ferrari on one of those escape ramps and get the hell out
of here."

Kevin nodded. "Let's go."

"Doug, you ride with Kevin," Mitch said. "No use in
both of us getting caught in this thing."

Doug, who had no problem with that, was in Kevin's
truck before Mitch had finished his sentence. Mitch peeled
out down the long driveway, slamming into potholes and
flying over ruts. Screw it, the Ferrari was doomed now. If he
couldn't sell it, what difference did it make if it got beaten
up? He pulled out onto the road, which was still dark and
lifeless. No other traffic, the only good thing about this
night so far. Less than half a mile down the road, Mitch saw
the first escape ramp, a patch of sand that ran off behind
some trees. He stopped, turned around, and drove as fast as
he could into the sand, grounding the Ferrari. He had gotten at least a hundred feet into the trees, concealing the
Ferrari from the road.

Mitch shut the car off, leaped out, and slammed the
door, then ran over to Kevin's truck, which was idling at the
end of the truck ramp. He jumped in and Kevin peeled off
in the same second. Mitch pulled the wildly swinging passenger door shut.

There was total silence in the truck. After a few minutes,
Kevin eased off the gas and drove normally. A few seconds
after that, two police cars, with their lights flashing, sped
past them in the other direction.

"Shit," Kevin said. "LoJack. Who woulda thought?" No one spoke, so he added, "I told you guys I wasn't a car thief. Dude, I told anyone who would listen that I wasn't a car thief."

"They'll sure believe you now," said Mitch.

After a few more minutes, Mitch put his head in his hands and said, "Shit, what a disaster."

"Coulda been worse," said Kevin.

"A whole lot worse," said Doug.

"That's the spirit," said Kevin. "Coulda been worse. Coulda been worse." He began repeating it like a mantra.

As they neared Wilton, the pumping adrenaline had ebbed and their lives began to seem normal again. None of them wanted to talk about the botched Ferrari job and Kevin, determined to talk about something positive, said to Doug, "Dude, I might have a job for you."

"Walking dogs?"

"No. I don't have enough dogs for three people. Dealing pills. Interested?"

Ordinarily, the answer would have been no. But business opportunities were scarce and clearly car-thieving wasn't going to be as lucrative as promised, so Doug said, "Awright."

"Do you know a lot of people who like pills? Because I can keep you busy. This guy I know, he's got tons of 'em."

"Awright," said Doug, who just a few weeks ago had been thinking of becoming a chopper pilot and just a few hours ago had been imagining himself a famous children's book author, and who was now realizing that the most realistic career choice at this point was felony trafficking. "I'm sure we can work something out."

Kevin pulled up to Mitch and Doug's apartment. He and Mitch briefly reviewed the dog-walking schedule for the next day.

"Wanna come in and smoke a bowl?" Mitch offered.

"Nah, I can't. Linda thinks something's up already. I gotta get home."

They said their goodbyes and Mitch and Doug went in and sat on the couch. No Ferrari, no money. Doug was partly relieved, Mitch knew, but he himself felt nothing but failure and rage. LoJack. He should have known better.

He folded himself into the couch, turned the TV on, and stared at it blankly.

8

CHAPTER

"WHERE DOES KEVIN keep going? I figured I'd ask you," Linda said cheerfully. She had picked him up that morning to take him to meet a restaurant manager who was looking for a sous-chef trainee, a contact she had made at the dress shop. Doug sensed she had made solving his unemployment problem a personal project, which was good, because his work search so far had involved daydreaming over the classifieds and listening to Kevin pitch a job selling pills. Which, to be honest, sounded better than working as a sous-chef, whatever that was. Despite having worked for four years as a corporate restaurant grill cook, Doug couldn't really cook and didn't have much interest in learning how. But Linda had obviously put some thought into his situation and he was touched by her concern. Too touched to mention that opening prepackaged bags of sauce and throwing meat on a grill and then removing it when it was done were the only culinary skills he had ever wanted to develop.

"I dunno," he said. Not only was he being driven to a job interview to apply for a job he didn't want, but he was also being grilled for information on the way. He had come along on this venture partly because he wanted a chance to talk to Linda, to confirm with her that what they had done was a terrible mistake and that it would never happen again. But Linda's mood was unconcerned, even breezy. It was as if she knew he was tortured and was enjoying it, and torturing Doug even more was the realization that she seemed to be suffering no remorse herself.

"The other night he said he was going to walk dogs, but when I was talking to you on the phone he was over at your place," she said. She had a bright smile while she was talking but Doug knew the smile was a feminine trick, belying the seriousness of the subject matter. Annalisa had pulled this one on him a number of times, beginning conversations about their future with an incongruous grin that caused him to let his guard down, to be equally lighthearted in his response. Women, Doug figured, instinctively understood that warning a male of an upcoming serious conversation would result in hearing a generic, prepared statement as a response, and generations of evolution had taught them all a disingenuous breeziness to avoid this.

"Yeah, he was there," Doug said. "We were going out to look for a Ferrari."

"A Ferrari? Really?" Linda nodded sagely and Doug hoped the conversation was over, but he knew it wasn't. His answer had opened up a host of other questions and he had not taken the time to prepare for them. He stared out the window hopelessly, resting his head against the cool glass as they drove down the main street of Wilton.

"Kevin likes Ferraris," he said.

"Yeah," Linda said, nodding thoughtfully, as if she were trying to solve a puzzle and had been handed information that was clearly irrelevant to the solution. "But why would he tell me he was walking dogs and then go over to your house and talk about Ferraris?"

"Why don't you ask him?" Doug snapped, taking himself by surprise. "I mean, what's with this? You act like you want to help me out, taking me to a job interview, and then you start grilling me for information. That's bullshit."

"I'm not grilling you for—"

"Just let me out," Doug said. "Just pull over and let me out right here. You know what? Fuck that guy, this chef or whatever he is. Maybe you could have asked me first, you know? Like, have I ever said I wanted to be a chef?"

Linda pulled the car over to the side of the road. "I'm sorry," she said, her voice soft and reasonable. "I was just trying to help. I just thought . . ."

Doug got out, slammed the door, and stepped in a puddle of freezing water which came up past his ankles. "Goddamit," he yelled in shock as the water flooded through the holes in his worn tennis shoes. Then, turning around, he saw his reflection in the car window. He looked pathetic, lost. He opened the car door and got back in.

"What are you doing?" Linda asked.

"Let's just go," he said. "Let's go to the interview."

"I don't want to waste your majesty's time," Linda said, the gentleness gone from her voice. She pulled the car out into traffic and made a U-turn in the middle of the road to take him back home. "I wouldn't want you to miss your afternoon bong hit. I'm sure there are so many other useful things you could be doing right now if only I wasn't forcing you to try to get a job."

"You're not forcing me," he said. "It . . . it was nice of you—"

"Fuck you." Linda began driving faster, speeding up to blast through a light that had just turned yellow. "Why don't I just drop you off and you can get together with Kevin and that jerkoff roommate of yours and smoke pot all goddamned day for all I care. And if you see Kevin, you can tell him to go and fuck whoever he wants and not to bother coming home because I don't need his sulking, moaning, bitching, lying ass around the goddamned house anymore."

Wow. Linda was usually so soft-spoken and cheerful. Doug was trying to absorb everything she had just said to determine which of the many points she had just brought up needed to be refuted first. Did she really just call Mitch a jerkoff? Did she really think Kevin was fucking someone else? Wasn't it a little hypocritical to attack him for that, all things considered? Perhaps that would be the point he brought up last.

"How come you think Mitch is a jerkoff?"

"I have had it with you guys," she continued, ignoring him, her face filled with rage, an emotion Doug had never seen on her before. "What do you think I am, some kind of fucking . . ." She trailed off and Doug thought the anger was subsiding, but it turned out she was just searching for the right word. " . . . middle-aged goddamned English teacher trying to get you to sit up straight and not chew gum in class? I just don't want to see all the people I care about flush their fucking lives down the toilet, but oh, no, I guess that's just not cool, is it? No, anyone with a sliver of common sense is just a boring old nag."

Doug was about to tell her she wasn't old or boring, but fortunately for his sake, he never got the chance because she started up again. "You know what I'd like to do? I mean, I'm sure nobody gives a fuck, but you know what would really make me happy right now? If I could take Ellie and go back to my mother's and get away from this . . . everyone in this . . . in this . . . goddamned . . ."

She appeared to have run out of steam and Doug felt the nicest thing he could say was to finish her sentence for her. "Town?" he ventured.

"Shut up," Linda snarled at him. She was still driving fast, whipping around curves, and they were almost back at Doug's apartment. She continued her rant without even looking at him. "You know why I don't? Because I don't want Ellie to have to start up in a new elementary school. Despite everything, with the pot and everything, I . . ."

And then she stopped talking, a bit too suddenly. Doug merely noticed that she'd fallen silent at first but after a few seconds the fact that she had stopped talking began to seem curious, so he reviewed the last things she had said. Ellie, new elementary school, pot. What did Ellie have to do with pot? The abruptness with which she had finished her rant seemed to indicate some kind of secret link which she had accidentally revealed before stopping herself.

"What are you talking about?" Doug asked, not really sure if he was imagining it, or if Linda's demeanor had changed. She seemed suddenly defensive.

"Ellie." Linda snapped. "I have a daughter. We, Kevin and I, have a daughter. Though you wouldn't know he's a father from the way he behaves." This last bit she said almost by rote, as if she had said it before, and she probably had, Doug thought, to the women she worked with at the dress shop. The rage was gone; the rant was over. She was phoning it in.

"Yeah, I know you have a daughter," Doug said. "But what does that have to do with pot?"

Linda took one hand off the steering wheel and waved it frantically, as if fanning herself. "Nothing," she said. "Just ignore me." Her voice was softer now but Doug thought she looked stressed, not cleansed by the catharsis of rage as he would expect.

"No, no, no," Doug said, leaning forward in his seat with the look of a TV detective who had stumbled upon a clue. "You mentioned Ellie and then you started talking about pot. What does Ellie have to do with pot?"

Linda pulled up outside his apartment and stopped the car but left the motor running. She stared out the window and sighed. Doug wasn't sure if this was his cue to get out of the car, as if his question didn't deserve a response. Maybe it didn't. Maybe he was just being even more of an asshole than she already thought he was. He fumbled for the latch on his door but just as he was about to open it, Linda said, as if she was clearing her throat to start a long speech, "OK."

"OK what?"

"There are some things I didn't tell you."

Doug nodded. "Like, uh, what?"

Linda sighed again. "OK," she repeated. "Don't be mad."

Despite himself, Doug chuckled. "What would I be mad about?"

"Well, um, you know how Kevin is always . . . um, thinking that you might have turned him into the police?"

"Yeah," Doug said slowly, his brow furrowing now.

"Well, I know you didn't."

"Yeah. I know. We talked about that."

"No, I mean I actually know you didn't. I don't just know it because you're a cool person, or whatever, and I have good instincts. I mean, I know why Kevin got busted."

"Really." Doug was trying to piece things together. If she

knew why Kevin got busted, why didn't Kevin know why he got busted? Why did Kevin always have it at the back of his mind that Doug had something to do with it? Why hadn't Linda just provided him with this tiny, yet extremely important, piece of information? "Why did he get busted?"

"Because Ellie brought some pot leaves into school for show-and-tell," Linda said, and started giggling. "She thought they were pretty. She went down into his grow room and picked some leaves and told everyone in her class that her daddy grew these in her basement."

Doug started laughing too. "Why didn't you just tell Kevin this?"

Linda stopped laughing. "Because Ellie asked me not to. She was very upset."

Doug nodded. "So, wait. My friend has been walking around thinking I turned him into the cops for a year because you didn't want to upset a six year old?" He wasn't laughing now either.

"It's worse than that." She sighed heavily and continued. "I didn't want Kevin hanging out with you guys. I knew he was suspicious of you after he got arrested, and I thought, maybe he'll start acting like a responsible adult now. So, I just let him go on thinking that."

Doug let that sink in for a second. "So you think we're a bad influence?"

Linda said nothing, confirming it.

"You know what I think? I think Kevin's a bad influence."

Linda looked quizzical. "What do you mean by that?"

"You know what we've been doing for the last two weeks? He's not having an affair. We were stealing a Ferrari and it was his idea."

"WHAT?"

Doug had hoped to see relief in Linda's eyes now that he had confirmed that her husband wasn't an adulterer, but instead was confronted with what appeared to be shock and rage. Exhausted by the seriousness of the conversation and his inability to control it, he burst out laughing and was glad when Linda started laughing too.

Doug told her the story, slowly, so as to prevent further outbursts of surprise. When he got to the LoJack detail and the Ferrari being dumped on a truck ramp, Linda had her head in her hands but her mood had perceptibly improved. She was laughing at her husband's idiocy and Doug's own idiocy for accompanying him, but laughter was better than screaming, Doug figured. He felt some sense of accomplishment for having calmed her down.

"So that's Kevin the good influence," Doug finished.

Linda was quiet for a moment as they listened to the car idling. "I'm sorry," she said.

Doug lit a cigarette. "Whatever. It's water under the bridge."

"What are you gonna do? For work?"

Doug was on the verge of telling her about Kevin's pill-selling scheme, but decided that he had confessed enough for Kevin for one day. "I dunno. We'll see. I don't think cooking is really in my blood right now."

She leaned over and kissed him, not passionately but affectionately and accompanied with a little head rub intended to denote frustration. He squeezed her hand. In that second, Doug had the thought that the reason she was upset at Kevin for stealing the Ferrari was not that it was a felony and it risked their livelihood, but because she had not been included. Linda felt left out. Or maybe not. You could never tell anything with women.

"I'll call you," he said as he got out.

"Stay out of trouble, will you?"

"Yeah."

"I mean it."

"I . . ." He didn't want to make any promises he couldn't keep. "I'll do my best."

• • •

MITCH WAS WALKING an excitable German shepherd named Ramone and thinking about the business of dog-walking. Kevin had just given him his first paycheck, and it was slightly under $400. He had worked two weeks but had clocked less than forty hours. He couldn't pay his bills with an income of $800 a month, and his car insurance would be the first bill to not be paid, because, let's face it, life wouldn't really change that much if he didn't have car insurance. It *would* change if his electricity or heat got cut off and it would certainly change if he stopped eating or smoking pot, but car insurance? Nah. There were times when a kind of financial triage became necessary, when things like car insurance and unkeefed Canadian kind buds, once considered a necessity, suddenly became luxuries, and one of those times was fast approaching.

However, this meant that if he got pulled over while driving from one dog to another, his car would be impounded and then he'd be making zero a month. So, much though he loved dogs and enjoyed walking them and enjoyed working with Kevin and enjoyed being able to go to work high and see into the dog's true nature and not have to put up with Bob Sutherland staring into his eyes asking if he had allergies, this job wasn't going to last unless something changed. He needed more dogs.

He would bring this up with Kevin later, but he knew that Kevin was already giving him all the business he could afford to give. Which meant maybe he should get a part-time job of some kind. But it was the nature of dog-walking that you could have no other real commitments, because dogs needed to be walked at all different hours of the day, depending on the client's needs. So if he got a part-time job, he would be of no use to Kevin, and just having a part-time job would do him no good. He already had a part-time job walking dogs. Argh. Out of one shit situation, into another.

Besides the dogs, one of the things Mitch liked about the job was spending time in rich, quiet neighborhoods. The apartment he shared with Doug was just a mile from the metal-refinishing plant, where the rents were cheapest and the roads and houses were covered with soot and grime. Tractor trailers roared by at any time of the day or night. Mitch had never noticed how unpleasant the noise was until he had begun spending his days experiencing the total silence of the exurbs. Rich people, unable to spot his incongruity because he was, after all, walking a dog, were actually friendly to him. Who but a local would walk a dog in their neighborhood? Back at home, people shuffling to and from the convenience store never made eye contact, unless it was to bum a cigarette or some change.

He turned the corner onto Westlake Avenue and began walking Ramone up to the Westlake shopping district, a quaint row of completely useless stores which gave any passerby a quick hint as to the local property values. There were two antique shops, a store that sold delicious-looking pies covered with glazed strawberries for thirty dollars (Mitch had asked the price once when the munchies were kicking in and had wound up buying Twinkies at a convenience store a few moments later), and another store that sold futuristic furniture for so much money Mitch just looked and laughed. A three-thousand-dollar chair that looked like it had been designed for George Jetson—that would go smashingly in their living room, Mitch thought, next to the broken vacuum cleaner that had not been put away in so long that it had actually become their centerpiece. And finally there was a health food store–slash–flower shop–slash–art gallery, a combination of three businesses for which Mitch had no use at all.

And across the quiet street, there was a bank.

Mitch had noticed the bank the week before, when he had seen an armored car pull up out front and watched the guards, one ancient and one obese, struggle with two huge sacks of money. To Mitch's eyes, these were the worst-protected sacks of money he could possibly imagine, but he had not really thought about it at the time because the Ferrari mission was occupying the criminal portion of his brain. Now that that had ended in disaster, he was free to imagine new schemes and this little bank with its poorly protected delivery looked like a promising prospect indeed.

The downside of walking through the business district was that Ramone couldn't really pee on things. It was one thing to walk him up the tree-lined streets, where plants and shrubs and mailbox posts covered in the scents of other dogs provided an abundance of urinary possibilities, but quite another to have the dog pissing on parking meters and ornamental shrubs, spraying the ankles of matronly passersby. Despite the fact that a sign said dogs were welcome in the shopping district, Mitch had enough sense to know the purpose of the sign was really to allow the matrons to take their Lhasa Apsos and Shih Tzus into the antique stores, rather than to welcome a monster like Ramone to splash a quart of urine all over the Lillington Daisy display. So Mitch had to time his reconnaissance of the armored car precisely, because there was no way to linger without drawing attention.

The armored car pulled up in front of the bank at exactly the same time it had the previous week, which excited Mitch. Despite his career arc, he had a great respect for punctuality. He watched the old guy, tall and white-haired and bony, get out of the passenger side, noticing the caution with which he moved. Mitch thought he could almost hear the man's bones rubbing together. The obese guard remained in the driver's seat doing paperwork while the ancient one slowly opened the back door of the armored car.

The heavily armored door creaked like a castle gate as the guard swung it open. From where he was standing, Mitch couldn't see into the back of the vehicle, but he figured if he crossed the street quickly, he could get a look inside, making sure not to get too close to the guards, where they would notice him and possibly reach for their guns. His fears turned out to be unfounded, however, because as he approached the old guard, the man noticed Ramone.

"Ah, he's a big boy, isn't he?" the guard said cheerfully, seeming to forget about the bags of money behind him. "I used to have a shepherd. Long time ago."

Ramone, sensing he was being discussed, began to wag his tail and moved toward the guard with a burst of energy. Mitch had to hold the leash tight to prevent him from leaping up and putting his giant paws on the old man's shoulders, which would probably have knocked him down. As

Mitch restrained the dog and the guard bent down to pet him, he got a clear view over the man's shoulder. The inside of the armored car was empty but for four large canvas sacks of what Mitch could only assume was money.

The obese guard came around the side of the truck, wheezing and red-faced, apparently from the effort of climbing out of the driver's seat. He nodded curtly to Mitch, then opened the doors wider and grabbed one sack, and pushed another toward the older man. From this action, Mitch got a glimpse into the relationship between the two. The fat guy was businesslike and unfriendly, most likely the boss of the two. The older guy, whose mind seemed somewhere else, perhaps on the retirement he could not afford, was the affable one. Mitch imagined that the fat guy often complained to his supervisor about having to work with the older guard, and the supervisor told him to just play the hand that was dealt him.

Mitch also noticed they both had guns on their belts. And Tasers. For two unathletic fellows, they could do some damage.

"You guys have a good day," he said, pulling Ramone away from the old guard, who was ready to turn his attention back to the heavy bags. As Mitch walked off, he overheard the fat guy talking roughly to the old man. Fat prick, he thought.

Ramone had forgotten about them already and was sniffing an ornamental shrub outside the bakery, while the staff and customers gazed at him, critically, Mitch felt. Then Ramone lifted his leg and, with at least five people watching, unleashed a pulsating torrent of urine all over the sidewalk. It was unending. By the time he was done, the sidewalk was thoroughly drenched, as if it had been washed with a hose. Mitch saw the owner of the bakery approaching the door to talk to him. Through the glass, he gave her a quick friendly wave and dashed off, pulling Ramone behind him. The dog soon overtook him. He enjoyed any opportunity for a run.

• • •

WHEN HE GOT home, a downpour had started. The winter downpours always reminded Mitch of the opening scene in *Taxi Driver*, where Travis Bickel talked about the rain washing the scum off the streets. From his battered back porch, piled high with broken and disused plumbing equipment, Mitch could watch it doing exactly that. The thin layer of filth that accumulated on everything, courtesy of the metal-refinishing plant, actually created a black sheen on the water puddling in the yard.

He cracked a beer and didn't look up when the door opened and Doug came out onto the porch. Were it not for the cloud of pot smoke still around his head, Mitch would have sworn he had just gotten up.

"Hey dude," Doug said, sitting heavily on a wooden bench and rubbing his eyes, which were as red as a bunny's. "While you were out, I got ahold of some reefer."

"So I smell."

"I picked up an eighth for you too."

"Thanks. How much was it?"

"Fifty."

"Cool. I'll pay you in a minute."

"Whenever." Doug sat there for a moment more, perhaps just stoned, but Mitch sensed he was tense or upset.

"You all right?"

"Man, I just don't know what I'm gonna do about a job. I really don't want to work at a fast food place."

Mitch watched the rain cascading off the porch roof so hard he was getting a little bit of spray in the face. Now would be the time to bring this up, he figured. "I know how we can make a million dollars in forty-five minutes."

Doug laughed. "I don't know what I'm gonna do with my life," he said.

"I'm serious."

Doug looked at him and realized he was. "A million dollars?"

"Maybe."

"What's maybe? A million dollars or not?"

"Four bags of money."

Doug sat up straight. "I'm listening."

Mitch was pleased to see Doug's reaction, having expected the same moaning and groaning that had accompanied the Ferrari mission. Maybe a few weeks without any paychecks at all coming in had reshaped his attitude, given him a whole new respect for crime. Rather than considering the Ferrari fiasco proof of the stupidity of criminal behavior, perhaps Doug was considering it hands-on experience, which Mitch figured was a much more effective way of looking at things.

"Where are these four bags of money?" Doug prodded.

Mitch explained everything, making sure to stress the age and obesity of the guards. Doug was nodding thoughtfully. The Ferrari mission had been good tactical experience, Mitch decided as he was talking. They had learned a lot. For instance, it was important to dress for the weather. When they took down the armored car, there wasn't going to be any business-suit bullshit. And they had learned to consider the possibility of radio tracking devices, or more relevantly, to expect the unexpected.

When he was finished explaining, Doug nodded. "Shit," he said, lighting a cigarette. "Kevin's coming over in a few minutes to bring me a box of pills to sell. Let's ask him what he thinks."

"Sounds good."

"When opportunity knocks, make lemonade," Doug said.

"I don't think that's the expression. I think it's when—"

Doug laughed, as he often did when he said something stupid, leaving Mitch unsure as to whether he had said it for laughs or if he genuinely didn't know the expression. Mitch knew that most people underestimated Doug's intelligence when they first met him, partly because Doug would make comments like that one, subtly encouraging them to. "Let's just rob an armored car," Doug said.

Mitch nodded approvingly at the new, aggressive Doug. "All right then. One robbed armored car, coming right up."

• • •

OVER TIME, THE pot smoked in the house had begun to stain the walls up near the ceiling, but it was only noticeable if you lay on the couch and looked up, which was the first thing Mitch usually did after smoking pot in the house. So whenever he took a few quality bong hits, the first topic he introduced was how they should immediately buy some paint and freshen up the living room to avoid losing their security deposit.

"Dude, you say that every time you get high," said Doug.

"Stoner," said Kevin.

They were splayed out across the living room, a thick gray cloud of pot smoke in the air, the type you didn't notice if you were in the room when it was created. Sometimes they would be sitting and watching TV and smoking away, and a newcomer to the room, such as a pizza delivery guy, would comment on the cloud, reminding them that it was there, which would trigger more stressed mumbling from Mitch about the security deposit.

They had been discussing the Great Plan all afternoon, but eventually the marijuana had overtaken the conversation and turned it into a silent reverie. Yet the Great Plan, as it had developed in a haze of smoke, seemed surprisingly solid. They were to acquire a car for parts from the classifieds and somehow get it running. That way they could have a getaway vehicle which was unregistered and uninsured.

One of Doug's three superpowers, in addition to being able to identify and recite the effects of any pill and being able to name the performer of any rock song from the 70s to the 90s, was an ability to tinker with things and get them running. Once they got the car running, they would slap the old Nevada license plate on it and park it in the street across from the bank and wait, hoping that no cops showed an interest in the plate. There was, they decided, no other way but to take that small chance. It was Mitch's job, each time he walked Ramone, to monitor the police activity in the neighborhood, to make sure that the chance that some cops would drive by and notice their illegal plate was minimal.

When the armored car showed up, Mitch and Doug would simply push the old guard aside, grab the money, leap into the getaway car, and drive a mile and quarter to an old access road. There, Kevin's truck would be parked. They would remove the old Nevada plate, roll the junker car into a ravine, and drive back to Wilton with the money.

As the Great Plan would take place in broad daylight, it depended on the element of surprise. There would be witnesses, so ski masks were a must, but as long as there were no police, everything would go smoothly. They would buy a Taser, they decided, so they could "subdue" the guards if any problems arose. But definitely only as a last resort. Mitch liked the word *subdue*.

It had been discussed as much as their pot-soaked brains could handle, and finally the energy the subject inspired had petered out, and they had stretched out on the sofas and begun discussing the décor.

"Man, every time someone moves out of an apartment, they paint the place," said Kevin. "The security deposit is just for shit like holes in the wall or destroyed carpet."

"I'm just saying," Mitch said. "We should keep the place looking decent. I mean, look up there." He pointed lazily to a gray patch next to the light fixture, and Doug and Kevin dutifully looked but said nothing, frustrating him more.

Despite having neither a great respect for authority nor much interest in paying his bills, Mitch had a genuine respect for landlords which went beyond fear of eviction. His father had, during a slow season in the Smoke-Eeter selling business, tried his hand at property management, and Mitch remembered his tales of horror about how badly people treated rental property. He would come home and relate how some tenants had ground dog shit into a carpet rather than clean it up, because they knew they were moving out soon, or just bailed out on their tenancy and left a refrigerator full of rotting food. So in his efforts to be the perfect tenant, Mitch demonstrated a passive obedience to his landlord, an agreeableness he showed to no one else. And he took abuse for it.

"I think Mitch has a crush on the landlord," Doug said.

"Are you gay for the landlord, Mitch?" Kevin asked.

"I think that's why we stole the TV for him from Accumart. Because Mitch wants some landlord dick."

"Will you guys shut the fuck up? Seriously. I mean look at these walls, man. They were white when we moved in."

"*Mitch wants the landlord,*" Doug sang merrily.

"Fine," Mitch snapped. "Let's just leave the place a mess. Hey, why don't we just . . ." He paused as the marijuana temporarily interrupted his thought processes, then finished a moment later without any of the intensity. "Burn the place down," he said and yawned.

Time passed. How much was hard to say because everyone was stoned, but long after Mitch thought the subject was forgotten, Doug finally said, "I think you're right. We should paint the place. After we rob the armored car."

"It'll look a lot nicer," Mitch said. "You'll appreciate it."

"And we can get some new furniture," Doug added.

"What're you guys, interior decorators? I thought we agreed not to spend any of the money on anything but necessities for sixth months." Kevin sat up straight and looked at them both. "That's the plan, right? We have to stick to that. We just sit on the money for six months."

"Yeah, man," Doug said, nodding to placate him. "It's cool. I meant six months after we rob the armored car."

"No you didn't. We gotta be serious about this."

"We're serious, man."

"Because everyone in town is going to be looking for three guys who are suddenly acting like millionaires," Kevin said. He, too, began to lose intensity and he slumped back down on the couch.

"It's cool," said Mitch. "No spending money on anything but necessities for six months. That's the deal."

"That's the deal," Doug said.

"Bullshit," Kevin sighed. "I'm gonna come over a week after the robbery, and there'll be, like, a construction company putting a swimming pool in the backyard, and there'll be two Ferraris in the driveway. I know you guys, man."

"Definitely not a Ferrari," Mitch said. Then he adopted a British accent and added, "Frankly Douglas, I wasn't that impressed with the Ferrari, were you?"

"Decidedly not, Mitchell. I do think perhaps a Rolls-Royce though. That would be splendid."

"And a butler. We must hire a butler."

"Oh, we just must."

"You two are fuckheads," said Kevin, standing up, shaking his head slightly to get the cobwebs of dope and relaxation off his brain. "I gotta get home. Linda's gonna be wondering where I am."

"Later," Doug said. "I'll see if I can drum up some interest in those pills."

"Hey," Kevin said. "I have an idea." Then he paused for long enough that Mitch and Doug both figured the idea had disappeared into the marijuana wasteland and he would just turn to leave. But he continued. "You guys do that British accent thing pretty well."

"Yeah. So? What's the idea?"said Mitch.

"Well, when we rob the armored car, man, we should all wear ski masks and talk with British accents. You know, like . . . uh . . . the guys in *Reservoir Dogs*. Remember, they were all calling each other Mr. Pink and Mr. Green? Well, we'll talk with British accents."

"Cool," said Doug.

"Splendid," agreed Mitch.

"All right, I'm outta here," Kevin said, turning to go.

"Cheerio, then," said Mitch.

"Ta-ta," said Doug.

9

LIKE ALL GREAT plans, the Great Plan required an initial down payment. Cars, even junk cars, weren't free. Neither, for that matter, were Tasers and ski masks. The money was to be acquired by Doug, who would be selling pills. When he heard this, Doug reminded Mitch and Kevin that pill-selling could be quite a profitable enterprise and that the original plan had been for Doug to keep all the money, as he was taking all the risk. Therefore, the pill-selling money was technically his and should be repaid upon receipt of the huge bags of bills. As Mitch and Kevin figured Doug's total input would be in the neighborhood of five hundred dollars, and the take from the robbery would be in excess of a million, they put up no argument. Doug didn't seem to understand that when they were splitting up a million dollars these distinctions wouldn't matter so much. So they surrendered the point and agreed that Doug would first take out his five hundred, and then they would split up the million.

But Doug began having trouble right away. He had put word out that he had pills the day Kevin had told him of them, but still, six days later, no phone calls. Even the cooks from the restaurant, who used to come in hungover every morning and loudly proclaim a wish for pain pills, had not called. Perhaps they had prioritized their expenses and found that, after being laid off, there simply wasn't enough money around to pay for a pain-pill addiction. Doug decided he needed to find a richer clientele.

He called Mitch's cell phone. "Dude, we gotta go to a fancy club or something," he said when Mitch answered.

"Why?" Mitch was walking Ramone, keeping a close eye out for the police. He had been cheered to see that they didn't seem to be around.

"I need to get rid of these pills. Man, we can make hundreds of dollars a night and really get this thing moving."

"I'm not going to a club, man. Those places suck. They closed all the clubs in Wilton anyway."

"We might have to go someplace else. Out of town."

Mitch rolled his eyes, imagining Doug coming up with this idea as a convoluted way to get him to drive for an hour to see one of those shitty bands he liked so much. "Dude, just talk to some people around here. I'm not going to a club. No way."

Holding the phone to his ear with a raised shoulder while

watching a muted TV, Doug could hear Mitch rolling his eyes. Mitch didn't get bands like Left Outlet and Portishead, and Doug secretly thought it was because Mitch was insensitive, even deaf to some of the world's more obvious vibes. He rolled his eyes in turn and wondered about Mitch's value system, whereby it was OK to Taser a seventy-year-old man but in no way was it OK to visit a dance club.

"Dude, I've asked, like, everyone I know. Nobody can afford pills."

"All right then," said Mitch, adopting his commando persona. "But we're gonna have to sell *some* pills so we have money to go to a club."

"I can't sell *any* pills, man."

"Are you sure we'll be able to sell them at a nightclub?"

"Better bet than around here."

"All right, man. I'll put it on my credit card." They said goodbye, and it began to snow as Mitch walked Ramone back to the house. Dammit, the last thing he wanted was to run up more debt, especially at a freakin' dance club. Nobody but Guidos and losers with gold chains around their necks went to those places, bathed in cologne and perfume, reciting hackneyed pickup lines to each other. Mitch hadn't been out to a bar for any reason other than to watch a Steelers game in years, and the last time he had been to a dance club he had felt like he was watching a Discovery Channel nature special on mating rituals. Doug, he knew, was a music lover and wasn't opposed to dancing, and he had the vague feeling that Doug was just trying to get a financed night out of the house. Fine, if that was how he wanted to play it, Mitch would make him drink water at the bar. While he sipped martinis, which he didn't even like. Yeah, he'd see how Doug liked that.

Then it occurred to him that he had been walking all over Westlake for half an hour and had not seen a single police car, and he suddenly knew that this thing, if done right, was going to net them some serious cash. Hell, maybe Doug really did need to go to a club to sell those damned pills. When it came to the retail of contraband materials, he seemed to know what he was doing. And he was one of the team. Mitch decided that Doug could have a martini too.

• • •

THE NEAREST CLUB that was worth going to was all the way down near Pittsburgh, an hour's drive away over winding country roads and then a brief stretch of interstate. Mitch noticed the roads getting wider as they got closer to the city and he had a sudden urge to stay, to find work here, to never go back. As he merged onto Interstate 79, he saw the same endless rows of buildings and parking lots and fences that you found in any Pennsylvania town, but here they had an air of victory about them, as if they had triumphed over the landscape. In Wilton, it seemed like nature was always fighting back, and winning. Raised in Queens, Mitch always had the feeling that the endless walls of trees which lined the roads outside Wilton were plotting to retake the town, to evict the environmentally irresponsible inhabitants and grow back over the land that they had been cleared from by the original developers of the town. Here, though, in the suburbs of Pittsburgh, it was obvious that the trees had given up.

"It's ugly," Doug said, looking at the night landscape, a sprawling view of strip malls and carpet outlets illuminated by the yellow glare of streetlights. Mitch had been thinking just the opposite. It pulsed with energy, figuratively and literally. Wires and transformers and relay boxes and traffic lights and cell phone towers, every one of them representing a job, a person needed to maintain it, an opportunity. There were *things to do* here. Why would anyone want to go back?

"After we get the money, let's move to Pittsburgh," Mitch said.

"No way, man," said Doug, and even as he was saying the words, Mitch became aware of a gulf between them and knew that this, more than anything, was the reason they would likely one day stop being friends. Doug had grown up in Wilton and liked the familiarity, and even though he frequently spoke of leaving, Mitch often noticed he had no real interest in the rest of the world, or even the rest of the country. He would travel to another city to see a Phish show, but not to see the city itself. He would talk of relocating to places like Aspen or Monterrey or any place with

cliffs and girls in bikinis that he saw on the Travel Channel,
sometimes with great enthusiasm. But the enthusiasm would
quickly fizzle, and then he would hunker down and stare out
the window at the warm glow of the metal-refinishing plant.
It was an issue they had discussed only in the most superfi-
cial way, but it represented a difference between them that
was beyond compromise.

"Tree-fucking hippie," said Mitch.

"Sorry, I don't like soot and trash and grime," said Doug,
referring to big cities, apparently unaware that he was also
giving a fairly accurate description of Wilton.

He must look around Wilton with rose-colored glasses,
Mitch thought. To Doug, it was home sweet home, but the
thought of going back there empty-handed tonight gave
Mitch a stab of anxiety.

To quell it, he asked, "You really think we can sell a box
of pills to strangers?"

"There's no telling," said Doug, not providing the words
of comfort Mitch was looking for. "Selling anything is a
crapshoot."

"But you think there's a possibility?"

"Of course, man. I wouldn't have suggested this if there
wasn't a possibility."

Mitch nodded. Doug had what Mitch considered a rare
social gift, a genuine enthusiasm for meeting people. When
they went to parties or concerts, Doug would often disappear with random people he met and be found hours later,

having had soul-searching conversations with strangers which he would claim had enlightened him somehow. And before Kevin had been busted, Doug had managed to parlay this openness with strangers into a thousand-dollar-a-week business. Since it had been so long since Mitch had seen Doug using his gifts, he had forgotten there was a creature with insight and energy inside the stoned blob of protoplasm who now spent his days on the couch, a remote control in hand.

The club was exactly the kind of place Mitch dreaded: a neon-lit, garish, New York City–wannabe dance club, where the crème de la crème of Pittsburgh's northern suburbs could buy eight-dollar drinks and spend the evening pretending they were Eurotrash. Mitch groaned as he pulled into the parking lot and saw two Italian men in silk shirts opened to the navel going in the front door.

"Aw, come one, man. This is the best place you could think of? Look at those guys. I don't wanna go in there."

"We're here to sell pills, right?"

"Yeah, but . . ." Mitch sputtered. "This is Guidoville. Isn't there, like, a country bar or something around here?"

"Since when do you like country music?"

Mitch groaned again and banged his head on the steering wheel. Doug knew how he felt about dance clubs; they had discussed it a number of times and never reached agreement. Dance clubs were supposed to facilitate meeting women, but for Mitch they did just the opposite. He was good at conversation and bad at dancing, and the loud music in the clubs robbed him of his weapon. These clubs, he felt, gave the advantage to dumb people who couldn't carry on a conversation about anything except shopping but who looked good gyrating.

"Man, you just gotta chill out," Doug said. "We'll have a good time."

"This is a sacrifice," Mitch said. "I'm sacrificing here. I'm taking one for the team."

As he parked, two women in tight miniskirts and high heels walked past the car. Mitch watched, open-mouthed, as they went in the door, suddenly aware of how long it had been since he had seen a real, live, attractive woman in the flesh. He *had* to get out of Wilton. "Shit, man, who knows?" he said, suddenly cheerful, eyes riveted to the marching asses. "Maybe it won't be so bad."

● ● ●

INSIDE, THE CLUB was exactly what Mitch had expected. Thumping, raging sound—he hesitated to call it music— filled every inch of the place like dirty floodwater, and there wasn't enough square footage to accommodate all the patrons, a situation that apparently made the business "happening." People crushed together was the club owner's dream, but to Mitch it looked like a fire marshal's nightmare.

"This place sucks," he told Doug conversationally, who

nodded, unaware of what had just been said. Doug made the motion for drinking and pointed Mitch toward the bar. Then, with the calculating gaze of a sniper, he surveyed the terrain, looking for people who appeared to want pills.

And he found them. He grabbed Mitch's arm to make sure he had his attention and pointed to two guys standing by a rail. They were holding beers but didn't seem interested in the women or the dancing, and they were scanning the crowd with the same sniper intensity that Doug had just displayed. One of them was bald-headed and muscular, wearing a tight T-shirt, and looked more like a bouncer than a patron. The other was just a normal-looking guy, perhaps a bit underdressed, like Doug and Mitch.

Mitch would never have noticed them. Doug pointed to them and nodded, then pointed to the bar again, instructing Mitch to go and buy beers. Mitch began to push his way through the crowd, feeling the driving beat from the speakers vibrate in his gut. He hadn't had this much fun since he had been stuffed in the back of an armored personnel carrier in the army, bodies pressed against him, the rifles and entrenching tools of the other soldiers poking him everywhere, comfort impossible. The endless monotony of the beat reminded him of the thumping of the APC's engine. All that was missing was the diesel fumes coming up from the floorboards. People paid a cover charge for this, he thought.

The crowd at the bar was three deep and customers were

holding their money high to get the bartenders' attention. Mitch was wondering how long it would take him to run out to the parking lot, drive to a beer distributor, and get a beer there, and considering whether or not that would be a time-saving alternative when Doug tapped him on the shoulder. He had the two guys with him. Doug motioned that they should go outside, which was cool with Mitch.

Mitch was amazed; Doug had been able to pick these guys out of a crowd. That had to be some kind of a marketable skill. He was a human drug dog, able to detect a possible customer in a crowded room. In the parking lot, they made their introductions and Mitch shook the two men's hands and instantly forgot their names, as usual. Then they went to sit in their car, a luxury SUV. Mitch stretched out, enjoying the comfort of the seat, assuming his role was the heavy, the henchman. If the deal went bad, he was supposed to watch Doug's back. But these guys seemed enthusiastic about the pills and perfectly friendly, so Mitch stared out the window and listened to the conversation.

"These are the good ones," Doug was saying. "They're seven-point-fives. This is about the strongest shit you can get, except for the tens, but those suckers are impossible to find anymore." He sounded professional, like he was giving a presentation in a boardroom. Mitch almost expected him to start pulling charts and graphs out of his pocket and review the strengths of hydrocodone tablets with a laser pointer.

The bald-headed guy rolled a pill around between his thumb and forefinger for a few seconds, then asked if he could take it. Doug nodded. "Sure, man. It's cool when the buyer takes a pill 'cause it means you're not a cop."

Eager to prove that he also wasn't a cop, the other guy reached into Doug's little box and took a pill too.

"How much you want for 'em?" he asked.

"I can get five bucks a pop for these, no problem," Doug said. "It depends how many you want. If you buy in bulk, you'll get a price cut."

Doug, Mitch realized, was a good businessman. He had a thousand pills in the box, and the shifty doctor who gave them to Kevin only wanted two dollars a pill. So Doug had started out the negotiations with a possible three-thousand-dollar profit.

Staring out the window, oddly excited by the whole thing, Mitch listened as they haggled. The final price they agreed on was $2,800, which the bald-headed guy produced by just reaching into his wallet. This guy carried around more money than Mitch had seen in months. The only time Mitch ever had a stack of hundreds in his hand, he was on his way to the post office to get a money order for rent. These two didn't look rich, yet they had a luxury SUV and three grand in cash. He was tempted to ask questions about their lives: What did they do for a living? Who were they? Did they have families? But he was smart enough to know that a parking-lot drug deal wasn't the occasion for exchanges of real information.

The deal completed, they said their goodbyes and shook hands again as they got out of the car. Eight hundred dollars, just like that. Mitch felt a surge of adrenaline as they got back into their car.

"Holy shit, dude, that was awesome! You're the man!" He punched Doug's shoulder. "Eight hundred bucks! We can get a great car for that."

"We have to get ski masks and Tasers too," said Doug, who was hunched in the passenger seat, counting the money.

"I can't believe it was that easy. Dude, we ought to do this full time."

Doug shrugged. "Do you want to? I mean, do this instead of robbing the armored car?"

Mitch started his car, mulling the idea over. Today had certainly been easy money but he knew that every day wouldn't be that easy. They had just gotten lucky. And besides, Doug had all the skill, knowledge, and bargaining ability. Mitch really didn't bring much to the table.

"Nah," he said. "I mean, it was impressive and all, but you did everything. All I really did was give you a ride."

"I could do this full time," Doug said. "Maybe we should do this instead of robbing the armored car."

"Are you having doubts?"

"I don't know. I'm getting kind of scared about the whole thing," Doug said. "I mean, I just need a little bit to live off. I don't need to be rich and shit. I don't need millions of dollars. Money doesn't buy happiness."

"Sure it does," said Mitch cheerfully.

"Look at Kurt Cobain."

Despite the giddiness of the moment, Mitch felt anger welling up. He hated this logic on which so many people operated, the quaint, pat little platitudes they used to comfort themselves, the bumper stickers and refrigerator magnets that supposedly summed up all their struggles. Money doesn't buy happiness. God has a plan. It will all work out in the end. It was brainwashing, calculated and perfect, the final bitch-slapping to top off a lifetime of stocking shelves or filing papers or answering phones. If he was going to spend his life making money for someone else, Mitch thought, that was fine. It was inevitable. But don't insult my intelligence by trying to convince me money is worthless, just so you can keep the whole fucking pile to yourself.

He knew that Doug was a man of simple needs and that he really would be happy with very little. So, for that matter, would Mitch. But it wasn't all about the money. It was about Accu-mart, about the army, about Doug's car getting impounded. It was about everything that had ever made him feel small, that had given him the message that he owed someone something, that he had to do more, that his behavior wasn't good enough.

"Kurt Cobain was a drug addict," Mitch snapped. "All the people who killed themselves when they got rich were drug addicts. Janis Joplin, Hendrix, Jim Morrison. Money doesn't buy happiness for drug addicts because they can buy so many drugs all of a sudden that they just freak out. Then rich people look at that and they say, 'Money doesn't buy happiness, fuckers. See what happened to Kurt Cobain? So stop asking for more money, 'cause it ain't gonna help.' They just use that bullshit as an excuse to not give us raises. Then *they* take the money and laugh on the beach in Bermuda. Dude, fuck that. If money doesn't buy happiness, why do guys guard it with guns?"

He drew a deep breath, then continued his rant while Doug sat in the passenger seat staring at him. "They *expect* us to eat that shit up. They expect us to say, 'Wow, money doesn't buy happiness. Boy, I'm sure glad I don't have any money. Otherwise, I'd just overdose on all the drugs I could buy. Yessiree, it's much better if the rich people keep all the money, 'cause if I had any of it I'd just spend all day jamming heroin into my arm.'"

"Wow, dude," Doug said, taken aback by Mitch's sudden ferocity.

"Money buys happiness for everyone else. You fucking bet it does. It gives you mental peace, man. You know why? Because if you got money, you stop worrying. And not worrying all the time is happy enough for me."

"You worry?" Doug asked. He sounded innocent, like a little boy, and Mitch felt a twinge of regret that he had cut short their celebration of the successful drug deal with an outburst of bitterness. But he hated seeing his friend act . . . brainwashed.

"Of course," Mitch said. "Don't you?"

"No," Doug said softly. "I just figure everything will work out in the end."

Mitch gritted his teeth. "I worry all the fucking time," he said. "I worry about bills, about the rent, about not being able to ever afford anything. I can't go anywhere or do anything. Shit, even any of that stuff you see people doing during the commercials in football games: mountain-biking, traveling, going to the beach, concerts, vacations. It's like there's this great big fucking world out there full of all this great shit, and man, we're never gonna be a part of it. We can't even have a little taste, you know? So, yes, I worry."

They pulled onto the interstate, and as Mitch brought the car up to highway speed, he wondered if Doug's silence was disagreement or contemplation.

"It's like we're all in this big beehive, man," he continued, "and we're just these worker bees. And all we're ever gonna do is bring honey to the queen."

"Hmm," said Doug, which didn't really clear up for Mitch whether Doug agreed with him or not. He didn't feel he had made his point well. *Honey for the queen.* That was pretty damned poetic and Doug didn't appreciate it. He knew Doug wasn't as angry as he was but Mitch felt he ought to be. He'd just been laid off, for chrissake. It was like the dude never got mad

In reality, Mitch knew that the reason he wanted Doug along for the armored car robbery was because it was going to be a part of his life, and he knew that if something important to him was not also a part of Doug's life, they would start drifting apart. Lately, Mitch had been getting an increasing sense of their eventual separation's inevitability.

There was a long stretch of silence as they focused on the road, the lights of the city fading behind them, and Mitch tried to think of the perfect sales pitch to get Doug to commit. He knew he was terrible at sales. The truth always burst out of him at inconvenient moments. It was one of the reasons his attempt at working in the corporate world at Accu-mart had ended so badly, and he had the sense to know that any further forays into corporate life would end the same way.

They crested a hill and Pittsburgh became just a muted glow in the rearview mirror. The gentle thumping of the concrete road cast a hypnotic spell in the car, like white noise. Mitch's voice was softer when he spoke again. He had decided on the positive approach.

"I'm looking forward to robbing this damned armored car," he said. "I'm actually looking forward to it, like we're going on vacation or something. You know why?"

"Why?"

"'Cause ever since I was in school, everyone has been trying to teach me a lesson, you know? Accu-mart, the army—always someone telling me to sit up straight, quit smoking pot, do this, do that. Stop getting in trouble for stupid shit."

Doug nodded.

"Well, I've learned my lesson. I'm not going to spend any more time getting in trouble for stupid shit. No more. You understand? No fucking more. I don't want to be the guy who is always getting in trouble for stupid shit. Next time I get in trouble, it'll be for something serious."

"Hmm," said Doug.

10
CHAPTER

"THIS IS IT. This is the place," said Kevin, pulling into a driveway that was little more than frozen mud. At the far end of the driveway, by a garage that looked like it was a day from total collapse, was the car they had come to buy, a 1980 Chevy Impala which had been listed in the paper for $300.

They had been excited after reading about the Impala, because in a big old car like that, there was plenty of room to work on the engine. Kevin was always ranting about how cars nowadays crammed everything in so tight, all the computerized gizmos and gadgets, so that you practically had to remove the engine block to check the oil. But not on these old babies. You could crawl under the hood and sleep in there after your wife threw you out, he said, a comment which made Mitch and Doug look at each other in concern.

"I just meant there's a lot of room in there," he explained, noticing their reaction.

The plan was to check the car out, maybe do some work on it, and get it running—all without registering it. The Impala, with its eight-cylinder engine and bulletproof appearance, was the perfect getaway car. They would slap the Nevada plate on, drive it to the bank, then drive with the money to a preselected spot in the woods where they had parked Kevin's truck. Then they would push the car into the ravine (the preselected spot required a ravine) and speed off, rich men.

It was important, therefore, to give the guy who sold them the Impala fake names, in case the cops ever found it in the ravine and traced it back to the last registered owner. They had practiced their fake names so there would be no slipups. Doug had even suggested wearing fake mustaches and wigs, but after consideration, that suggestion had been discarded because none of them knew enough about applying a fake mustache to be able to guarantee that it would work. The possibility of a mustache falling off while they were talking to the guy who was selling them the car was too great. Anyway, the town where they were buying the Impala was fifteen miles from Wilton and over twenty from West-lake, where the robbery was going to occur, so they figured they'd just take their chances.

Before going to look at the car, they had also reiterated the final part of the plan, the aftermath: Absolutely, positively, no spending any of the money for at least six months. The money was to be buried in three packages, one for each of them, in the exact same spot where they had parked the Ferrari on their most humiliating night of crime, a location chosen because it was neutral ground that they all knew well and also because burying money there would be a symbol of their new status as successful criminals, as opposed to bungling ones. It would be like giving the finger to the LoJack company and their fine product.

"Dude, this car stinks," said Doug, who was sitting in the backseat. Kevin had driven Linda's car because all three of them had decided to go and look at the Impala, and Mitch and Doug were sick of being crammed in the pickup. Linda's car had a backseat, and to Doug, it smelled like something really bad had happened in it quite recently. "Do you think Ellie, like, had an accident back here?"

"She's nearly eight, douchebag," Kevin snapped. "She doesn't have accidents anymore."

"It reeks back here," said Doug.

"Whatever."

"Remember our names," said Mitch, becoming the embattled paratroop commander again. They were bitching about smells while he was trying to get into character as "Rick." Rick, his Chevy Impala–buying alter ego, was a devoted employee of a major discount retailer, and Mitch was eager to try out this new fake personality on the man who was selling the car. He was disappointed that neither Doug nor Kevin had bothered to fabricate any details to go with their fake names, and he wasn't even sure if Doug remembered his. They didn't seem to think the fake identities were important, but screwing up something like that would be as bad as a fake mustache falling off while you were shaking hands. They were acting like amateurs.

Mitch went up to the front door and knocked. There was no answer. He had spoken to the guy on the phone not more than an hour ago, and he had sounded very old. Perhaps he had just hung up the phone and gone out and forgotten all about them.

"Dude, I'm telling you, it reeks. There's something in there," he heard Doug saying. Standing on the front porch, Mitch rolled his eyes. They were still bitching about whether or not Linda's car smelled. Obviously the car smelled. It had nearly made Mitch gag on the ride over, but so what? Couldn't these guys see the need to focus? He wondered how they were going to pull this robbery off if they kept getting sidetracked and bitching about trivial shit.

"Come on, you guys," Mitch said, deciding that he had to be the leader of this crew. They hadn't even gone over to look at the old Impala. Instead, Doug was digging around under the driver's seat of Linda's car and pulling out a bag.

"Ohmigod," said Kevin. He had turned pale.

"What are you guys doing?" said Mitch, but he was alarmed enough now by Kevin's reaction that he was no longer angry.

"God, this bag REEEKS," said Doug, holding it at arm's length. It was a heavy, dark green trash bag that unfurled as he held it out, and as it was upside down, the contents fell out and landed with a thud at Doug's feet.

It was Scotch Parker.

Doug yelped and hopped away from the dead terrier's little body. Released from the trash bag, the full odor of the rotting carcass hit all of them at the same time, and Mitch gagged and felt his eyes water. He looked over at Kevin, who had covered his face with his hands, seemingly more ashamed than disgusted.

"Dude," Doug croaked. "Why are you driving around with, like, a dead dog under the seat?"

Kevin was strangely silent.

"Seriously, man," Mitch said after a second. "That's a good question."

They all stared at the little terrier's body, bloated and gray. Mitch took a deep breath and went in closer to get a better look. The dog's eyes were half open, his tongue hanging out of half-open jaws, his tiny teeth exposed. For most people, the sight of a dead body of any species was a cause for emotion, so seeing a dead animal that he had never known in life was a rare opportunity to study death in a neutral context. Then he breathed and got a whiff of the decaying carcass, and he gagged again.

"Kevin, man, we gotta bury this thing," he said.

"His name's Scotch," Kevin said, his voice flat.

Mitch was taken aback by Kevin's tone and turned to Doug. "You wanna help me bury it?"

Doug nodded and walked over to the half-collapsed garage. Leaning against some rotting firewood was an old, rusted shovel.

"FUCK!" Kevin screamed.

Doug and Mitch, who were about to start digging a hole by the pile of rotting firewood, flinched.

"FUCK, FUCK, FUCK!" Kevin was screaming at the top of his lungs. He walked over to the front of Linda's car and began savagely kicking a headlight. This isn't good, Mitch thought. The whole aim of this transaction was to keep everything cool, to pay cash for a junk car and leave, and not be remembered.

"What the hell is his problem?" Doug asked Mitch.

"I dunno," said Mitch, looking equally mystified. He handed Doug the shovel and ran over to where Kevin was screaming. "Dude," he said, putting his hand firmly on Kevin's shoulder. "What are you doing? What's the matter with you?"

Kevin seemed to run out of energy and slumped forward. "Fuck," he mumbled.

"Is this about that dead dog?"

Kevin suddenly lurched forward, full of fury again, and kicked the bumper. "FUCK!" he screamed. Mitch tried to hold him back.

"Settle down," said Mitch softly.

"I've got . . ." Kevin said, panting from the effort of his outburst, "a goddamned dead dog under the seat of my car." He threw his arms up and turned around to face Mitch. "That's like the story of my fucking life."

"Well . . ." said Mitch, trying to think of something helpful to say, "I wouldn't go that far. But as long as we're on the subject, *why* is there a dead dog—"

"I'VE GOT A DEAD DOG UNDER THE SEAT OF MY CAR AND A FERRARI IN A FOREST AND A FUCKING DRUG-DEALING DOCTOR MAKING ME SELL HIS PILLS FOR HIM!" Kevin was bellowing like a wounded animal and Mitch's only thought was that he was glad they were in a neighborhood where the houses were fairly far apart. If he'd had an outburst like this back where they lived, neighbors would have been peering out their windows and calling the cops by now.

"Dude, keep your voice down!" yelled Doug from over by the garage, where he was dutifully digging a hole.

"Goddammit! Fuck my life! Fuck my fucking life!" Kevin kicked the front of the car again, but the burst of energy was gone, though the fading rage seemed all the more heartfelt. "Fuck, dude," he said to Mitch, as if imparting a profound piece of wisdom. "I mean, *fuck.*"

Mitch nodded.

"I can't do anything right. Not one fucking thing." Kevin sounded like he was about to start sobbing. He was wearing a frozen half-smile, though, and Mitch wasn't sure which of his senses he should be guided by. "I mean, I leave a goddamned dead dog in the car and let my wife and my daughter

drive around with it in there for a fucking week and . . . and
. . . they fucking poisoned him with antifreeze, man."

"Poisoned who?" Mitch ventured, trying to piece the
rant together.

"ANTIFREEZE!" Kevin screamed and Mitch flinched,
realizing the tirade wasn't nearly over. "And the cop
wouldn't do a goddamned thing about it, and he said I
could investigate myself for five hundred dollars. Five hundred dollars! Do you have five hundred dollars to investigate . . ."

Kevin seemed to be pausing for breath so he could bel-
low some more incoherent syllables, but Mitch put his hand
up, almost as if he were requesting a turn to speak in class.

"Dude," he said. "It's OK. We're going to rob an
armored car."

Kevin considered that for a second and Mitch thought
how odd it was that robbing an armored car was the only
hopeful thing he could offer. Maybe things really were that
bad. "I'll probably fuck that up too," Kevin said, but more
softly, and Mitch thought the outburst really was over.
Thank god the old guy wasn't home.

"We're not gonna fuck it up, man. We're gonna do it
right."

Kevin stared into the grass of the old man's yard for a
moment, then looked up, suddenly cheerful. Suddenly
enough for Mitch to be a little alarmed. The switch in emotion was almost psychotic.

"OK," Kevin said, brimming with energy. "Let's do it."

"You wanna have a look at the Impala?" Mitch asked cautiously.

"Yeah," said Kevin, his eyes now insanely bright. "Let's have a look at the Impala."

"You OK, man?" asked Doug, who had just finished burying the dog by the garage. He tamped down the last piece of earth and put the shovel back against the woodpile.

"I'm great!" said Kevin, with an enthusiasm that made Doug and Mitch glance at each other. Mitch shrugged. They opened the hood and looked at the Impala's engine, which was in surprisingly good condition.

There was the sound of footsteps behind them and Mitch was startled to see an old man dressed in jeans and a flannel shirt standing there.

"Hey," Mitch said, trying to hide his surprise. "I didn't see you there. Where did you come from?"

The old man appeared annoyed. "Came out the back door. To see what all the commotion was. You fellas wanna buy this thing? It's three hundred dollars."

"I'm Rick," said Mitch, extending his hand. The old man grabbed it and then let go. This grumpy old bastard was barely looking at them, so the subterfuge was, hopefully, unnecessary.

"You wanna buy this thing? It's three hundred dollars."

"Does it run?" asked Kevin.

"Yeah it runs. It runs OK. What do you want, a goddamned

new Cadillac? It's three hundred dollars, for chrissake. Get it outta here."

You had to love grumpy people, Mitch thought, because they didn't ask questions. Foul, grumpy people were the opposite of nosy neighbors. If only there were more of them.

Doug pulled three hundreds out of his pocket and gave them to the man.

"You a dealer?" he asked Doug as he was counting the bills.

"Nah, man. I just have long hair. It doesn't mean anything."

The old man looked at him, confused.

"I think he means a car dealer, dude," Mitch said. Doug burst out laughing, which only irritated the old man more.

"Get this damned thing outta here, and you go too." He began to walk back into the house. "Making all that commotion. Disgraceful. Goddamned disgraceful."

Well sonofabitch, Mitch thought, watching the old man climb the steps back into his house. That was easy. They had a getaway car.

• • •

THE GETAWAY CAR, it turned out, had a top speed of about fifteen miles an hour and labored mightily up even the slightest grades. As the Wilton area was nothing but steep grades, it became apparent to them that the getaway car wouldn't get them away from very much until it had a tune-up or, at the very least, some new sparkplugs.

"I can do that," Doug said. "But for a tune-up I'll need to buy a timing light. That's going to cost, like, two hundred dollars."

"Dude, this time next week we'll have hundreds of thousands of dollars."

"I'm just saying, man. When we count out the money, I want to get repaid for all this."

"OK, fine," snapped Kevin, whose glum mood returned after they left the old man's yard. "We'll have a million fucking dollars to split, but we'll pay you an extra thirty-five fucking cents or whatever you want."

"Chill out, man," said Mitch, hoping this wasn't going to degenerate into a full-blown fight, leaving the goal of the whole partnership, the robbery, forgotten. He had decided he was the leader here, based on the fact that he didn't have dead dogs stuffed in his car, like Kevin, and he wasn't prone to flights of fancy, like Doug. "Let's all relax," he said, trying to sound soothing.

"Dude, fuck you," said Kevin. "We've got dogs to walk." He tapped his fingers on the steering wheel of Linda's Toyota, indicating a desire to go.

Doug hadn't responded, which was in keeping with his recent respect for everything Kevin said, as if he owed the guy something. Mitch thought maybe he was overdoing the leadership thing. Maybe nobody was really ready to accept him as the leader yet. So instead of trying to mediate, he suggested they all go inside and smoke a bowl. Doug accepted the offer.

"You've got to walk Duffy," Kevin said. "I've got dogs to walk too."

"We'll just smoke a bowl, then I'll walk Duffy."

"You do what you want. I gotta go." Kevin peeled off.

"I'm worried about him," said Mitch.

Doug said nothing.

Inside, they went over all the necessary details as they packed the bowl. The car had to be kept in the grass lot behind their house, away from prying eyes, they agreed. All the work Doug did on it would have to be as secretive as possible, and in the event he wasn't able to fix it, they agreed they couldn't take it to a garage because a mechanic would remember the car. An old car like that was just too distinctive.

"I'm worried about Kevin," Mitch said again, after he had smoked. Again Doug said nothing. Mitch was also worried about Doug for that matter. Whenever they smoked, they would trade a few bits of deep philosophy or random thoughts, and lately the thoughts Doug was having indicated an awareness of death, or at least change. In the old days, he would come up with such gems as, "Why do we only use the word *recess* in court and elementary school? Why don't we take recesses at work?" Recently his pot ramblings had been more along the lines of, "It would suck to have to be identified by your dental records."

Doug took a deep, slow hit and leaned back on the couch. "Man," he said. "If we get shot during the robbery, I hope the car doesn't blow up and burn us beyond recognition and shit. I'd hate for someone to have to identify me by my dental records."

"Not again," said Mitch. He took a long hit himself and lay on the floor, looking up at the ceiling. "Man, the ceiling's gray," he said. "We gotta paint this place."

"Not again," said Doug.

They both chuckled. "We need a change," Mitch said. There was silence and the comment hung heavy in the air because they both sensed that change was coming.

• • •

THE NEXT WEEK was a one of busy preparation. Doug used his free time to get the Impala running better, which required a fuel filter change and some new sparkplugs. He was going to give it a tune-up, but as they intended to drive it two miles and then push it into a ravine, he decided to save the money it would have cost to buy a timing light and instead invested it in a car stereo that he bought from a junkie who lived behind the Dumpster at the convenience store. Then, instead of getting the sparkplugs to fire in perfect order, he spent the day installing the stereo so they could listen to tunes while waiting for the armored car to show up.

Kevin and Mitch devoted time between dog walks to

finding a ravine in a forest near the Westlake branch of the First Susquehanna Savings Bank. There was plenty of forest. There was even a great dirt road that led back into the forest not a mile from the bank, but the road was flat all the way back, no ravines on either side. There was a small drainage ditch at the very end of the road, but it would scarcely conceal the Impala and might well cause water drainage problems for the farmer who lived there, who would most likely be out to investigate after the first rainfall. So no good.

"What we need is a rock quarry we can push the car into," Mitch told Kevin.

"Man, all the quarries are twenty miles over on the other side of town."

"We can't drive this thing twenty miles."

"No way. Lucky if we can get five miles out of it at a reasonable speed."

"Goddammit. Everywhere you look around here there's a ravine. Then, when you actually need one—"

"How about burning it?"

"No way, dude. That's all we need, a giant tower of smoke over Westlake. Then if . . ." Mitch was going to say "if we get caught" but searched for a different phrase, not out of any sense of superstition, but because successful people did not entertain ideas of failure. "If . . . if. . . . We want to avoid the possibility of an arson charge. That's serious shit."

"I think all of it is pretty serious shit," Kevin said.

It was, indeed, serious shit, but starting a forest fire after you robbed an armored car was the type of thing that could make news from here to Pittsburgh. "No fire. What else?"

Kevin nodded. "Drive it into a creek?"

"Nearest creek is six or seven miles away."

They stood looking over the drainage ditch. Damn, it would be so perfect, if only it were a ravine.

"How about parking it back behind those trees over there?" Kevin said.

"Someone'll find it. Hunters, kids, all kinds of people come back here."

"How about burying it?"

"What, digging a hole big enough for that thing? Fuck that. We'd need a fucking backhoe to make a hole that size."

They laughed.

"Shit," Kevin said, lighting a joint and handing it to Mitch. "How about burning it?'

"Dude, we just talked about that."

"Yeah. Right."

"Tell you what," Mitch said after a moment. "We park it back behind the trees and leave it there. It might be a day or two until anyone finds it. Then they trace it back to that old guy. Shit, he doesn't know anything about us. He didn't even ask our names."

"We have to wipe our prints off everything," Kevin said.

"Everything. We don't even go into that car without gloves on."

"We should tell Doug. He's working on the engine. He'll leave prints on the fuel filter."

"We'll tell him."

Kevin looked dubious. "I think we should find a ravine."

"Dude, there aren't any ravines around here."

"We need to keep looking."

They continued to stare into the drainage ditch.

"Linda's talking about a divorce," said Kevin. "She said she's going to file papers."

"Dude, that sucks," Mitch said, handing back the joint. "I'm sorry."

Kevin shrugged. "Dude, do you think things'll change after we get the money?" He had a forlorn expression Mitch hadn't seen on him before, an utter hopelessness, as if he just wanted to sink to his knees and sob.

"Yeah, man, everything'll change," Mitch said, putting some brightness into his voice for Kevin's sake. "Whose life doesn't change when they suddenly become millionaires?"

"Man, it's weird," Kevin said. "I think Linda knows about the Ferrari. I mean, I have no idea how she found out. But you know what she said to me yesterday?"

"What?"

"She said that she won't come visit me in jail. Because she knows that I'll tell her that I did whatever I did for her and Ellie and she doesn't want to hear that."

"You're not going to jail," Mitch said.

"But don't you think it's weird that she knows so much?"

"She's your wife," said Mitch. "No, it isn't weird,"

"How about covering the car with brush? You know, like camouflage."

"Dude, let's just wipe it down, no prints, and we'll be fine. That old dude'll never be able to find us. He didn't even want to transfer the title over to us. He just gave us a car for cash. We'll be fine."

Kevin nodded thoughtfully, the despair of a moment before now replaced by an energetic interest in his work. "OK, then. That's what we'll do. No prints."

"No prints."

"I'll park my truck right here," he said, pointing to a cleared piece of solid ground. "That's only four and a half minutes' drive from the bank. The cop cars, when they come, will probably come up Westlake Avenue, behind us, from the other direction. So we're good. We'll be in that old junkbucket for as little as five minutes."

"We need a tarp in the back of your pickup so we can throw the money bags under it," Mitch said. "Those things are pretty big, and there's not a lot of room in the cab."

"Tarp," Kevin said. "I'll take care of that. I'll throw some work equipment in the back too, maybe a leaf blower and some rakes or something. So we look like landscapers. Did Doug get the ski masks?"

"Not yet."

"Well, he needs to get 'em," Kevin said. "What does he do all day?"

"He sells pills for you," Mitch said pleasantly, trying to avoid any more confrontation.

"Right," Kevin said, getting the message that picking on Doug's unemployed inactivity was off-limits, at least until the mission was carried out. "Man, I think we should try to find a ravine."

"There are no ravines," said Mitch, walking back to the pickup. "This is the best we can do."

"What is a ravine, exactly, anyway?"

"It's like, a big hole in the ground you can push a car into." Mitch flicked the joint into the drainage ditch. "And there aren't any around here."

Kevin watched the joint land in a little puddle of water and circle around. "Are we really gonna do this?" The question hung in the air for a few seconds and Mitch figured it was a genuine invitation to discuss backing out of the whole thing. He also figured that Kevin was worried about going back to jail. Of the three of them, he was the only one who knew what the worst-case scenario actually entailed.

"You're not going back to jail, man."

"You think everything will be fine?"

"You won't go back to jail. I guarantee you."

Kevin started the pickup's engine. "Come on. Let's get outta here."

11
CHAPTER

THE NEXT DAY, Mitch went down to the Wilton Mall and looked around in the bookstore for books on leadership. There were dozens of them but most of them were full of advice for middle-management professionals. Dressing professionally was a common theme. Red ties were encouraged. So was drinking water, lots and lots of it, while constantly showing a positive attitude. Great leaders must smile and pee a lot, Mitch figured, as he put the last of the books back on the shelf. He decided to try looking for something more practical, but nothing offered advice on robbery.

That was the problem with crime: there was very little helpful literature on it. A simple manual would have been invaluable, written, say, by a guy who had pulled off an armored car robbery. But obviously, anyone who had successfully done that would be trying to lay low and would not want to attract the attention of the publishing industry.

The only place you could find people willing to discuss such matters was in jail, where one would be able to find an authority on every aspect of robbery except how not to get caught, which was the most important part.

So he tried to rent a movie about robbing an armored car. After a half hour in the video store, the only film he could come up with was *Heat,* which he had seen in the theater when it first came out. The guys in that movie just made Mitch feel inadequate. They had thousands of dollars worth of equipment: radios, complex codes, night vision goggles, and M16s. The Robert DeNiro character lived in a beach house. Mitch wondered why people who could afford all that shit didn't just invest the money rather than rob an armored car. If he had his own beach house, he and Doug would just toke on the deck all day; screw all this robbery crap. Why risk freedom when freedom was great? Mitch estimated it would take him about a year to save up for an M16, let alone all the drills, pistols, duffel bags, and binoculars. He put *Heat* back on the shelf.

When Mitch got home, bookless and movieless, Doug was sitting at the kitchen table looking at a toothbrush in a clear plastic container.

"What're you doing, man?"

"I just applied for a job at Chicken Buckets," he said.

He sounded forlorn. Mitch felt that it was his job as unrespected gang leader to keep everybody chipper, but he was confused as to why Doug would try to find employment just a few days before they were going to rob an armored car. Robbing an armored car involved a great deal of uncertainty, but the one thing you *could* be certain of was that, whether things went really well or really badly, you damned sure wouldn't need a job at Chicken Buckets afterward.

"Why?"

Doug shrugged. "I dunno, man. I've, like, always had a job. Sitting around all day drives me nuts."

"What's with the toothbrush?"

"It's for a drug test," he said. "I filled out an application and they gave me this toothbrush to swab my mouth with. You don't even have to do it there. It's a take-home drug test. I guess they figured that if you made the guys do it on the spot, they'd never be able to hire anyone."

Mitch picked up the toothbrush. Instead of bristles, it had a little absorbent sponge.

"Cool, huh? They can test your saliva now," Doug said, taking the brush back. "The thing is, I don't even know anyone whose saliva I can use. They give me a take-home drug test, man, they're basically just asking me to cheat on it, and I'm still not gonna be able to pass it."

Mitch opened the fridge and cracked open a beer, then sat down at the kitchen table next to Doug and thought about it. Linda? No, she smoked occasionally. The landlord? You didn't want to ask your landlord to help you pass a drug test. Besides, he seemed a little freaky sometimes, wired up; maybe he dabbled in meth or coke. That would be all Doug needed—to get busted on a drug test for one of the few drugs he didn't use. "How about Ellie?"

"Kevin's daughter?"

Mitch shrugged. "It's human saliva, right? That's all they need."

They stared at each other. Mitch burst out laughing but Doug remained serious. He pushed the toothbrush, still wrapped in plastic, toward Mitch. "When you see Kevin tomorrow, can you ask him to have Ellie stick that in her mouth?"

Mitch was still laughing, snorting beer out of his nose. He nodded. He got up and went into the living room to watch TV. Maybe that was what leaders did. They solved other people's problems.

FEELING UNCHARACTERISTICALLY CONNECTED to the world, Mitch decided to watch the news. There was something about the idea of robbing an armored car that, rather than making him feel removed from society, made him feel accepted by it. While he walked dogs, he was devoting an unusual amount of his time to daydreaming about the good times that awaited him, the beers he and Doug were going to have on the beach on a Caribbean island, the island that always appeared in films, peopled only with thong-clad young women who loved to flirt. Then, upon his return home, the move to Pittsburgh, where he would find a nice apartment downtown, furnish it elegantly with a flat-screen high-def TV and a black leather couch, and finish his education. Maybe he'd get accepted to Carnegie Mellon or Pitt and actually get a degree in something like computer science, then go on to start his own company doing something computer-science related. He'd have money and a nice apartment and plenty of time to figure things out.

The news began to sour his mood, however. They were covering campaign speeches of various political candidates and Mitch amused himself by counting the number of times he heard the candidates say the word *freedom.* They all said it, no matter what they were running for. The city comptroller could get applause by saying, "FREEDOM." It was a magic word that instantly overstimulated any crowd full of gullible chumps, and what other kind of crowd went to see one of these yokels give a speech?

Freedom, Mitch thought to himself. Who would try to enslave us? We're a military powerhouse thousands of miles from anyone. Mitch imagined most countries in the world kept their heads down and hoped the U.S. wouldn't notice them, praying that a mineral or ore desperately needed for American creature comfort was never discovered on their soil. Freedom, my ass. The only real threats to freedom were the guys giving the speeches, even the city comptroller, who Mitch just didn't like the look of.

Doug came in, bringing the bong with him, and sat. "Wanna hit?"

"Maybe in a little bit."

Doug set about packing the bowl and Mitch watched him rather than the TV. Doug was careful and meticulous. The bowls he packed somehow always hit better than the ones Mitch packed for himself. Doug possessed an attention to detail that Mitch knew he would never master, some fundamental difference in brain function that probably would have been evident even in early childhood. But Doug would never have thought of, nor planned, the robbing of an armored car. Everyone had their skill set, Mitch decided. Perhaps he had been born for this very purpose, to rob armored cars. He sure as hell had never felt born for anything else he had tried.

"It's on for Friday," Mitch said. "We meet at two o'clock."

"Why two o'clock? I have to hand in my drug test at Chicken Buckets at three o'clock."

"Oh, for god's sake," Mitch groaned. "You're just gonna have to be a little bit late."

Doug shrugged. "OK."

That was cool. Mitch had been expecting an argument, which he would have interpreted as a sign of Doug's reluctance to join them. "Chicken Buckets," Mitch said with a half-smile. "That place sucks."

"Their chicken's not bad. They have a special deep fryer that, like, pressure-cooks it."

"Do you really want to work fast food? You'll have to wear a paper hat."

Doug shrugged again. "No spending money for six months, right? What the hell else am I gonna do?"

Mitch nodded, impressed that Doug was taking the plan seriously enough to have thought that far ahead. What at first he had interpreted as an unwillingness on Doug's part to accept that things were going to change was in fact a well-thought-out extension of their plan. Doug was a team player. No need to worry.

"It's going to be fine, man," Mitch said.

Doug nodded, not looking up as he readied the bong for the day's first use. "Hey man, could you change the channel? There's gotta be something else on. The news is bullshit."

• • •

THE FOLLOWING DAY, Kevin took over the walking of Ramone because he wanted to get a feel for the area outside the bank. Everything had to be planned down to the last second. Kevin felt a rush of excitement just standing in the spot where the robbery was going to occur.

There's where we'll park, he thought, looking at a place across the street from the bank. There was a recessed alcove between two buildings which would provide a small amount of cover. This is where Mitch and Doug will stand and wait for the armored car. It will park right here to unload. Kevin walked across the street, gauging the distance. It would take two, three seconds at most to run across the street with big bags full of money. *Big bags full of money.* He liked the sound of that. Then the Impala would fly off around the corner and onto the dirt road into the trees by the drainage ditch—a four-and-a-half-minute ride. He had timed it four times. Then into the pickup truck piled high with landscaping equipment. The big bags of money would go under the tarp. Ski masks and identifiable clothing would come off.

And away they'd go.

Speed was everything. It had to be fast. What were the variables, the factors that were out of their control? Maybe a cop would notice the old Nevada plate on the Impala. Couldn't do anything about that. He'd take care to park with the rear of the car up against another car, so the plate wasn't visible. What else? The time the armored car arrived. It was usually punctual, right at three, Mitch said, but it could be late. They'd have to be prepared to wait a few extra minutes. The ski masks might be a problem. Obviously, you couldn't put them on too soon or people would start getting weird. You couldn't stand around wearing a ski mask next to a bank. They'd have to agree on the exact moment the ski masks would go on and try to keep themselves as hidden as possible until that time.

Cold weather, or rain or snow, would really help. That would make heavy headwear less noticeable and reduce visibility. A good snowstorm might even delay the police's arrival, but it might also delay or even cancel the armored car's arrival, so it had to be just the right severity. There were always things out of your control that could help or hurt, Kevin thought. They'd have to be on the top of their game. Definitely no getting high before the robbery. They'd have to make that a rule. Kevin took out the little notepad he had brought with him and wrote *No getting high.*

Under that, he wrote, *Cold weather, rain, good.*

That was it. He was done. This thing was going to happen.

• • •

"THAT'S IT?" MITCH was looking at Kevin's notepad. "'No getting high'? 'Cold weather, rain, good?'" Mitch laughed as he tossed Kevin's attempt at scientific organization onto the couch. He noticed Kevin looked annoyed, even hurt, so, using his new leadership skills, which he was developing as he went along, he said, "Prints, man. We gotta write something about wearing gloves around the car at all times."

Kevin picked up the little notebook. *Prints* he wrote.

"Prints," said Doug.

"Dude, did you get the ski masks?"

"Not yet."

"You know it's tomorrow," said Kevin. "What the fuck are you waiting for? What about Tasers? Did you get them?" he asked, though he already knew the answer.

"Tasers might be a bad idea," said Mitch. "We've decided to go without the Tasers."

"Why? What if—"

"If we can't get the money without Tasers, we're just not getting the money," Mitch said. "I looked it up online. If you rob someone without a weapon, it's a whole different deal. It's, like, two years max. But if you're even carrying a Taser, it adds like three years to it."

Kevin thought about this for a few seconds, then said "All right."

There was a tense silence in the room, which had never happened during their planning sessions before. Within twenty-four hours, it would be done, over. Kevin, who had recently watched a documentary about D-Day, imagined that they were the Allied generals the night before the invasion. Nothing to do now except wait for the time to be right. And, of course, get some motherfucking ski masks.

He looked around the room at his partners as if seeing them for the first time: Doug, who seemed strangely distant, removed from the whole thing, as if he still hadn't made up his mind to go through with it, and Mitch, who seemed highly motivated, energetic, yet bothered about details. That was a good sign. He wondered what they thought of him. How did he look right now? Stressed? Distant? Determined? He realized what the mood in the room was—it felt like they were all waiting for another one to call it off, and no one would speak up. He felt the need to leave before anyone, most likely Doug, backed out.

"I'd better be getting home," Kevin said. "Linda has some errands to run, and I have to take care of Ellie."

"Hey man . . ." Doug said, rising from the couch. Here it comes, Kevin thought. He's going to back out. Fine. He and Mitch would do it and have more money to split. "Can you do me a favor?"

Kevin squinted at him. "What?"

Doug handed him the little toothbrush wrapped in plastic. "Can you get a swab from Ellie's mouth with that? I need it for a drug test."

Kevin looked at the toothbrush. "Yeah, sure." To make Doug feel better about asking, and because he thought Mitch was secretly laughing, Kevin added, "I had her pee in a cup once when I was on parole."

Mitch laughed out loud, a welcome sound in the tense room. "Get outta here, man. See you tomorrow."

The way he said it, the words had significance beyond their meaning. It really was as if they were all heading for the beaches of Normandy in the morning. Kevin liked the feeling of drama, the sense that everything insignificant now had historic and powerful meaning in their lives. Turning the doorknob. Was this the last time he would ever turn this doorknob? Going home and seeing Ellie. Would that be the last time he would see her? He cleared his mind. He didn't want to think about that.

"See you tomorrow, dudes." He slammed the door. Either way, this was his last night as either a broke man or a free man. Time would tell.

• • •

IT WAS SNOWING. That alone cheered Kevin up, especially as the Weather Channel hadn't predicted it. Kevin saw it as a good omen, a sign from god, and kept repeating how good it was until Mitch finally asked him to stop mentioning it.

"It's just snow, man," he said. Mitch, who was a practicing atheist, imagined that if god really did exist and actually took an interest in an armored car robbery, he would be more likely to side with the guards.

"Did you get the ski masks?" Kevin asked Doug as he climbed into the pickup. Doug wordlessly pulled from his pocket a handful of old, worn green wool caps, into which he had painstakingly cut eye holes. Kevin stared at them.

"Dude, are you fucking kidding me? Why didn't you just buy new ski masks?"

"What's wrong with using these? You can use them as ski masks."

"Was it because you were worried we weren't going to pay you back? For ten dollars' worth of ski masks?"

"Dude, those're fine," said Mitch, who was concerned that one of the others might try to pick a fight intentionally so that the whole plan would disintegrate. Now was not the time to bicker, couldn't they see that? But Kevin, who'd apparently had his heart set on black ski masks, wouldn't let it go.

"Would it have been so hard to go to the mall and buy a nice set of black ski masks?"

"I don't have a car anymore," said Doug. "So yes, it would. And at the end of the day, do you think we're all going to be sitting around going, 'Ya know, man, everything would have gone so much better if only our ski masks had been a different color.'"

"I'll drive the Impala out there," said Mitch, ignoring both of them. He was gripped by a fear that everything was going to fall apart, which made him talk fast and loud to drown them out. "I'll follow you," he said to Kevin, making firm eye contact to draw him away from the ski mask conversation.

"I'll ride with you," said Doug, getting out of the pickup. It might be better that way, Mitch thought, because it would put an end to the childishness. Kevin nodded, and Doug slammed the door shut.

"What's his problem?" Doug asked as they got into the Impala. "Excuse me, but I thought this was a robbery not a fashion show."

"No big deal, man. He just got hung up on details."

"But what the—"

"It'll be fine," said Mitch, cutting him off. "Put your gloves back on."

Doug had been idly pulling one of his gloves off, apparently forgetting that the night before they had spent an hour wiping down every part of the car that might contain a fingerprint—underneath the dash, the radio, the fuel filter, the wing nut that fastened the air filter to the engine, everything. All they needed now was to absentmindedly touch something and have to do it all over again.

"Dude, this car drives like shit," said Mitch, who was having trouble getting it up to fifteen miles an hour as Kevin sped off in front of them. "I thought you fixed it."

"The engine works fine," said Doug. "It's getting gas. You gotta let it warm up a little more."

Mitch floored the accelerator and the Impala bucked and chugged then shot ahead, banging Mitch's head against the headrest. Then the car began to buck and chug again, nearly smashing Mitch's head into the steering wheel.

"I put new gas in it, high octane," said Doug. "I figure it had been sitting for a long time, so the shitty firing was because there was water in the gas."

"How much gas did you put in? The needle's almost on empty."

"Two gallons," said Doug.

"Two gallons? Why didn't you fill the tank?"

"That high-octane stuff is expensive. Why throw money away? We're only going to drive it a few miles."

"This is our fucking getaway car? Jesus," Mitch snorted. He pulled over and called Kevin on his cell. "Dude, we gotta stop for gas."

"Didn't dipshit put any gas in the tank?" Mitch was

holding the phone close to his ear just in case Kevin said something like that. The last thing he wanted right now, when it seemed like things were actually going to happen pretty much as planned, was confrontation.

"OK," said Mitch, as if Kevin had said something agreeable. He hung up and they pulled into the first gas station, the one where the Mexican girl worked. It occurred to Mitch that Doug hadn't mentioned her in a while.

"You want to pay for it?" Mitch asked, thinking that giving Doug a chance to talk to the Mexican girl was doing him a favor, then realizing too late that he was basically accusing Doug of being cheap. Doug got out silently and went into the store. Mitch watched through the window as he paid the girl without talking to her, for the three hundredth time. Perhaps when you were on your way to commit a felony wasn't the best time to put your moves on a girl.

"Ten bucks," said Doug as he got back in the car. "That's all I got."

Mitch nodded and filled the tank with high octane. Funny, he thought, that Doug hadn't mentioned the Mexican girl in a while. He used to talk about her all the time, planning what he thought were clever ways to engage her in conversation. Something had been going on with him, something he hadn't been talking about. While pumping the gas, Mitch recalled other ways Doug had been acting weird—his nervousness around Kevin, his cryptic phone conversations. Then his mind switched to the conversation he had had with Kevin the day before. Linda knew about the Ferrari.

That was strange. Only the three of them knew about the Ferrari, and he knew neither he nor Kevin had told Linda. That left only one of them.

Holy shit. Doug must have told Linda.

He stopped pumping and stared into space for a few seconds while he tried to get his mind around why, exactly, Doug would have told Linda about the Ferrari. What could possibly have motivated him to do that? Why had he been hanging out with Linda at all, for that matter? Did the Doug–Linda connection have something to do with Doug not mentioning the Mexican girl? Fuck it, they were on their way to rob an armored car. Was it really the right time to start worrying about this?

When he got back into the car, he looked at Doug for a few seconds and Doug looked back.

"What?"

"Nothing." Mitch kept staring at Doug.

"Dude, you're freaking me out. What?"

"Nothing." He started the car. "Come on, let's go get this done."

12

T HE SNOW WAS beautiful. Not beautiful in the sense of aesthetically appealing, because Mitch hated snow. It was beautiful in the sense of making it difficult for police officers to chase and apprehend you. It was starting to stick too, which was even more beautiful. The only way this could not go perfectly now was if the bank closed early or the armored car never showed up.

Kevin parked the pickup on the dirt road by the drainage ditch they had been staring into just the day before, facing toward the road for a quicker exit. Mitch exited the driver's seat of the Impala and turned it over to Kevin, who got in wordlessly. Mitch liked the fact that no one was talking, as if they were commandos who had mastered their responsibilities so completely that words weren't necessary.

As Kevin pulled out of the dirt road, he asked, "You guys gonna talk with British accents?"

The British-accent thing had seemed like a brilliant idea at the time, but Mitch didn't really think that dialogue was going to play much of a part in the day's events. Besides, the mood that had spawned the British-accent idea, one of pot and partying, was absent in the car, where stress and fear and concentration had taken over.

"Nah," said Mitch. After that, no one spoke.

Kevin pulled onto Westlake Avenue and they passed the bank. He drove about a hundred yards down the street and then turned around. The street was deserted except for them, every parking space along the curb empty.

"Shit," Mitch said. "I hope the bank doesn't close."

"It's still open right now," Kevin said, "and if it's open, they're going to need a cash delivery."

Kevin looked at his watch. "Ten minutes, if they're on time. You guys want to wait across the street?"

"It's freezing," said Mitch. "I think we'll just stay in the car for a few more minutes."

"I need to stretch my legs," said Doug. He got out, slammed the heavy door of the Impala, and walked across the street without another word.

Kevin looked at Mitch. "Is he all right?"

"Is he ever?"

They watched Doug take up a position across the street, shivering in the little alcove by the antique store.

"Go tell him to at least pull his hood up," Kevin said.

241

"He doesn't have to pull his ski mask down yet, but it's probably best not to walk around bareheaded."

"Shit, there's no one around," said Mitch. "It don't matter."

Kevin was bumping his knee repeatedly into the steering wheel, so Mitch said, "Are you getting jumpy?"

"No," said Kevin, sounding more intense than Mitch had been expecting. "I just think you should go talk to Doug. There's something wrong with him. He's not talking and he's fucking standing in the street bareheaded when we all agreed to wear ski masks. The guy's been on the verge of fucking this up since day one, you know? First of all, he doesn't even do the one fucking thing he was given to do, which was buy ski masks, and now we gotta wear these fucking things." His eyes blazing with rage, Kevin held up the old wool cap with the eye holes cut out, his fingers sticking through the holes derisively.

"All right," said Mitch. "I'll go talk to him." He got out of the car and was aware of his feet crunching in the snow as he crossed the silent street. He wondered if instead of helping, the snow would serve as a hindrance, as it was recording his footprints for the investigators. He made an effort to grind his feet into the slush to make the footprints less distinct.

Mitch went and stood in the little alcove, shivering next to Doug. "You all right, dude?"

"I'm fine." Doug lit a cigarette and watched as an enormous SUV turned the corner and stopped right in front of them, blocking their view of absolutely everything. There were now two cars on the street, the Impala and the SUV, which was black and had tinted windows and was idling right in front of their little alcove.

"What the fuck is this guy doing?" Mitch asked.

"Dude, I don't know about this," Doug said.

Mitch had figured it was coming, but he had hoped that Doug would just keep his reservations to himself until the robbery was over.

"What do you want to do?"

"I don't need money this bad, man. I mean, I can work at Chicken Buckets. I should be at Chicken Buckets right now, handing in my drug test."

Mitch knew Doug felt this way and he had, in fact, always known. Every sign pointed to it, from the poorly prepared car with two gallons of gas in it to the cut-up ski masks, yet he had been denying it to himself, pretending Doug was still an enthusiastic team player. They should have left Doug out of it and he and Kevin should have been there alone. But it was a team effort and Doug was always part of the team.

"Well, shit, man. I wish you'd have said something before now." He lit a cigarette, aware that Doug was basically asking him permission to go. He didn't want him to. If Doug left, Mitch knew that nothing would ever be the same between them, that their friendship would basically be over. "Why'd you let it go this far?"

Doug began shifting his weight from leg to leg, and

Mitch could never recall seeing him more uncomfortable. For a moment, they watched the black SUV, in which, Mitch now realized, there was a teenage girl being taught by her mother how to parallel park. Over and over, the SUV lurched awkwardly toward a parking space at an extreme angle, then stopped, then jerked forward.

"I gotta tell you something," Doug said.

Right then, Mitch heard angels singing. There was a clanking and whirring of the heavy chains on the tires of the armored car as it turned the corner. And there it was, old, battered, and lurching, a monolith of scarred metal, parking right in front of the bank. Mitch could see, behind the windshield wipers, the familiar faces of the old guy and the fat guy. They were right on time, despite the snow. God, you had to love this company's punctuality.

"There's the truck. Look, is this about you and Linda?" he asked, hoping to move the conversation along. At the mention of her name, Doug looked like he had been punched. "I know about that," Mitch added.

"How, how. . . . Does Kevin know?"

"No, of course not. Dude, look, I've got to rob this thing, OK? If you want out, go ahead and take off. I'll see you later."

Before he could finish the sentence, Doug was running off into the street. Right behind the SUV, which inexplicably accelerated backward, knocking Doug down with a loud bang of metal and a yelp of pain.

"Awwww!" Doug screamed as he fell into snow. The SUV slammed to a halt. Mitch, who hadn't moved, saw the passenger door fly open, and a middle aged woman hopped out, looking panicked.

"Ohmigod," she was saying. "I'm so sorry. My daughter is learning to parallel park . . ."

Still standing in the alcove, Mitch saw the elderly guard come over to help Doug up. And then, right behind him, the fat guard, waddling over. From his vantage point, he could see inside the SUV, where a teenage girl was sitting with her head in her hands and appeared to be crying. But he wasn't thinking about that. He was thinking about the fact that *both guards* were helping a groaning Doug to his feet.

His legs moved before he could think about it. He darted along the side of the building, his feet crunching in the snow as he pulled his ski mask down. There they were—two big brown leather bags, just sitting in the truck with the door open. Mitch reached inside, wrapped his arms around them both, pulled them towards him, and, clutching them to his chest, ran over to the Impala.

"Go, go, go!" he yelled at Kevin, who was sitting in the idling Impala, wearing a ski mask. Mitch opened the back door of the Impala, threw both bags of money into the backseat, and climbed into the front passenger seat. Behind him, he heard someone scream, "Hey!"

"What about Doug?" asked Kevin as he put the Impala in drive. The Impala sputtered and lurched forward.

"Go, go, go!"

Kevin punched the Impala and they shot out into the street, where Mitch could see both guards running toward them. The fat guard was fumbling with the gun on his holster. Kevin drove right by him. The older guard slipped and fell in the street.

"Ouch," said Kevin as he drove by the old man. He pulled up next to Doug, who was standing next to the woman who had been in the passenger seat when the SUV hit him.

"Get in the fucking car!" Mitch screamed. He leaned into the backseat and tried to open the back door for Doug. The woman he had been talking to about the accident was staring into the Impala, now looking even more horrified than she had a few seconds before as she regarded two men in ski masks.

"British accents!" Kevin was yelling.

Doug didn't seem to be understanding that he should get in the car, so Mitch leaped out and in one smooth movement grabbed his coat, opened the back door of the Impala, and started to shove him in.

There was a gunshot and a yelp of pain.

"Jesus!" Mitch screamed. He looked over at the fat guard, who was crouching in a combat position back where the Impala had driven by him, a smoking pistol in his hand. Mitch knew that he hadn't been shot. Had Doug? Where had the yelp come from? He shoved Doug all the way in and slammed the door.

"Go, go, go!" Mitch shouted. Kevin gunned the accelerator and they skidded up to a stop sign. Mitch could feel the car sliding, tractionless, in the snow.

"Don't stop! What the fuck are you doing? This is a getaway!"

"I'd rather not be hit by someone coming the other way," Kevin said calmly, talking through the ski mask. He accelerated through the intersection.

"Owwww," Doug moaned.

"Dude, did you get shot?" Mitch stuck his head into the backseat, where Doug was lying on the bags of money, clutching his leg. He didn't answer.

"Man, I think Doug got shot," Mitch said to Kevin.

Kevin pulled up his ski mask. "No fucking way," he said.

"That fat bastard was shooting at us. I heard a shot."

"Yeah, I heard a shot too." Kevin looked into the rearview mirror. "Doug, man," he yelled. "Did you get shot?"

"Awwww," Doug moaned. "What are guys talking about? I got hit by a car. I think I broke my ankle."

Mitch leaned back over the seat, looking for blood, or a bullet hole. "You didn't get shot?" He began to pat Doug down, trying to find a wound. He felt relief welling up inside him as his search yielded nothing.

"Will you stop touching me?"

"I'm not touching you. I'm trying to see if you got shot."

"I didn't get shot, man. What the fuck are you talking about? I got hit by a car."

"You're sure you didn't get shot? You don't, like, feel funny?"

"Can you feel your legs?" Kevin shouted. "Can you feel your legs?" He started to crane his neck backward, and they nearly careened off the snow-slicked road.

"Dude, will you just drive?" Mitch snapped.

"Yeah, I can feel my legs. I can feel one ankle which feels like it's, like, fucking broken."

Mitch began to believe that Doug had not, in fact, been shot, and relief washed over him. He couldn't see any blood and Doug was being his usual self.

"We got plenty of pain pills," Kevin said. "When we get home, just take some pain pills."

"I intend to," said Doug.

Mitch sat back down in the passenger seat. "That's something you won't have to tell him twice," he said to Kevin.

They pulled onto the dirt road, which was now snow covered. Kevin parked the car as far back into the trees as he could.

"Man, I sure wish there was a ravine around here we could push this fucker into," Mitch said.

"This'll have to do," said Kevin.

"Awwwww," moaned Doug.

"Come on, you big pussy," Mitch said. They grabbed the bags and loaded them into the truck, under the tarp, then pulled the tarp tight to prevent anything from falling out.

Mitch peeked into one of the bags, but all he could see was another bag.

"Don't look now," Kevin said. "Later, later."

They got into Kevin's truck, with Mitch helping Doug, who was noticeably limping. Kevin cleaned the snow off the windshield. He fired up the truck.

"Ski masks off," Kevin said. "Make sure you've got your ski masks off."

Mitch was still wearing his. He pulled it off and nodded to Kevin. Doug had never had his on.

They sat for a second in the truck, listening to the country radio station to which Kevin left it permanently tuned.

"Dudes," Kevin said, before putting the truck in gear. "We did it."

• • •

THEY WERE SITTING in Doug and Mitch's living room, high on the adrenaline from the robbery. Doug's ankle was propped up on the coffee table, wrapped in ice, though Mitch thought he was exaggerating the pain as an excuse to eat more pain pills. The swelling didn't look that bad and Doug had never exactly been John Wayne when it came to minor injuries.

Mitch turned the TV on to wait for the five o'clock news as Kevin dumped the bags out onto the living room floor. Inside the bags were smaller, blue bags, made out of seemingly impenetrable plastic, with locks on them. They regarded the locks, then the bags, wondering which would be easier to cut through.

"We need bolt cutters for the locks," Kevin said.

"I bet I can get through the plastic with a steak knife," Mitch said. Then he tried doing exactly that until, after three attempts at stabbing the bag, he cut himself. "Fuck!"

"I have bolt cutters at home," Kevin said.

Nobody wanted to wait for him to drive home and back. They shook the idea off.

"This is like the shit they make bulletproof vests out of," said Mitch.

"Kevlar," said Doug helpfully.

Mitch stabbed the bag again. The knife just bounced off, cutting him again and spattering him with his own blood. "Fuck!"

"Dude, I bet you can rip that lock off with a wrench," Doug suggested. "Or two wrenches. I'll hold it, and you . . ."

Before he had finished, Mitch ran out to their cluttered back porch to grab as many tools as he could find. He brought back two wrenches, a razor knife, a pair of pliers, and a hammer and threw them onto the living room floor. Then he began stabbing and smashing everything that seemed to be keeping the bags closed. As he was doing this, he thought, What if we can never get these bags open? After all this, the Ferrari, the pill-selling, the planning, and the robbery, what if we end up just sitting here forever with god knows how much money on the floor, still in its indestructible bags? Maybe they would get busted and be national laughingstocks, a twenty-second-long bit on CNN about the three guys who robbed an armored car and couldn't figure out how to get the GOD-DAMNED MONEY OUT OF THE BAGS!

A lock snapped off in his hand.

"Thank you!" he cried in relief. He dumped the money all over the floor, and they looked at each other in surprise. There was a lot of it.

No one spoke. It was if they couldn't believe they had actually done this, accomplished their goal of successfully robbing an armored car. Until they saw the money, none of it had been real. In complete defiance of all logic, all three of them had been expecting something other than stacks of bills to fall out of the bag—promissory notes or letters of credit or rare coins—half convinced that today would be just another day that they got fucked by circumstance. But here it was. Money. Spendable American money.

"Shit," said Kevin, breaking the silence. "Look at that."

"Count it," said Mitch. "I'm gonna work on the other one." He grabbed the tools and began savagely beating the lock on the second bag. By this point he was bleeding pretty severely, soaking the blue plastic in streaks of red. By the time he heard a crunching of metal indicating the second lock might be giving way, the bag looked like someone had slaughtered a pig on it.

"Jesus, dude, go wrap that," Doug said. He limped over

from the couch as Mitch dumped the second bag onto the floor. More money. He stood up and regarded his living room floor, covered in bills of various denominations, Kevin studiously counting them and setting them in neat piles. Blood dripped from his hand onto the gray, matted carpet. He was panting.

"Go wrap your hand, man," said Doug again.

Kevin, sitting on the floor, counting to himself, said, "Get a calculator too."

· · ·

MITCH WENT UPSTAIRS and looked in the medicine cabinet for some gauze or Band-Aids and saw himself in the mirror. Except for the blood, he looked exactly the same. It surprised him. He had expected a fearsome monster to be staring back at him. He was a criminal now and he had imagined that his appearance would have changed accordingly, that his new status would be more obvious to the world.

The sink was turning red with his blood. The only thing in the medicine cabinet was a bag of hundreds of pain pills. He shrugged and took two, then winced, remembering the itching he had experienced last time. The hand didn't really hurt that much. He just wanted something to calm him down.

Looking at himself in the mirror, he was suddenly overcome with a feeling of dread. This couldn't keep going as well as it was going. Nothing in his life had ever gone this well. It was going to fall apart, and soon. He had to tell the others.

He wrapped his hand in toilet paper, which was turning red and soaking through before he could even finish, so he unwrapped it, held his hand up high like he remembered being taught in his first-aid class in the army, and did it again. It worked. By the time he had a decent bandage wrapped, the bathroom also looked like he had slaughtered a pig in it. He went back downstairs, the feeling of dread still with him.

"Did you bring a calculator?" asked Kevin. He was surrounded by money which had been organized into piles, perhaps six or seven of them.

Mitch shook his head. "Use your cell phone," he said. "Doesn't it have a calculator?"

Kevin nodded. "Good idea."

"What's with the piles?"

"Each one is twenty grand," Kevin said, going back to counting.

"Shit," Mitch marveled. Each little pile could buy a better car than he had even owned, or pay rent for two years, or . . . or anything. The possibilities were endless. He looked at Doug, who was sitting on the couch, similarly awed by the piles of cash.

"You still want a job at Chicken Buckets?"

"I'm thinking, maybe, like, fuck Chicken Buckets," said Doug cheerfully.

Despite himself, Mitch laughed, and sat down on the couch next to him. "I'm thinking about leaving town," he said.

"Why?"

"I've just got a bad feeling."

Doug said nothing. Then the news started, and Doug turned the sound up.

"Tonight, our top stories. The Pittsburgh Zoo might be getting a panda. And a daring daylight robbery in Westlake leaves an elderly man fighting for his life. Those stories and more, when we return."

"Fighting for his what?" Kevin had stood up and was staring at the TV.

"Dude," said Doug. "Fighting for his life? What, do you think he had, like, a heart attack or something?"

"And they're blaming it on us," said Kevin.

Mitch shook his head, disgusted but, unlike the others, not surprised. "I told you I had a bad feeling."

13

"**F**UCK THE PANDA! Fuck the goddamned panda!" Kevin was screaming as he paced back and forth, staring, enraged, at the television. They had sat through five minutes of panda news and he couldn't take it anymore. They knew more about pandas than they had ever wanted to. There had even been a special segment on their mating rituals and several slow camera pans of baby pandas being bottle-fed. "OK, I get it. Pandas are cute. Can we have some fucking news now?"

Mitch was sitting with his head in his hands, Doug silent, his injured ankle still propped on the coffee table. Kevin grabbed the remote and began flipping to the other news stations, which, incredibly, were also showing panda clips.

"I'm gonna strangle a fucking panda," said Mitch softly to himself.

"Dude, I just wanted to go to Chicken Buckets," Doug was saying to himself. "And now I'm wanted for attempted murder. Or maybe murder. Or—"

"Dude, shut up."

"And now, a daring robbery in Westlake leaves an elderly security guard fighting for his life." They shushed each other and cranked up the volume some more, so as not to miss a word.

"Finally," said Kevin.

"A daring daylight robbery in Westlake resulted in the shooting of Ames Security guard Francis Delahunt," the news anchor read. They watched the whole piece. At no point did the report actually say that it was the daring robbers who shot him, merely that the robbery resulted in his being shot. Then the news program cut to a detective standing outside the bank.

"This was clearly the work of professionals," he said as snow fell in his hair. The detective seemed uncomfortable with the microphone being held in his face. He had the look of a man who would rather get back to work. "They created a distraction and then hit the van." More babbling, then it cut to a cereal commercial.

"We're professionals," said Doug, flushing with pride. "I don't think I've ever been called a professional before." Then he remembered that he had just been implicitly accused of shooting someone and he fell silent.

"That was fucking smart," said Kevin, "jumping in

front of the SUV like that. Did you guys just think that up on the spot?"

Mitch and Doug looked at each other. "Yeah," Mitch said after a second.

"They know we didn't shoot that guy," Kevin said, scoffing at the report, but with worry still evident on his face. "They never actually said we shot the guy."

"Do you think somebody watching that report is going to figure that out?" Mitch snapped. "They deliberately tried to give the impression that we shot the guy. I mean, if someone gets shot during a robbery, it's pretty much a given that it was the robbers who shot him, don't you think?"

"This is fucked up," said Kevin. "I mean, we even decided *not* to bring Tasers. Tasers! Let alone guns."

"I think it's bullshit," said Mitch. "They're just saying he got shot so people will turn us in."

"I heard a shot," said Doug. "Didn't you guys hear a shot?"

"And a scream," Kevin agreed.

"I saw the fat dude with a gun," Mitch said, thinking hard and talking slowly. "He was the only guy there with a gun . . . and he fired it . . . and . . ."

"Fuck!" Doug yelled, his head in his hands. "I could have gone to Chicken Buckets this morning."

"Dudes," Mitch said, as if uncovering the Holy Grail, as if a ray of clear and brilliant light were shining on him, the light of logic. "If there was only one gun and one guy firing it . . . and one guy got shot, it must have been the guy with the gun."

"The guard," said Kevin.

"The fat guard shot the old guard."

Their thoughts began racing and they started finishing each other's sentences as they pieced the situation together. "And then he said—"

"It was us who shot the old guard—"

"Because he didn't want to get blamed for it—"

"But there's no fucking way. . . . They must know. . . ."

"They can do things with bullets, like ballistics tests and shit. . . ."

They stopped and stared at each other.

"I'm leaving town," said Mitch.

"Dude," Kevin said. "You can't leave town. We agreed we'd just sit tight for six months."

Mitch shook his head and sighed. "I know, but this shit changes everything."

"No it doesn't. Just calm down. Smoke a bowl, man. Everything will be OK. They've got no way to connect us with anything."

"I've got a bad feeling," Mitch said again.

Kevin stood up and looked at the piles of money on the floor. "Does this give you a bad feeling? Look at this." He looked at his cell phone. "There's sixty-six thousand, two hundred and forty-one dollars, each."

Mitch let the amount sink in for a second. Three years work at Accu-mart, just lying on the floor.

"We bury it, like we agreed," Kevin said. "For six months."

Mitch shook his head. "I've got a bad feeling," he said. "You guys bury yours. I'm keeping mine in a duffel bag."

"If he wants to keep his in a duffel bag," Doug said, "why isn't that cool?"

"Because if they search the house, they'll find it."

"Dude, if they're searching the house, it means we're fucked anyway."

Kevin sat back down on the couch, shaking his head. "I don't want to hear any more about your fucking bad feeling," he said. "We got away with it. We did something right."

Mitch looked at Kevin, the TV still blaring in the background. He was clearly unconvinced. "We need to make plans," he said. "Contingency plans."

"Contingency plans," Doug agreed. Mitch wasn't sure Doug knew what *contingency plans* meant, but he liked that Doug was backing him up.

"OK," Kevin said. "We'll make contingency plans."

• • •

DETECTIVE ROBERT SCOTT was wondering whether it was an act of genius to rob an armored car just as a snowstorm was starting, or a complete fluke. A lot of what these guys had done seemed like a fluke and he wasn't even sure if the supposed diversion the robbers had created, leaping out in the path of a car, had been intentional. How would that work, unless the mother, who had been teaching her daughter to parallel park, had been in on it? And clearly, she hadn't been.

And you couldn't arrange a snow storm.

Still, when he had spoken to the reporter, he had acted as if he were dealing with a group of criminal masterminds. It was always best that way. The more threatened the public felt, the greater the likelihood of someone turning the perpetrators in. That was why he had intentionally failed to mention that the idiot security guard had shot his own partner. As usual, the reporter just took down everything he said without asking any relevant questions and rushed to say it, word for word, in front of the camera.

The security guard hadn't wanted to admit he had shot his own partner. He had tried for at least thirty seconds to suggest that these guys had been armed, but that had fallen apart quickly when both the mother and daughter said they hadn't seen any of the robbers with a gun. The fact that the injured guard, getting loaded into an ambulance, had been repeatedly screaming "You stupid fucking moron!" at his partner, who had been trying, red-faced and pathetic, to keep his composure, also served to discredit the fat guard's claim.

A uniformed officer came up behind Scott, his feet crunching in the snow. "No tracks from the other vehicle, because of the snow," the officer said. "No prints in the

Impala. No info on the plate. Nevada DMV says, a thirty-year-old plate like that, we'll have to wait until Monday morning to get the info from Carson City. The government offices are already closed."

Scott gritted his teeth and shook his head. He hated when things happened at the end of the day on Fridays. Of course, most criminals knew this would slow down an investigation, which was why Friday afternoons were a particularly busy time.

"We could call the mayor of Carson City and get authorization," the officer suggested. "We can do that now. The new antiterrorism laws . . ."

Scott shook his head. "This really doesn't qualify. What about the VIN number?"

"The last time this vehicle was registered was in 1988. To a Reginald Wright, lives in Newcastle."

"Let's go talk to him."

The officer, a young man whom Scott only knew in passing, usually worked traffic detail and had almost finished his shift when the bank got robbed. He had already been kept past his end time for the three hours since they had found and printed the Impala, and Scott noticed a look of reluctance pass across his face.

"How about those guys over there?" Scott said, pointing to a few officers milling around the Impala. "Did any of those guys just come on shift?"

The officer nodded eagerly. "Peskey did."

"Send him over here. You go home."

"Yessir."

• • •

THE CONTINGENCY PLAN was not complicated. Doug and Kevin were going to take five thousand out for emergencies and bury the rest of their money where they had agreed: in the exact same place they had parked the Ferrari.

Mitch would take his money and stuff it in a duffel bag. He also made himself an emergency escape kit with all the things he needed to hit the road in a hurry: a few changes of clothes, his favorite bowl (a glass-blown piece of art he had bought off eBay), and something to fill it with. Everything else he owned he figured he could kiss goodbye, and it didn't amount to much.

Getting their story straight was another thing. They all agreed on that. Since Kevin had been the driver and had been wearing his ski mask, his name should never come up. In the event that Doug or Mitch, who might have been identified, got questioned, they would just say that the third guy was a mysterious stranger who ran off with all the money. Kevin didn't seem enthusiastic about being protected, but he did acknowledge that, as he had a wife and child and a criminal record, it might be best.

So the only one with a plan was Doug.

"We should both take off, man," Mitch said. "You gotta come with me."

But Doug knew he couldn't. It was all coming full circle, like some beautifully laid cosmic plan. He would be the one who would convince the cops Kevin wasn't involved. If he took off too, Kevin would get arrested. Now he saw how he could make things up to Kevin. Not by selling pills, because that had mostly been for him anyway. The only way he could make things right with Kevin, without telling him anything, was by going to jail for him.

Of course, that would only happen if the cops figured anything out. And as Kevin kept repeating over and over, and Mitch kept contradicting, that was never going to happen.

After The Contingency Plan had been made, they settled back on the couch and packed a bowl. Kevin called Linda and told her he was going to be late. He had dogs to walk.

"If Mitch leaves town," Doug asked, "can I walk dogs for you? I'd rather do that than work at Chicken Buckets."

"Sure," Kevin said. "But Mitch isn't going to leave town."

"Are you going to leave town, Mitch?"

Mitch said nothing.

• • •

"MR. WRIGHT? MR. Wright?" Detective Scott hammered on the decaying screen door again. The noise echoed back into the trees, shattering the peace of the gently hissing snowfall. Scott could hear a television inside and figured the guy was old or just nearly deaf. Judging by the look of the yard, which contained only things that had been bought before 1980, he guessed old.

Detective Scott knew from twenty-seven years on the police force that old people were hard to deal with. Civilians always thought it was young people who were rude to the police. It was certainly young people who committed most of the crimes, but old people were less likely to show respect, more likely to scream curses at you. Maybe they figured that, as death was relatively near, they had less to lose. Scott hoped this was one of the other kind of old people, the deferential, friendly kind, but something about the appearance of the house made him suspect otherwise.

The door flew open and an old man glared at them. "Whaddya want?"

"Evening, Mr. Wright. Are you Reginald Wright?"

"Whaddya want? Goddamn hammering on my door at this time of night."

It was only eight thirty, but Scott let it go. "Mr. Wright, I'm Detective Robert Scott of the Wilton Police Department, and this is Officer Peskey."

"Whaddya want?"

"Mr. Wright, do you own a 1980 Chevy Impala?"

"What? That's was this is about? I took the ad out of the paper. Sold it . . . last week."

"Did you transfer the title and get the paperwork—"

"I sold it, I tell you. What would the goddamned cops want a car like that for? It was a piece a' shit."

"Mr. Wright, we don't want to buy it. We want to know who you sold it to. When you sell a car, you have to do a title transfer and—"

"I'm eighty-four years old," said Mr. Wright.

"Well, that's actually not an excuse to not transfer the title."

"That's bullshit. All a bunch a' bullshit." Mr. Wright started to slam the door shut, but Detective Scott gently inserted his foot in the doorway to stop him.

"Mr. Wright, that car was used in a robbery. And if you don't talk to us, I'm going to assume you had something to do with it and have Officer Pesky here arrest you."

Mr. Wright, who was used to having his demeanor interpreted as lovable elderly dottiness, became lucid and agreeable in a hurry. "What do you want to know?"

"What did the guy who bought the car look like?"

"There were three of them. One of them looked like a hippie."

"A hippie?"

"Long-haired. You know. A damned hippie."

Scott wondered whether it was feasible to get this guy to a sketch artist with a snow storm developing and decided to leave it until tomorrow. This wasn't exactly the crime of the century. The guys had been unarmed and he didn't want to force either the sketch artist or this old guy to be out and about on icy roads at all hours of the night. He was about to suggest a visit in the morning, when Mr. Wright offered one last piece of information.

"They buried something. In my yard."

• • •

AFTER BURYING THE money, Kevin came home around midnight and noticed Linda's car was not in the driveway. He sat in his truck for a full five minutes before he resolved to go inside. It didn't necessarily mean she had left him. She could have just spent the night at her mother's.

In the dining room, there was no note, which was a good sign, but all of Ellie's toys and books were gone, which wasn't. He flipped on the bedroom light and went through Linda's dresser. All the drawers were empty.

It was over.

Sitting on the bed, he looked at himself in the dresser mirror. It was over. He had snow in his hair and he had just robbed a bank and his wife and daughter were gone. How long had he been playing the role of father and husband without actually being one? Almost from the beginning, his family had been an afterthought. He had married too young, for all the wrong reasons, he decided. He had been envying Mitch and Doug, as they sat around baked and bunny-eyed in front of their TV, for the last few years. Maybe that was what adult males needed—a few years of baked, bunny-eyed behavior before they took on the roles of father and husband. He had rushed into things without ever taking the time to decompress from his teens.

Fuck it. He felt relief rather than regret, or at least, he told himself he did. It was too much for one day. First an armored car robbery and then your wife leaves you on the same damned day. He'd have to figure out what he felt later.

Was it fixable? Could he have everything back the way it used to be, after they had first been married? Possibly, he decided. It would take a lot of work. But with $62,214 and eleven cents, he might actually have the time and resources to work things out. The thought gave him a lift.

In the meantime, he would just enjoy having the house to himself. Then a thought occurred to him. The reason Linda had left was because he was always living in the meantime. He had secretly wanted the house to himself for eight years. Obviously, it had shown.

He was thinking too much. He would deal with everything tomorrow. He went down to the basement, got his bong and little stash, took it up to the bedroom, and smoked. Couldn't do that with Linda and Ellie there.

He exhaled a long, slow stream. Nobody to criticize him. Freedom.

•   •   •

THE NEXT MORNING, as so often was the case after a big storm, it was sunny. The snow was melting fast, the icicles hanging from the gutter of the back porch dripping furiously over the disused plumbing equipment, splattering Mitch's socks as he tried to smoke a cigarette. The bad feeling from after the robbery had returned full force. Mitch kept having to stifle the urge to grab his prepared bag of money and sundries and tear off without even saying goodbye to Doug. Couldn't these guys see anything coming?

There was a knock on the door and Mitch froze. Jesus Christ, this was it. He began to tremble and watched the cigarette shake in his hand as he wondered where he had left his bag. Could he get to the bag and over the neighbor's fence before the cops kicked the front door in? He tiptoed to the edge of the porch and peered around the side of the house and saw Kevin's truck.

Shit. He was going nuts. He exhaled, surprised at his panicked reaction. He answered the front door, hoping that his little fear episode wasn't still evident on his face.

"Dude, hope I didn't wake you up," Kevin said cheerfully. "I gotta walk some dogs today and I was hoping you could spot me a bud or two."

"Sure." Mitch went to get his bag of weed and a baggie. "Why are you walking dogs on a Saturday?"

"A couple of clients are out of town for the weekend." As an afterthought, he added, "Linda left me last night."

Mitch didn't know what to say. He felt he should offer something supportive, but the only comment that came to him was that a blind man could have seen that one coming.

"That sucks, dude," Mitch said finally, not sure if Kevin

even agreed. From his cheerful demeanor, he looked like he had shed a burden rather than lost a family. Some marriages were better ended, Mitch thought, aware that he knew nothing of the subject and didn't really intend to find out.

Doug came downstairs, sleepy-eyed and bed-headed, and nodded to them. Mitch handed Kevin the weed as Kevin's cell phone rang.

"Dude, you want some coffee?" Doug called from the kitchen.

But Mitch was watching Kevin. "Yeah," Kevin was saying into the phone. "I took him in my car and we buried him. I mean, *I* buried him. In a yard."

Mitch could hear the other person talking; Kevin was nodding. Then he hung up. "That was weird," he said.

"Do you want coffee?" Doug called again.

"What do you mean 'weird'?" Mitch stood up.

"The cops found Scotch Parker's body. He had a collar on him with a phone number. That was Mrs. Parker. She wanted to know why the cops came to her house this morning asking about her dog being buried in that guy's yard."

"The cops came? Over a dog?"

"Huh?" Doug shouted from the kitchen. "What's this about a dog?"

Mitch felt his heart start thumping again, like it had a few moments before. He searched for an excuse that would make everything all right. "Maybe the guy was just pissed . . . about the dog being buried in his yard. Maybe . . ."

"She said there were three cops. They were very serious."

Doug came out into the living room and saw the looks on Kevin's and Mitch's faces, confused, yet worried. "The cops went to that old dude's house?" he asked.

They began finishing each other's sentences again. "Which means—"

"They found the car."

"Fuck!" yelled Kevin. "I told you we should have found a ravine. You gotta have a ravine. You can't just leave a getaway car just sitting there."

"But . . ." said Mitch slowly, still piecing things together, " . . . they knew to go to the lady who owned the dog."

The three of them stood in the living room in silence while this information sank in, staring at each other, each hoping another would say something obvious and comforting which would make everything OK.

"And the lady must have given them your number," said Mitch.

"She did," said Kevin.

"We are fucked." Mitch sat down heavily on the couch.

"After all that. A fucking dead dog," marveled Kevin. "I shoulda just thrown his body out the fucking window."

"OK, we're fucked," said Mitch, his paratroop commander persona taking over. He jumped up and flung open the closet door and took out his coat and started looking around for his shoes. He found them and put them on. "Here's the deal," he began while hurriedly tying them.

"You give us up. We'll be ready for it. All your money's hidden. Just say you drove us out there to buy the car and that was it. Go walk dogs."

Kevin turned to go. "Sorry, dudes," he said.

"Sorry, man," said Doug, still holding a coffee pot in the kitchen doorway.

"Later, man." Mitch was a blur of activity, flying around, getting everything together. He opened his duffel bag and saw the money, the socks, and the underwear. He tried to decide if he needed another pair of jeans. Fuck it, he had enough to buy a new pair if it came to that. Kevin was still standing in the doorway.

"Gimme that weed back, man," Mitch said. "The cops'll be going through your shit later."

Kevin, whose hand was noticeably shaking, handed the little baggie back to Mitch.

"Get outta here. Go walk dogs."

As they heard Kevin's truck pull out of the driveway, Mitch turned to Doug, who still hadn't moved.

"Dude, last chance. I'd come with me if I were you."

Doug didn't look panicked or even slightly freaked out. He was standing in the kitchen doorway, coffee pot in his hand, with a serene smile on his face. "Nah, man. I'll be OK."

"You know you'll go to jail. You'll wake up in jail by tomorrow morning."

Doug nodded. Mitch went over and shook his hand. "Later, dude."

"Later."

Mitch turned to leave, then turned back. "I gotta be able to get in touch with you, to pay for a lawyer."

Doug shook his head. "I'll have Kevin handle that." They stared at each other for a few seconds, then Doug asked, "Where are you gonna go?"

"I dunno."

"Good luck."

"Same to you." The door slammed, and he was gone. As he was running down the steps and out into the street, Mitch thought, Guess I'm not going to get a chance to paint the ceiling.

14
CHAPTER

THEY CAME FOR Kevin when he returned from walking dogs. The whole time he was walking Duffy, the St. Bernard, he had been expecting cop cars to come screeching up to him. But they had just sat outside his house waiting for him to come home.

They were very polite and Kevin was very prepared. He was expecting to be wrestled to the ground and have his face pushed into the wooden floor of his porch, his mouth filling with paint chips, as had happened when they busted him for pot. But the detective was the kindly looking older man he had seen on TV and he just showed Kevin his badge and asked a few questions.

"How are you today, Mr. Gurdy?" the detective asked.

Kevin nodded. "Is this about the dead dog? Because Mrs. Parker just called me," he said, looking at the three police officers. "I'm really sorry. I didn't know there were all these laws about dog burial."

The detective gave him a skeptical smile and nodded. "Where were you yesterday afternoon at about three P.M.?"

Kevin gave the prepared answer: walking dogs. He described the schedule exactly. He had, of course, walked his dogs an hour early that day. Once again, the detective looked skeptical.

"When you bought the Impala, who was there with you?"

It hurt to do it, but it had been the plan all along. Kevin gave them Doug and Mitch's names. He stressed that Doug had just been laid off from his job and that his car had been impounded, and he tried to think of other things to say which might give the cops a better impression of the two. Then he remembered to ask the question that only a guilty man would forget to ask. "What's all this about? We just buried a dog."

• • •

DOUG WAS SITTING on his couch watching television when the cops arrived. After Mitch had left, Doug made the coffee and tried to figure out the only thing he still had control over—what exactly he would be doing when they came for him. He imagined a few different poses. He could be reading. He could be smoking pot. (What difference would it make at this point?) He could be watching TV. He could be cleaning the apartment, but clearly there was no point to that, as he would not be around to enjoy the cleanliness. Why go through the misery of cleaning unless you could enjoy the fruits of your labor?

It struck him that it might be a good day to go down to the convenience store and ask out the Mexican girl. He realized that the reason he had never done it before was that he lacked the confidence of a man who knew what he would be doing tomorrow. Today, he had that confidence but he decided not to bother because it just seemed like a bad way to start a relationship.

Perhaps she'd still be there when he got out.

He finished his coffee and smoked a bowl, then hid all the bongs and bowls, and put the last of his stash in the garbage. It hurt to throw the pot away but he decided he was in enough trouble as it was, so why make it worse?

Then he settled in to watch television, one ear tuned to every vehicle turning onto the street.

Around noon, he heard it and knew right away. Two cars, both with large engines, but not large enough for them to be trucks. They were driving slowly, as if checking addresses. Doug turned the sound down on the television, which he hadn't really been watching, just staring at it as if it were a campfire. He felt strangely serene.

The engines stopped. Doors were opened and closed.

He clearly heard one police officer walking around to the back of the house, trying to be quiet about it, but his feet crunched in the new-fallen snow. That, Doug figured, was in case he tried to bolt out the back door.

There was a hard knock on the door and he got up and answered it. A kindly faced older detective and a younger, uniformed officer stood on the front step, both looking extremely serious.

"Are you Douglas Keir?"

"I am," said Doug. He opened the door wider to allow them in and noticed that the action caused the two policemen to look at each other, surprised. They came inside.

"Is Mitchell Alden at home?"

"Mitch left."

The plainclothes detective turned to the young officer and said, "Check upstairs."

As the officer walked up the stairs, his gun unholstered, the older man turned back to Doug. "Can you tell me where you were yesterday afternoon, around three P.M.?"

"Three P.M.," Doug said thoughtfully. He screwed up his face, as if thinking very hard. The younger officer came down the stairs.

"It's clear," the officer said. "No one up there."

"Yes, I remember," said Doug. "At some point around three P.M. I think I was, uh, like, in Westlake."

"What were you doing there?"

"I was, uh, like, robbing an armored car."

• • •

CABS, BUSES, AND trains. He caught a cab from the convenience store to the bus station, a bus from Wilton to

Pittsburgh, and from the Pittsburgh train station he got the Amtrak to Cleveland. As he was buying the ticket with cash, making sure to crumple the bills in case they looked too fresh, Mitch congratulated himself on an act of sly genius. He doubted that anyone in the history of the world had ever before fled to Cleveland.

Why, he wondered, as snow-covered Ohio farmland shot past, does security go apeshit checking your luggage at airports but just let you take any damn thing you want onto a train? You could get on a train with a ticking suitcase with wires sticking out of it and no one would care, but you couldn't get on a plane anymore with a bottle of water. He wondered if there was some hidden agenda he wasn't seeing. Maybe the security was all for show, the shoe removal and the metal detectors just an act in a piece of terrorist-prevention theater. As he hugged his duffel bag full of cash to chest, he figured that having everyone scared shitless was always good for whoever was running the show.

Mitch was giving the issue thought because it was making it necessary for him to take trains rather than planes. No Homeland Security doofus was going to go rifling through his bag of money, no sir. But this meant that a trip to Cleveland would take seven hours rather than one, and Seattle or LA, if he decided to go there, would take days and days. And he couldn't leave his duffel bag alone, even for a few moments, so eating on the train was out. Still, no matter how much the ride sucked, Mitch figured that it had to be better than what was happening to Doug.

He wondered what to do when he got to Cleveland. He would get a hotel room, maybe buy some clothes and get a haircut so he looked a little more professional. Then he'd try to get most of the cash turned into traveler's checks. He needed to see about getting a fake ID from somewhere, though that could be risky. Maybe he'd just get a job for a few months that paid under the table, wait until everything died down, and then figure something out. Maybe he'd go to Canada. Maybe to Seattle.

Despite having a bag full of money and an open road in front of him, Mitch didn't feel as free as he had imagined he would.

AFTERMATH

SCREW MITCH AND Doug, Kevin thought. Mitch had blown town and Doug was in jail, so it was easy for them to keep their promise and not spend money in Wilton for six months. It had taken Kevin just one month of having to pay alimony, child support, and a mortgage on a dog walker's salary before he was parked across the road from the hidden bag of money with a shovel in the back of his disintegrating pickup truck.

The rain was hammering down, so anyone who passed by would be concentrating on driving, and Kevin had taken care to park back behind the trees where the pickup wouldn't be visible from the road. Rain made people uninterested in anything except getting home safely; it also made the ground soft for digging. He stepped out of the truck and was soaked almost immediately by the near-freezing rain, making him gasp for air. Before he even reached into the back for the shovel, the water was dripping off his eye-lashes, making it hard to see. He laughed.

Ducking back through the trees, he felt a sudden rush of freedom. Despite everything, he knew when he got home to his empty house, nobody would be there to ask him where he had been. Nobody would demand that he explain why he was soaked to the skin. Linda was a good person, most likely a better person than he would ever be, but Jesus H. Christ could she ask a lot of questions. Every day with her had been like a visit to the parole board. Where? Why? With whom? Now, tell me again?

He slammed the shovel into the soft earth, pleased to see that the ground where the cash had been buried didn't look disturbed. There had been so much rain and snow in the past few weeks that not even a professional tracker would be able to see that someone had dug a hole here. Which was good, because it was deer hunting season, so most of the people likely to walk past the spot would actually be profes-sional trackers. He was careful not to throw the dirt, laying each shovelful gently beside the hole. After about ten or twelve loads of dirt, he felt the sharp edge of the shovel drive into the trash bag. Damn, he thought, we really didn't bury it very deep. What if animals had burrowed into it? What if a mudslide . . . He shrugged. Sometimes you just had to leave things to chance. He threw the shovel down and sat on a rotting log as he pulled open the bag.

Money. The first handful of cash he extracted was a

wrapped brick of twenties, and as he looked at it in his lap, he was shocked to feel his eyes welling with tears. It was so unexpected that he put his head in his hands and let the money fall to the forest floor. More tears came, mixing with the freezing rain running out of his hair and down his cheeks. Within seconds, he was sobbing, so mystified by the emotion that he made no effort to stop it.

After a few moments, he became aware that even under the canopy of the trees, rainwater was dripping into the open bag of money, and he leaned over and twisted the top shut. The action allowed him to regain his breath and he looked down at the cash he had dropped on the ground. He was glad that looking at it again didn't induce another burst of emotion. He picked it up and put it in his pocket. He figured it was about three thousand dollars. He grabbed two more bricks of similar size, tied the bag closed again, and carefully replaced the dirt, making sure to scatter sticks and brush around the tamped earth. Within moments, the driving rain had made the dig marks invisible.

When he got back in the truck, he tossed the money on the seat of the pickup and stared at it. What had that been about? He hadn't cried since he was a teenager, and a young teenager at that. What was the last thing that had made him cry? He thought back. Frustration, probably. Ever-present frustration.

Then he looked at the money on the seat, so soaked

that water was dripping off it and pooling by the vinyl backrest. It was his. That was what had made him cry. He had earned it. Sure, he had stolen it, but he had done it successfully. After dropping out of college, getting kicked off the football team, failing as a husband and a father, and screwing up as a marijuana grower, he had finally, as the prison counselor had advised him, set a goal and achieved it. This dripping money on his passenger seat represented the first damned thing in his whole life that he had done right.

He was turning into a decent businessman too. The dog-walking thing was really taking off.

It was time to reward himself, Kevin decided. He hopped out of the truck, grabbed the shovel, and went back for ten thousand more. He would buy a new truck. A guy who did things right didn't drive around in a twenty-year-old pickup truck. His life was turning around and he wasn't going to hide it.

• • •

"MY LAWYER IS a con," Doug said into the telephone, looking through the glass at Linda. "He served five years for attempted murder, so he knows all the COs. He's totally hooking me up."

"That's nice," said Linda. Since she had arrived for her visit, she had appeared strained, as if fighting off sobs, which was making Doug uneasy. Before Linda, Doug had just had a fifteen-minute conversation with his lawyer, who had, through code, basically implied he could get the guards to bring him pills, weed, or anything he wanted. Rather than a Harvard lawyer, Doug now understood, an inmate needed a lawyer who knew the guards.

His lawyer had studied law while he had been in prison and supposedly turned his life around. (Though not enough to refrain from suggesting that he arrange drug deals for his clients.) Pennsylvania didn't require lawyers to go to school, a little known fact that inspired Doug to follow in his lawyer's footsteps. His first week in prison, he had resolved to become a lawyer, then noticed that, in a building where everyone was going to trial, the law books were always checked out. The only remaining skills book he could find was on cooking. He couldn't escape it. Maybe he would just break down and become a chef. Or a dog walker for Kevin.

Doug had the feeling that Linda really wanted to nag him, but she had figured that if you were talking to someone in an orange jumpsuit, nagging clearly wasn't necessary. She looked so, well, sad, that it was making him feel bad. Did he look that pathetic? "When I get out, Kevin said I can walk dogs for him," Doug said, trying to add some cheer to the mood.

"When will that be?"

"My hearing's on Thursday. My lawyer thinks eighteen months. It was going to be five years but he said if we agree not to talk to anyone about the guard shooting the other guard, then the armored car company wouldn't push for a stiffer sentence. Man, it's weird. It's like that's all they care about. Not embarrassing themselves. That, and the money. They said I could get out next week if I told them where the money was."

"But you're not going to?" Linda's voice rose in surprise. "Doug, you could be free."

Doug leaned forward and lowered his voice as he spoke into the phone. "I'm freer in here with money than out there without any. Besides, eighteen months for sixty grand? I figured it out. That's like three times what even a manager makes at Chicken Buckets."

Linda laughed, despite herself. Doug liked her smile. He felt the urge to say something romantic like, I miss you, but squelched it. To squelch it further, he asked about Kevin.

"He's fine. He's walking dogs. Business is good, I hear. Last I saw him, he had a new truck."

"He was supposed to wait six months before . . ." Doug said, then he realized that Linda might not need to know their prerobbery plan and quickly changed the subject. "You guys not getting back together?"

Linda shook her head. The buzzer went off, which Doug had learned was the signal his visit was over. Linda knew what the buzzer meant and looked around the metal- and cinder-block room as if relieved. The atmosphere in there was not inviting. Few people could tolerate more than their fifteen minutes.

"It's not so bad in here," Doug said cheerfully, hoping to get another smile. He got a sad one as she said goodbye. She waved as she left slowly, still looking at him, and Doug was afraid she was going to cry.

But it isn't so bad in here, Doug thought. He wasn't lying for her sake. He had a CO who could get him better drugs than he'd had on the outside, and he didn't have to feel stressed about not getting on with his life. You *couldn't* get on with your life in there; that was the point.

There was no pressure. That was the beautiful thing. No one expected you to make anything of yourself. A good day in jail was when you didn't get into a fight. You actually got credit for that. How cool would life be on the outside if, every week that you didn't get into a fight, a government official came by and complimented you, then gave you a reward? All you had to do was be nice and everyone was happy with you.

With no pressure and with his drug and alcohol counselor frequently praising him for being good-natured, Doug felt he could finally get his life back on track. He didn't know how yet, but it would come to him. The chopper pilot thing seemed like a stretch, even to the eternally optimistic counselor, but Doug was still thinking about writing a children's book. He was sure that he could write about a lobster who could stay off drugs and not stab anyone. Prison was the perfect writing environment. Hadn't there been a famous novelist who wrote from prison? Charles Dickens or Oscar Wilde, one of those English guys? Doug definitely remembered his English teacher in high school mentioning something about that.

Doug went back to his cell and the automatic lock closed behind him. His roommate, Mikey, who was in for "terroristic threats," was snoring away on his cot. One of the guys in the mess hall had told Doug, in a conspiratorial whisper, that terroristic threats had nothing to do with terrorism. It was most likely a sentence for stalking a girl. It was hard for Doug to imagine Mikey doing illegal things, because he seemed like such a quiet, sleepy guy. Severely overweight and soft-spoken, Mikey liked playing chess and humming to himself. It had been Mikey who had first clued Doug in to the secret of prison—it wasn't so bad.

Sure, there were no girls, and the black guys listened to shitty rap music all the time, but it was only for eighteen months. He could just hang out, relax, meet people. If there were some women and some Allman Brothers, Doug figured jail would be a pretty cool place.

Maybe after he got out, he'd take his sixty grand and go live somewhere like jail. And get a job as a sous-chef. Or a writer or something.

It was all cool.

• • •

POURING ROAD TAR was hot. The tar was hot; the metal machinery that heated it was hot; the tools were hot because they were always in contact with the tar or the machinery. Even the towels you had to have so you could touch the tools became hot a few hours into the shift. Mitch's hands were covered in burn scars after only a week on the job. He was spending twenty dollars a week on skin lotion, and it wasn't even summer yet.

Mitch had found a job working road construction in Cleveland. His plan had been to work for anyone who didn't ask for ID and a Mexican woman at the day-labor service had told him about the road crew. She had mentioned it in passing, figuring that a white guy wouldn't be interested, and had been surprised when Mitch enthusiastically copied down the number. He had been there a month before anyone even asked him his last name, and when they did, he lied. He got paid cash on Fridays.

As the only guy on the crew who was not Mexican, Mitch found himself learning Spanish fairly quickly. As the only guy who could read and write English, he found himself a foreman after two weeks. An illegal citizen in charge of illegal aliens. The bosses suspected something about him but he showed up on time and worked hard so they didn't care.

Sweeping the tar smooth on an exit ramp on I-90, Mitch looked around at the brick warehouses on either side of him. The buildings were covered with decades of highway grime, most of the windows broken. Cleveland was dying but it still had some time before it reached the death spiral that had enveloped Wilton. Here there were the usual boarded-up businesses and homeless people and trash strewn streets, but there were echoes of life mixed in. There was a bar scene. There were art galleries. He didn't go to them but they existed. It was comforting.

The tricky part had been finding a place to live. He didn't want a roommate, because he had a duffel bag with sixty thousand dollars in it, but he had to find a place that wouldn't do a background check. Despite his attempts to appear nonthreatening, everyone he talked to eventually asked for ID or mentioned a credit check. Mitch would say he forgot his wallet, then disappear into the ether. Just when he was about to give up and was considering hitting the road again, he saw a small ad in an independent newspaper for a room to rent.

The room was in a neighborhood called Bratenahl. Mitch knew right away it was what he wanted: Bratenahl was neither seedy nor flashy, just the kind of place you should live if you were trying not to be noticed. The door was answered by an old woman with a German shepherd, which reminded him of Ramone. For a brief moment, he was nostalgic for Wilton, for that comparatively secure life of dog-walking and pot-smoking and hanging out with Doug and Kevin. Then he remembered Accu-mart and the metal-refinishing plant. Things were better now. He had what everyone who lived a successful life had: secrets and money.

Mitch and the dog, named Lucy, hit it off right away, which turned out to be all the ID Mitch needed.

"What brings you out here?" the old lady asked as he was carrying his bags up the stairs to his room.

Mitch was going to make up a tall tale, something about a lost love or an undercover police mission, but decided to stay as close as possible to the truth. You had to be careful with old people. Some of them acted like they had no memory just to see if you were the type of person who would take advantage of someone with no memory. "I got laid off in Pittsburgh," he said flatly. "Managed to find work here on a road crew."

"Yes, times are tough," the old woman agreed. "My James, when he was alive, he was a union electrician. He got laid off six times in forty-seven years. You never know."

But when she left, she gave Mitch a look, which he understood perfectly. The look said, "I know you've done something and there's some story as to why you're renting a room in a town you've never been to before. But my dog likes you and that has to be worth something."

•   •   •

MITCH BROUGHT HOME $320 a week for forty hours of splattering himself with boiling toxins. He didn't really need the money, of course, and sometimes he thought he only kept the job so his landlady wouldn't be suspicious of him. Because the money he earned was all extra, he blew it in bars, buying drinks for girls. Going out, enjoying himself, and talking to women were all things he hadn't done in Wilton. And he owed it all to his Little Bag of Security.

"Let's take a smoke break for a couple of minutes," Mitch yelled to the Mexicans over the roar of the traffic. The noise was the worst part of the job. Sometimes, falling asleep in his room, he could still hear the cars whizzing by, an endless parade of traffic in his head. He liked it more when the work caused a traffic jam, because the idling, creeping cars didn't make as much noise. But then you had to work faster, or else the people stuck in traffic would call the company and complain.

Fucking people.

The Mexicans, who were furiously sweeping the tar flat, looked over at him. They liked working with him because he took a lot of breaks. The oldest one, Jorge, who could speak good English, came over and bummed a cigarette.

"You like party?" he asked Mitch.

"Do I like to party? I think so. What exactly do you mean? 'Party' means different things to different people."

"No. You like to go to party?" Jorge made dancing motions. "*Fiesta.*"

"Oh, fiesta. Yes, I like fiesta."

"My wife birthday. We have a party tonight. You come?"

Well I'll be damned. It had been a while since anyone had asked him to a party. His social calendar had been a blank slate for the last few years. Why yes, he decided, a party would be just excellent. He nodded enthusiastically at Jorge.

When a man is waiting for the statute of limitations to expire, Mitch thought, a man ought to enjoy himself.

• • •

WHEN HE FIRST got to the party, Mitch was overwhelmed by feelings of nostalgia and loss. He sat in the corner while samba music blared and thought morosely of better times. He remembered hanging out with Doug at the community-college parties they had crashed, laughing at the host's lame CD collection, trying to spot the slutty girls with the hearts of gold whom they both openly yearned for, hoping they might take them somewhere to enjoy the White Widow that was reeking in his pocket. Now Doug was in a cage and Mitch was fresh out of English-speaking friends, a foreigner in his own country.

There were plenty of girls here, as Jorge had promised him. But as far as Mitch could tell, none of them spoke English, and on the few occasions they made eye contact with him, Mitch sensed suspicion rather than the hot-blooded Latino lust he had been hoping for. He had the vague feeling that before his arrival, his attendance had been discussed, and he imagined Jorge announcing to the crowd that a white guy was coming, and they all had to be nice. This paranoid thought, combined with the language barrier, was what was giving him his first pangs of homesickness for Wilton.

"Meesh," Jorge yelled jovially, slapping him on the shoulder with a huge grin. "You have fun?"

Mitch had been studying some family photos on the living room mantel with far more attention than they deserved, as if he were so engrossed by the fading photo of an elderly Mexican woman that he had become unaware of the dancing and drinking all around him. As he turned to face Jorge, he got a face full of hot, tequila-laden breath

"Yeah, man," he said, holding up a bottle of beer, as if that were all that was required for a good time.

"Come meet my uncle. He want to talk to you."

An uncle? Mitch had been hoping for an introduction to a niece or a sister, but even an uncle was preferable to staring at more pictures of Granny. He nodded and followed Jorge through the house, past amorous dancing couples and chatting housewives, their eyes glazed over with an early evening buzz, their voices louder than usual. Some of the children turned to look at the gringo, but to the adults he was simply invisible. Outside of this house, in the streets of America, he knew, it was the other way around.

Jorge took him out into the yard, which was a few square feet of weeds and dirt with a small garage at the back with an unpainted, broken door. Jorge pushed the door open with a great deal of effort and they stepped inside. The gathering here was all men and the atmosphere was very different from the festivities and dancing going on in the house. Four young men, tattooed and aggressive-looking, were sitting around the garage on buckets and rusted metal chairs, and they stared hard at Mitch with what he felt was deep suspicion. Mitch tried to hide his unease by nodding cheerfully to everyone. No one returned his greeting.

An older man with a potbelly was sitting on a torn green vinyl couch. He stood up as Jorge closed the door behind him and unsmilingly offered Mitch his hand. "I am Armando, Jorge's uncle. You are Meesh?"

"Yeah, hi," Mitch said. Maybe is was just unpronounce-able for these guys. *Meesh* would do fine.

"Jorge tells me you know banks."

Whaaaaat? Mitch hoped his reaction didn't show and he exhaled slowly, trying to preserve his cool. He looked quizzi-cally at Jorge, who was looking down at his shoes. How . . . who? As long as he had been in Cleveland, he hadn't men-tioned a word of anything to anyone.

His shock and confusion must have been visible to Armando, because he broke into a smile, and even one of the brutal-looking tattooed young men sitting on a bucket allowed himself a flicker of amusement.

"Banks?" asked Mitch. He wanted more information before he told them anything. How had they come to this conclusion? Was his picture in the post office? He had fig-ured that his little crime, for what it was worth, had been swept into the morass of the decaying social fabric, forgot-ten with yesterday's news cycle. His current life had depended on this. How had they found out?

"Come on," Armando said cheerfully. "Who wants to

spread tar with Mexicans except a guy who's wanted? I can tell you don't rob liquor stores or bodegas. You're smart. You go where the money is. You do banks."

This logic confused Mitch. Apparently, all the time he had thought he was invisible, they had been sizing him up. He had thought his guy-who-just-got laid-off routine was working like a charm. He shook his head. "No," he said.

There was a moment's silence in the garage while they looked at him, disappointed either in his refusal to come clean or their own error of judgment. Mitch cleared his throat. "Armored cars," he said finally.

"Ah hah!" roared Armando and the young men sitting around also laughed. Mitch had the feeling he was on stage and giving a killer performance. He smiled sheepishly, unused to the attention.

Armando pushed forward an overturned bucket and motioned for Mitch to sit. His demeanor was suddenly serious. Everyone had their own version of the embattled paratroop commander. "So what do you know about security systems?"

"Security systems?" Mitch shook his head. "Not much." He sensed that he might lose the crowd with this confession and that a full explanation of his crime would provide more amusement than respect. But he wasn't sure. Wasn't there an element of learning to all crime? He had, after all, successfully robbed an armored car. He doubted anyone else in the room could say that.

"I don't know anything about all that technical shit," Mitch said. "I just know that a security system is only as good as the people who respond to it." He sat down on the bucket and pulled it up next to Armando, surprised by his own intensity. He was realizing that he did have knowledge, and a work philosophy, and experience, all the things he had faked at Accu-mart. "It's all about efficiency, about timing. If you can do what you have to do and get back in your car in ninety seconds, the security system doesn't matter."

He looked around the garage and saw expressions he wasn't used to. Respect. People were actually interested in what he had to say. He knew enough to stop talking and sat back on his bucket, waiting for a response from one of the others.

There was a moment of silence while looks were exchanged. Then one of the tattooed men in a white T-shirt pulled his bucket up next to Mitch and glanced at Armando, as if to give approval.

"We have this thing we're working on," said Armando, leaning forward, his voice low to accent the gravity of his disclosure. "You might be interested?"

Mitch leaned in too, keeping his own voice low. "Yes. I might be."